RAFE MARTIN

SCHOLASTIC INC.

New York Toronto London Auckland Sydney
Mexico City New Delhi Hong Kong Buenos Aires

Arthur A. Levine Books hardcover edition designed by David Caplan, published by Arthur A. Levine Books, an imprint of Scholastic Inc., October 2005.

ISBN-13: 978-0-439-21168-0
ISBN-10: 0-439-21168-9

12 11 10 9 8 7 6 5 4 3 2 1 7 8 9 10 11 12/0

Printed in the U.S.A. 23

First Scholastic paperback printing, February 2007

For the wing we each have.

It was on the last day of the six years during which she was not to speak or laugh if she hoped to free her brothers from enchantment, that her own sentence was to be carried out. Five of the six shirts were done, but the last and littlest was still missing its left sleeve. As they led her to the stake and the fire was about to be lit, she looked up and saw six swans flying through the sky. Her heart leapt with joy at the sight of them. The swans touched the ground before her and with lowered necks walked forward. Quickly she threw the shirts over each of them. At once their swans' skins fell off and there, once again, stood her own brothers, strong and handsome. Only the youngest and littlest lacked a left arm, and in its place there remained a swan's wing.

"The Six Swans,"
THE BROTHERS GRIMM

The Story

Rain pelted heavily against the narrow, glazed window. Lightning flashed, vividly illuminating the room. Then a heavy wooden door creaked slowly open and torchlight brightened the darkness.

Ardwin looked up from his bed, eyes wide.

The old nurse, Marjorie, set her torch in an iron ring bolted to the wall. "It's all right. I'm here," she said softly. "And you are safe in your own room in the castle. Nothing can harm you."

"The storm woke me. I couldn't sleep," Ardwin said.

Lightning flashed again. The crashing *BOOM!* of thunder was now very close. Desperately Ardwin looked around the stone-walled room with its heavy, hanging tapestries. Was there a way out?

Marjorie saw this and said again, "There is nothing to fear. I will stay. There is a guard at the door."

She came forward and steadied a cup to his lips — water mixed with honey, to which extracts of valerian, hops, hyssop, and skullcap had been added; a drink to bring restful sleep. *Poor thing,* she thought. *Gone these six years and now come back like this. He'll have a hard road all his life.*

Ardwin finished. There was a soft rustling from beneath him as he rolled to one side and seemed to stretch out beneath the covers.

In a calm voice, old Marjorie sang:

> *"Safe from storm and wind and wolf,*
> *Safe from tooth and bitter clime,*
> *Safe from claw and fire and steel,*
> *Safe from harm, on my arm,*
> *Old Marjorie stays until you heal."*

She looked down. Ardwin was staring up at her. "Tell the story," he said.

She sighed. He was strong-willed and it was more an order than a request, but she tried to avoid his command. "It's too long," she answered. "And it is late. Another time. I am weary."

"No," he said, insistent. "I can't sleep. Tell it. You tell it best."

I tell it best? He was clever too. *I tell it best!* The rascal! Trying to butter her up like that! Well, maybe he'd soon fall asleep if she began. She might as well. After all, he *was* the prince. "All right," she said. "But then you must promise to try to sleep."

Ardwin nodded his head and settled himself under the covers. Again, the rustling — almost like the sound of dry leaves. Marjorie sat on a chair by his bedside. She straightened her skirt, then cleared her throat. If she delayed, maybe the sleeping draft would have time to work. Then she could to go to sleep herself. She poured a cup of water from the pitcher on the nightstand. She drank, looking down at the boy over the cup's rim. No use. He was wide-awake and waiting. *No rest for the weary,* she thought. She sighed again. And she began:

"So, there was a king out hunting and he got lost in the dark woods. The sun began to set and the king shivered to think of a night all alone there. Though he did not like to do it (after all, he was the king), he called for help. An old woman stepped from behind a tree, her head bobbing and wagging as if it might fall off.

" 'I will help — on one condition,' she said.

"The king hated *conditions.* What he liked was freedom — wasn't he the king? But he wanted to go home. So he said, 'Name it.'

" 'My daughter,' the old woman answered, 'is very beautiful. Make her your queen and I will guide you from here. If you refuse, I will abandon you. Ravens and owls will peck out your eyes. Wolves will eat your flesh and gnaw your bones. Rats will crawl —'

"'That will do,' said the king, interrupting. 'I understand perfectly. Let me see her.'

"Then, with her head still bobbing on her scrawny neck, the old woman led the king, by tangled and twisting paths, to a cottage. At a loom sat a beautiful young woman, dark-eyed and raven-haired, with skin white as bone and lips like blood.

"'All right,' said the king, who was a widower. 'I will marry her. Now lead us from here.' Yet as he spoke, his heart warned he should be wary."

"Yes," came the voice of the boy from the pillow. "If only he had."

"Then the daughter flung a black cloak over her shoulders, and the king took her up before him on his great horse, and the old woman led them by more secret ways to the edge of the wood. The moon was rising and the stars shone like pearls. Wild geese flew and made mournful cries. All at once the king knew exactly where he was. It was as if a mist had lifted. His castle stood before him. He turned to the old woman, but she was gone. He spurred his horse forward, and the two rode home, and were married.

"Now the king had seven children from his first marriage, six sons and a daughter. And, while his new wife was beautiful, he never felt at ease with her, so he never told her about his children. Perhaps he sensed that she wanted all his love and would not share it. Or perhaps he thought that if he and the new queen ever had a child, she might kill his children to give her own child the throne. Dark thoughts, mayhap, but he could not shake free of them. So he hid his children deep in the forest in a lonely castle.

"So well hidden was that castle, and so twisted and tangled the paths that led to it, that the king himself could never find it, if not for a magic ball of yarn. When he tossed the yarn to the ground, it unrolled and led him to the castle.

"Soon the queen became suspicious. Where did the king go for hours on end? He must have no secrets, not from her. She must know, and control all. The servants would at first say nothing. Then she showed them a certain closet filled with nastily bubbling potions, mummified bodies of cats and frogs, shriveled claws, carnivorous plants, dried skulls and bones. One trembling old fool of a servant — a plague upon him — broke down and told her all, of the yarn, the hidden castle, and the children. But the fool kept at least a bit of his wit, for he spoke only of six sons and said nothing of a daughter."

Ardwin shifted under the covers, and once again Marjorie heard that soft rustling sound. Ardwin nodded. "He did. He kept that back. It helped."

Marjorie agreed. She reached for the cup and took a sip.

"The wicked queen fashioned six shirts," Marjorie went on, "and into the fabric she wove secret designs. Then she took the ball of yarn and left the palace when the king was away. She tossed the yarn and followed it as it unrolled. Soon, she stood before the hidden castle. The gate of the castle swung open and six boys ran out."

"Yes," said Ardwin, half raising his head from the pillow now. "That's what happened, Marjorie. But it was a mistake."

Marjorie nodded. "Indeed. The boys thought it was their father who had come for them, but they were wrong."

Ardwin lay back down. "Very wrong."

Marjorie waited a moment, and sipped more water. "As they ran toward her," she said, "the queen tossed the shirts, one onto each boy. With that, the boys fell to the ground, turned into swans, and flew away. The king's daughter awoke and, looking from the window, saw it all.

"When the king returned home, his beautiful queen welcomed him warmly. The next day he took his ball of yarn and went to the hidden castle. But only his daughter ran to greet him.

" 'Where are your brothers?' he asked, looking around with growing dread.

" 'Father,' she sobbed, 'a pale woman with raven-black hair and bloodred lips turned them into swans. They flew away.'

" 'Dear child, such things happen only in dreams, bad dreams,' said the king.

" 'No, Father,' sobbed the girl, and held out her hand. In it were six white feathers. 'Here are feathers from their wings. It was real!'

"A nameless terror gripped the king. 'Come,' he said. 'I will protect you. If the worst has already happened, it cannot be helped. But perhaps you are mistaken and they will soon return. Come now with me, back to my castle.'

" 'No. I will not,' she said. 'If my brothers return I must be here to greet them.'

"The king saw she would not yield. So he said, 'You may stay here alone for one night. But tomorrow I will come for you.'

"Then the king, in great sorrow and with great misgiving, rode from the hidden castle back to his palace.

"The next morning, the princess put a loaf of bread and a jug of water into a knapsack and set off into the forest. 'I will find my brothers and save them,' she said to herself.

"When the king and his men came galloping to the hidden castle's gate, the girl was long gone. Though they searched, they found no trace of the princess. It was as if the dark woods had swallowed her.

"The king slumped to the ground, hid his face in his cloak, and wept.

"The brave princess walked and walked. Toward nightfall she came to a cottage. She knocked, and when no one answered, she pushed open the door and stepped inside. She found six beds and, on a sturdy wooden table, six round plates and silver spoons.

"She was so tired and the place so lonely that she stretched out on the hard wooden floor (it would not do for her to lie upon a downy bed, all muddied and dirty as she was) and fell fast asleep.

"When she awoke it was already dark, but a small lamp was lit, and by its yellow light she saw two swans fly through the open window. Four others already stood in the cottage. The six swans lowered their long necks and began to hiss and blow at one another. And what was this? Why, their feathers flew off, whirling like snow. And there stood her own dear brothers, in shirts of swanskin.

"When her brothers saw her they cried, 'How have you come?' And, 'Ah, sister! Sister! You must go!'

" 'Go?' she exclaimed. 'Never. I have sought and found you. I will stay. We shall live safely together here. No one will find us."

Ardwin's voice rose from the semidarkness. "She was bold and brave. But she did not understand."

"True," concurred Marjorie. "You know better than I. Shall I continue?'"

Ardwin nodded.

"So, then. 'Alas,' said the oldest brother, 'if it could only be. But you cannot stay.'

" 'Why not?' asked their sister.

" 'We can only be human for a small portion of each day,' answered the oldest brother. 'Only enough time is given us to eat and rest. Then we must become swans again. And soon, when the wild swans fly away, we must fly too. You will be alone.

" 'Then I will stay here and you can return as you are able.'

" 'No,' said the eldest unhappily. 'Robbers live here. When we see a lamp lit, then even we dare not come inside. No,' he said, shaking his head, 'you cannot stay.'

" 'There must be some way to free you from this evil spell!' she insisted.

" 'There is,' admitted the oldest reluctantly. He looked at his brothers, then at his sister. 'But it is too hard. We cannot ask it.' The others nodded."

"We cannot," said Ardwin, repeating the words with Marjorie.

Marjorie did not pause.

" 'Tell me,' said the princess. 'What is it?'

"The brothers looked uncomfortably at one another. Then the eldest, whose name was Bran, said, 'The witch told us that there is only one way we could be set free. She told us in order to torment us, for she laughed and said no one could do it.'

" 'I'll do it,' said the girl. 'Tell me what to do.'

"Bran sighed. Then he said, 'For six years you must not speak, laugh, or cry. And you must weave six shirts of star-wort and nettle. The starwort will fall apart, and the nettles will scratch and sting. Your hands and arms will be cut and blistered. They will turn rough and red. You may not reveal the reason for your silence to anyone, ever. When the six years are done, we will fly to you and you must fling the shirts upon us. Then we will be ourselves again and swans no more. In that way, and that way alone, can the spell be broken.'

"The princess looked at her brothers, youngest to oldest. 'I will do it,' she said again."

"Alas, sister," said Ardwin, speaking from his pillow. The room was getting darker, the torch burning down, the light fading. Marjorie could no longer see him clearly.

Marjorie continued with the story. "When the princess arose the next morning, her brothers were gone. She cut herself a staff and set off deeper into the forest. In time she came to a clearing where starwort and nettles grew. She began to gather plants. The nettles scratched and stung. Weeks and months went by. It was bitter toil. For food she steamed nettles and gathered wild nuts, berries, and grasses. For a house she had a hollow tree. When the weather was warm, she would climb up into its branches and sit and weave, but when it turned cold and wet, there was a knothole and the tree was so huge, she could slip inside. Moss grew around the entrance, making a curtain. And there she slept. And there too, through the chill of fall and bitter cold of winter she stayed, weaving her brothers' shirts. Often, just as a sleeve was done, or when she was about to sew some last bit in place, the shirt crumpled and fell apart. And the poor girl, without uttering a word or even a cry (for that would ruin all), began again.

"Spring came. The princess was weaving in the branches of her oak when she heard horses. She climbed higher and slipped into her shelter, from where she peered down. Three horsemen approached. Two were clad in forest green, wore leather jerkins, and had bows and quivers. The central rider wore scarlet and gold, a golden circlet was around his red hair, and a gold chain hung over his shoulders and chest. As for weapons, he had a fine horn bow and a fine quiver, and a gold-hilted sword.

"The three horsemen rode beneath her tree. The rider in scarlet glanced up. He reined in his horse. The others stopped and lifted their bows. 'No, no,' he said, and laughed. 'Look!' Now the riders saw her, too.

" 'Come down!' called the one in scarlet. 'Come down, for you are beautiful. Do not be afraid. I am the king of this land.'

"The girl shook her head no! So the young king climbed the tree until he was face-to-face with her. 'What is your name?' he asked. Again she only shook her head. 'Come,' he said gently. 'Tell me. I mean no harm.'

"But she would say nothing.

"After a time, the king coaxed her from the tree. Her clothes were in rags. Her hands were rough and scratched and blistered. Her hair was tangled and wild, yet her bearing was regal. In fact, despite the roughness of her appearance, she was the most beautiful young woman he had ever seen.

"'Come with me,' he said, 'and be my queen.'

"The princess nodded and, taking the partially completed shirts and a basket of starwort and nettle, rode with the young king to his palace, where they were married.

"The princess was happy. Yet her happiness was blighted. Though she loved her husband, she also loved her brothers. So she did not speak, and day and night she wove. How could the young king understand? Still, he let her weave and he spoke kind words to her, and she answered with soft looks and nods. In this way he knew that her heart was his. And he was content.

"But his mother, the old queen, hated the girl. 'She is mute as an animal come out of the wild wood, and no fitting wife for my son. She's hardly human! As for her constant weaving, why, she must be mad!'

"A year went by. When the princess gave birth to a son, she was torn between laughter and tears, but remained silent. Even a single word, a single soft coo of love, and her brothers would be forever lost.

"The young king was overjoyed with his new son. He laughed and sang enough for two.

"That night a cloaked figure climbed into the princess's bedchamber, lifted the newborn baby from the mother's side, daubed the princess's mouth with blood, and vanished. When the princess awoke and found her child gone, she nearly screamed but, remembering her brothers, she remained silent.

She ran to her husband. His mother was already at his side. When the matter was made clear, the old queen exclaimed, 'Gone? No! Eaten is more likely! Look at the blood on her mouth! She has eaten her own child! Kill the witch!'

"The king protested, saying that it could not be so. Still, though the palace was searched top to bottom, the child was not found. Days, weeks, months went by. The tragedy stifled all joy. But day and night, the princess furiously wove.

"Then a second child was born, another son. He too was stolen away and blood dripped on the princess's lips, and again she was accused of foul murder and witchcraft. The king would not believe this second time either. He even sought to silence the rumors, threatening to execute anyone who spoke openly of them. But he could not stop the whispers that spread like a stain through palace and countryside.

"Time went on and, in its fullness, a third child was born, this time, a girl. Guards were posted around the bedchamber of mother and child. But late in the night, a secret panel slid back, a cloaked figure slunk to the bedside, and this third child too was gone, and blood left on her mother's lips.

"In the morning there was such a clamor! The old queen was screaming, 'Burn the witch! My grandchildren are dead! Burn her, the devouring witch! Burn her till her evil heart shrivels and she is dead!'

"And this time the king could not protect his wife, for the judges were called in, and sentence passed.

"The poor princess bowed her head and madly wove the last shirt. The six years were up that very day, and whatever else might happen of sorrow and of evil, she knew she might still be able to redeem her brothers. They bound her, leaving her hands free to weave, for the king, her husband, insisted on that. Then they brought her to the courtyard, where a wooden stake stood waiting, surrounded by a tangle of dry branches and wood.

"The executioner held his torch in readiness to set all ablaze. They tied the young queen to the stake as still she feverishly strove to finish the last shirt."

"Yes," said Ardwin. "The last and littlest shirt."

"Indeed," said Marjorie. "How the poor, young king, her husband, now wept and sobbed. 'She is innocent!' he exclaimed. 'I know it!' And he refused to give the final, fateful command. The old queen pushed him aside. 'Light the wood! Burn the witch!' she screamed.

"The executioner in his black hood bent down with his torch, when *whirr whirr whirr, flap flap flap,* six white swans flew from the sky! They circled the pyre and beat at the soldiers, the executioner, and the old queen with their great white wings. The torch was knocked from the executioner's hand, his wrist broken by a single, powerful, winged blow. Then, as all watched in fear and awe, the six swans landed, lowered their necks, and approached the young queen. Swiftly she flung a shirt over each of their backs.

“And what was this?

“Why, at once the swans turned into tall, broad-shouldered, handsome youths who drew their swords and, rushing forward, cut their sister’s bonds and surrounded her with a ring of sharp steel.

“Then at last the girl cried, ‘Free! My brothers are freed from enchantment, and I can speak! I never harmed my babes. I am innocent!’ She told all. And when the king heard her tale, he drew his sword and put it to the executioner’s neck and said, ‘Tell all you know. If you hesitate, I will end the pain of your injured arm swiftly. For I shall take your head.’

“And the executioner cried, ‘Sire! I was ordered to steal the babes.’

“ ‘By *whom*?’ roared the king.

“ ‘B-b-by your mother!’ stammered the executioner. ‘But, Sire, the babes are safe, not dead. I have seen to that.’

“Then the six brothers and all the people too clamored for justice, shouting that the old queen must make use of the stake, the sticks, and the flames. The judges stood apart and conferred. And they agreed. So all was done as demanded, the older boys binding the witch-queen and knotting her ropes tight.

“Then the princess and the young king embraced. The six brothers embraced their sister too and thanked her for not failing them despite her anguish and trials. The three babes were brought from hiding, hale and healthy, and so all was finally, and once again, well.

"Almost all. The princess had not had the time to complete the sixth shirt. The left sleeve was missing. And so, when the youngest and littlest brother became human again, instead of a left arm he had a wing, there, on the left side, the side closest to the heart."

Old Marjorie nodded, signaling that the tale was done, but there was no response. She peered down. In the dim light she could just see that Ardwin's eyes were closed. She could hear him breathing rhythmically. The potion had worked at last. *I could have ended the tale sooner,* she thought, *and saved my breath. Ah well, what's done is done. If I had stopped too soon, he might have waked and then I'd be up all night telling him tales.* She rubbed her elbow, always stiff in damp weather. Her eyelids grew heavy and slowly drooped shut. Her head swayed until her chin settled on her chest. The torch stub gave off one last, dying puff of smoke, then guttered out. Marjorie began to snore.

But Ardwin was not actually asleep. He was drifting back and forth, like a leaf in the tide, between the world of his bedroom and the world of his dreams.

It always began in the marshes, with him feeding beside his five older brothers.

Lifting his beak from the weeds and muck, he'd say, "We have no house, but we have wings. Let's see how high they can lift us! Who will come?" When the others showed no interest, he went alone.

He set off, wings beating, running along the surface of the water. When he treaded only air, he tucked his webbed feet under his body and began climbing. Stretching his long neck, he pushed on, flapping his wings, rising higher still, up and up to where the air was cold and thin and the horizon spread forever. Mountains rose from beneath the world's rim and grew tall and forbidding. The wind roared. Still he flew on, striving higher.

Thousands of swans, looking like white midges, swarmed over the blue sea far below. The pale marshes looked like sea foam; the glacier glistened like a blue-green gem. Even the highest mountaintops were beneath him, pennants of snow rippling from their peaks, white and sheer.

Black spots swam before his eyes. His lungs burned, yet he was filled with joy. At this great height, the world seemed his alone. He felt like a god, wild and free!

For a time he floated, wings outspread, the world below. Then he dove. The wind clawed his eyes, buffeted his shoulders and chest, and bent his wings dangerously. He folded his wings in tight, lest the hollow bones break, and then he plummeted like a stone.

In warmer, rising air, he began a series of shallow dives to bleed off the terrific speed. He glided down until rivers again foamed over rocks, the blue sea splashed against a solid shore, the glinting marshes formed his narrow horizon, and the tiny specks he had seen from so high above were once more his own swan brothers. Back down he flew, landing among them with a *splash,* exhilarated and exhausted.

Once he had been caught in a powerful storm. An updraft flung him high into the great black thunderhead, boiling overhead. His rain-soaked wings were soon glazed with ice. Nearly frozen, he was tossed about helplessly by the furious winds. He was bruised, battered, and terrified. Lightning seared the air, and thunder split the sky with an ear-shattering *BOOM! My wings will be ripped off! My bones will shatter!* he thought in panic. Then, somehow, by the merest chance — or was it? — the madly churning winds tossed him free. He flew on, dazed, ears ringing. When he made it back down, he collapsed on the shore of the lake. It took him days to recover.

Ardwin lay in his bed now, half awake, trying to recapture that world of mountains, forests, rivers, and seas that had been his, so recently, and once upon a time.

Outside his window distant thunder rumbled faintly, and lightning flickered. The storm had almost drifted away.

Old Marjorie's snores were fading too. Ardwin, letting go at last, tumbled into sleep.

Apprentice

One spring morning when Ardwin was fourteen, he said to his father while they were eating breakfast together, "I've been home for four years now and there are things I must learn to do. I want a brace so I can strap on a bow. And I want to learn how to really race a horse, not simply ride. Others my age can do these things. It's my time now."

King Lugh lifted a slice of bacon and crunched it. "I admire your spirit, Ard, I really do. And I can sympathize with your impatience. But you're still learning to master so many things." He reached across the table and tapped Ardwin genially on the arm. "Patience! One step at a time. If you want to shoot, go to the smith and have him forge what you need. Old Peter, the master archer, can train you. He worked with Bran for a time too. Next year you can focus on horse racing. Now pass the toast and jam like a good lad, will you?"

Ardwin wasted no time. The next morning he went to find old Peter Sharpshins, the master bowman, and said, "I need you to teach me to shoot."

"Drop your cloak from your shoulder," answered the old man.

Ardwin dropped his cloak. The white swan's wing, strong, broad, and thickly feathered, stood out from his tunic, which had been cut loose on the left side to give it room. The old archer rubbed his grizzled chin and pushed back his hood, eyeing the wing. "I taught a man," he said, "whose left hand had been chopped off. We made a brace for the bow, and he became a decent shot. Your wing will be harder, both to fit and to work with. It will catch any breeze and throw off your aim. You'll have to be determined and willing to work hard if you expect to gain any skill."

"I am willing," said Ardwin. "I'll do whatever you say."

"Hmmm," grunted the old bowman. "Your brother Bran said the same thing. Then he went off and did as he pleased. He never listened to me, or to anyone. He had the eye and the talent, but not the patience. Bran was happier with the sword and the lance, anyway. He said he liked to hit things and feel the blow."

"That was my brother," said Ardwin. "Not me."

"All right. We'll have the smith make a brace. He has your measurements?"

Ardwin nodded.

"If you have some ability and hard work suits you, I'll take you on. Otherwise you can ask one of my assistants. They won't mind wasting time."

Ardwin left the practice yard. *To become merely "a decent shot" will not be good enough,* he thought. *I can do better than Bran. I* have *to!*

That night he couldn't sleep. He lay in bed picturing a bow clamped to his wing. He imagined its weight and heft and the awkward way the wing would have to bend in order to set an arrow to the bowstring. In his mind he saw himself facing a distant target. Then a breeze blew, pushed at his wing, and shifted his stance. He waited till the feathers merely ruffled idly, then released the shot. It sped to the target, stabbing the center with a satisfying *thunk!* He imagined it over and over.

It was windy when he returned to Peter Sharpshins. Dust whirled and bits of grit and straw blew. The old archer sat in a sheltered doorway, holding a longbow with an iron brace attached. A quiver of gray goose arrows leaned against the door frame. "Try this," he said.

Ardwin slung the cloak from his shoulder and lifted the bow. He set the brace, a kind of open clamp padded with leather, over the long, thin wing bone, and tightened the clamp. As he turned the screws they pinched his skin. It was just bearable, but lifting the wing was hard. The bow with the iron clamp on it weighed more than he had expected.

"Take these," said the archer, handing Ardwin the quiver.

Ardwin put the strap over his shoulder, and they set off through the yard where cooks and stable boys, carpenters and maids were all within arrow range. The archer's old, one-eyed hound, Gander, and Marjorie's brindled cat, Micebane, lay sleeping in the sun beside the stone wall. As they passed, Gander opened his single eye, yawned, stretched, then rose and ambled after them.

They went out the postern gate, into the field where targets had been set at distances from thirty to one hundred yards.

"Take your stand," said the archer, nodding to a bare spot ahead. "Plant your feet. Face your left shoulder toward the target. Start by aiming at the closest and let's see what you can do."

Ardwin went to the mark, set the arrow to the string, and drew the nock to his cheek. He had imagined it well. But then the breeze gusted, and the wind caught his wing and pushed him so that he staggered, and the arrow leaped from the bow and sped off too wide and too high and too close to the face of the old master archer, who drew his head into his hood, turtlelike, and exclaimed, "Hunhhh!" The arrow disappeared into the grasses far to the right of the target and twenty yards beyond. Gander, who had been lying in the grass, looked up and whined.

Ardwin began to sweat.

"Again," said Peter Sharpshins, pushing back his hood. "Shoot again."

Ardwin drew another arrow from the quiver. Already his shoulder ached from holding the bow with its heavy clamp. The pinched spots on his arm were raw and they hurt too. The breeze blew again. With his wing raised, it was like holding out a great white sail to the wind. He felt he would blow over, but he stood his ground and, when the breeze passed, let fly.

The arrow flew straight, but way too low, and stuck into the earth ten yards short. From far off among the trees a raven croaked and cackled and maniacally chortled. He was being laughed at. Through the power of the wing he could still sometimes understand what animals, especially wild ones, were saying. The raven's cry was clearly derisive.

"Again."

Ardwin shot. This time the wind did not blow and the release was perfect. Now the arrow rose up and continued well beyond the first target, then dropped and stuck point-down, closer to the third.

Again came the raven's crazed, mocking laugh. Then it flapped its wings and flew from the trees. Circling overhead, it loudly *caw cawed* (which Ardwin understood as *ha-ha!*), then flew away.

"Pay attention!" said Peter Sharpshins. "Now, again!"

When the arrows were gone, he said, "Retrieve them."

With the bow rubbing his feathered skin raw and almost dragging the thin shoulder bones from their socket, Ardwin dutifully went into the field and retrieved the spent arrows. He had hit two targets, one on the outermost rim, one on the third ring. The other arrows had gone into the grass and dirt. Ardwin was sweaty and tired. His arm hurt and he felt humiliated. *I am not much of an archer,* he thought. *I have no talent for it. Master Sharpshins will send me to an apprentice. At night, when the archers gather to drink their pints, they'll all make jokes about me and the wing. I can just hear them.*

He pulled each arrow from the dirt, grasping the shaft carefully, up near the point, so it would not break and so the stiff feathers would not be damaged. Then he pulled the two arrows from the targets, turning the shafts slowly back and forth to release them from the cloth and straw without loosening the points. He brought back the full quiver, then, hopelessly, once more took his stance.

"No need," said the old archer. "Let's go. I'm hungry and thirsty with all this work."

Ardwin let out a breath and unclamped the bow. He swung the wing to relieve the buildup of blood, and rubbed the raw marks where the clamp had pinched the skin against bone.

They walked in silence. Bugs rose from the grasses, skimming effortlessly on the breeze. The wind came up and blew the wing, tugging at it to regain the sky. Ardwin plodded heavily along.

"Tomorrow," said Peter when they reached the gate. "Same time. We'll meet here. No need for the yard."

"You'll . . . you'll take me?" exclaimed Ardwin. "You'll take me as your student? Why? I was terrible!"

"Yes, you were. But you have perseverance, Prince Ardwin. You kept at it despite your lack of success. What's more, you made no complaint against the wind, and you damaged no arrow. When you failed, you made no moan. Bran broke a bow over his knee when he began, so frustrated did he become. Now put some ointment on those sores and, tomorrow, pad them with a folded cloth. I'm off to have lunch, and I recommend you do the same."

Ardwin almost floated back to the castle. Bran had been awful! But he, Ardwin, had perseverance! He could hardly wait for the morning.

Conditions

Within a year Ardwin could outshoot anyone except a certain minister's son named Conrad, who egged him on to a shooting contest.

A wooden wand was set upright at a distance, and where Conrad's arrow nicked or moved it, Ardwin's split the wand exactly. The king, delighted, slapped his thigh and cried from the viewing stands, "A cunning shot!" Old Peter Sharpshins pulled at his mustache ends, his blue eyes twinkling with pride from inside his green hood. At bull's-eyes, Conrad might set a clear center shot, but Ardwin, his bow held firmly in its brace, sent an arrow into Conrad's nock, shattering the shaft and bringing roars from the crowd.

Then the moment came. "An eye," Conrad said coolly, pointing to a flock of geese flying overhead. Drawing his bow, he paused, sighted along the arrow, and let fly. His arrow flashed skyward. One goose gave a shrieking cry, then tumbled in an ugly, gyrating heap to the ground. A page ran forward, then jogged back with the bird in his arms, the neck dangling loosely, an arrow sticking through the head. "The eye!" he would call, holding the goose high for all to see.

It nauseated Ardwin, and Conrad knew it.

"Shoot well, son," the king called encouragingly, waiting for the moment when Ardwin would win and be honored.

The crowd sensed it and, caught in the unfolding drama, leaned forward as one.

Then, as more geese flew over (Ardwin had made the king pledge that swans would never be used as targets), Ardwin seemed to aim carefully, shot — and missed entirely, his arrow sailing off many feet distant from any of the large birds. He couldn't harm them, not when he knew their lives so well.

The crowd exhaled.

"The winner is Conrad," the herald announced, and the king sighed. The old master bowman shook his head. Conrad stepped forward smugly to receive the silver arrow. "Nerves, Prince *Hardwin.* Nerves of steel," he smirked and smiled crookedly. Then, beneath his breath, he added, "Archery is no game for *chickens.*"

"Idiot," Ardwin muttered back. "I do not miss because of nerves. I miss because I do not choose to take such easy targets."

Year after year it was the same.

Conrad's needling got under Ardwin's skin. Skye, the daughter of the king's physician, and a good friend to Ardwin, said reassuringly, "Don't let Conrad bother you, Ard. Something within is always pinching at him. He's pitiful, really."

Ardwin nodded. "Yes, you're right, Skye. Thank you."

But Conrad saw Ardwin's resolve to ignore him as a challenge. He became expert at cunning jibes and jokes about flight, wings, swans, geese, and feathers.

In swordplay as in arm wrestling, Ardwin shone. No one near his age could stand against him, not even his friend Stephen, the chief minister's son, who stood taller than Ardwin by a head. Ardwin's right arm, backed by muscles built up over six years of daily flying, simply shredded all defenses. Conrad never even entered the lists against him. "It's pointless," he sniffed. "Mere brute strength is so crude. There is no skill involved."

Ardwin knew Conrad was wrong. *It's only common sense for people to build on their strengths,* he thought. *It's Conrad who is the crude one.* Still, the words stung and, try as he might to ignore them, or to defend himself against them, Ardwin couldn't. They got to him.

Then he discovered that the spear and javelin required a keen eye as well as strength. He took them up, worked hard, and soon could hit any target, even the farthest. There was something about watching a spear fly that greatly pleased him.

His pleasure never lasted. Sooner or later merchants or emissaries would arrive at his father's court, nudge one another, and crane their necks to sneak a look at "Prince Freak." As he rode through the town, people turned their backs, afraid of catching the evil eye. "Witch-spawn," he heard some mutter, and saw them cross their fingers and spit into the dust, while others, more sympathetic, merely shook their heads. The wing itself might embarrass him by suddenly flashing out and striking a passerby; at dinner it might tip a cup and spill the wine. Once it knocked over a candle and started a fire.

And there was always Conrad. One day, Ardwin, returning from the woods with his spears over his shoulder, rounded a corner and came upon Conrad walking with a companion. Immediately Conrad said, "Watch your step, my friend! You wear new boots. There may be goose droppings on the path." Then, as if suddenly seeing Ardwin, he added, "Ah, Prince *Hardwink*, I mean, *Ardwin.* My, but my tongue seems to be something of a *cripple* today. You must excuse it. Beautiful morning, is it not?" And with his friend sniggering at his side, he walked on.

Fortunately Ardwin had Stephen and Skye as friends, and they more than made up for Conrad. Stephen even convinced Ardwin to learn to swim, though not without dangerous trial and error.

One hot summer afternoon Stephen jumped into the river

and Ardwin followed. Even though Ardwin had paddled on rivers, lakes, and even out on the sea, he had never learned to swim as people do. He had only been a child of three and a half when his stepmother cast her spell. Now, when the water closed over his head for the first time, he panicked. He sank down into the cold and the dark, to where weeds curled like fingers around his feet and he couldn't kick free. He could see the sun glinting and wavering overhead, bent and distorted by the watery glass through which he looked. Bell-like dollops of air burbled from his mouth. He was drowning. Then Stephen's white, anxious face was before him. A pale arm reached out and grabbed him by the hair and dragged him back up into the light and air and warmth. He broke the surface wheezing, coughing, gasping for air, and Stephen dragged him to shore.

"Don't," gasped Stephen as he pulled Ardwin up onto the bank, "ever scare me like that again!"

"Right," muttered Ardwin, coughing and retching. "Absolutely right." He waved his drenched wing toward Stephen in thanks. The wing, gone wild now that it was back in the air, whacked Stephen hard in the face, bloodying his nose. Stephen rolled away groaning, but laughing. "Don't thank me! *Please!* I mean it!" he protested. *"Don't!"*

"Sorry," said Ardwin, embarrassed.

The wing was built for rowing and sculling, not through water but through air. Ardwin pitied anyone standing near him when the flocks were migrating. Some unsuspecting soul was sure to get whacked when the wing sprang toward the sky. The air was its true home. It was not much use thrashing around in, on, or under water. Its hollow bones and feathers, too, were lighter than the muscle and solid bone of his arm, making him float on his heavier, right side like a beached whale.

Still, he kept at it and finally learned to swim, sidestroke. When he accomplished that, there seemed nothing he couldn't do if he put his mind to it.

At sixteen Ardwin was broad-shouldered and strong, with a shy wildness about him. He was skilled with bow, spear, and sword. He was an excellent horseman and he could shoot, swim, and row. And he could often understand the language of wild things. Sometimes he felt he still lived in that world in which everything had its place, and every creature could talk. One afternoon he told Stephen as they hurled spears, "I've been thinking. I'd like to go back to the swans for a time and reclaim my roots. I think it would help me sort things out — and it would be an adventure. Are you interested?"

"Definitely," Stephen said. Which helped Ardwin think more seriously about it, as well as feel less lonely.

Still, in the spring or fall, when Ardwin heard the flocks calling, *"Come away, come away!"* it was hard not to feel abandoned and stuck. In dreams he visited snowcapped mountains, glaciers, and bays white with swans; saw seals dive and whales spout. He could see his swan brothers, Bran, Seth, Rory, Dan, and Emery, flying before him, their feathers gleaming white in the moonlight as they balanced, shifting and tilting, skillful as sailors in the crosswinds. Far below, the lights of farm and castle shone like pinpoints in the darkness. Stars burned overhead, and all around them, thousands of swans flew in great white skeins stretched across the sky. There were swan warriors and swan wives, swan lads and maidens. As they flew on and on, cities, towns, even frontier outposts were all left behind. Then there was only wilderness, darkly forested or bright with snow and ice. And there was . . . certainty. As a swan, he had been sustained by the calls that linked all the swans together, whether in darkness, or in storm. He understood barking foxes, howling wolves, and the shrill, piercing cries of eagles and hawks. Even the moon and stars seemed to whisper wordless messages from the sky.

Yet each morning, when he awoke, he was back in the nightmare of his waking life, shut in his room in the castle — a freak, isolated and different.

On hot, muggy days, Ardwin sat on a flat stone in the garden, near the wall. He set down a dish of water mixed with milk and honey and waited. The trick was to let his jumpy, human mind slow. If he remained patient and still, then . . .

It was like a door opening.

The grass grew greener, the song of the birds sweeter. The rock wall before him revealed the thoughts of its builders in patterns left by their hands. The smells of the earth and of growing things became like a perfume. He could hear grains of soil crumbling and shifting, tumbled by the busy feet of ants. Magnetic, vitalizing currents streamed from the sun.

The wing *awoke.*

Then a slender, green, enameled head slid from a chink in the wall, and a flickering tongue lapped the milk and honey. As the snake stared up at Ardwin with black, jeweled eyes, its throat working as it took his offering, its cool thoughts came to him. He saw long tunnels and tall, wet grasses, and felt himself become swift and sharp as lightning before a storm. The bright, hot day seemed to cool too, and the glaringly bright skies seemed to darken and grow ozone-rich, as if the long-awaited rain was about to come. Then Ardwin knew he was ready.

"Good day," said Ardwin politely.

The snake lapped the water, milk, and honey, its throat rippling as it swallowed. "Good day," it answered courteously. "And thank you. It'sss good."

"I'm glad. Is there anything else I might bring you?"

The snake reflected. "Eggss," it quietly said. "Yesss. Eggss."

"I'll do that," said Ardwin. "Is it cooler underground, down in the dirt? It is broiling up here."

"Underground?" answered the snake. "In dirt? Isss that how you sssee it? My friend, I pity you. I live in a jeweled cassstle. Itsss roof isss like the night, full of gleaming bitsss, like ssstarsss. I have magnificent ssstairwaysss and corridorsss. It isss comfortable, never too hot or cold. Of courssse, when the sssnowsss come, the cold putsss me to sssleep, ssso I know little of winter. But it isss very beautiful where I live." The snake lifted its head and looked around. "Not ssso bright and glaring. Though thisss isss nicesss too," the snake added, looking at the green leaves hanging overhead. Then it returned to its dish.

"Would you mind if I brought friends to see you?"

"To sssee me?" The snake looked down along its shimmering green length to where its tail disappeared into a hole beneath the wall. It seemed pleased by what it saw, for its mouth curved in a shy smile. "Yesss," it said. "Bring them."

"Look," Ardwin said to Stephen and Skye.

"Oh!" exclaimed Skye when the smooth, green head emerged.

Stephen jumped back and fingered his dagger.

"No," cautioned Ardwin. "Relax. Watch. Wait."

They crouched beside the stone wall radiating its awful, midsummer heat. The sun blazed, beating down. There was not a cloud in the sky. The snake emerged and drew itself elegantly forth. It raised itself up, the long, slender body swaying gently. The black eyes regarded them solemnly, but glints of quiet humor shone in the depths.

"We have come, as I said," Ardwin said, and set down the dish.

"Welcome," said the snake.

Then it lowered its head and the flickering tongue quietly lapped the saucer.

"I feel cooler," whispered Skye.

Stephen whispered uneasily, "Me too."

"His presence is like that. It comes from his thoughts," whispered Ardwin. "I can't read his mind. But sometimes, when I'm near him, I catch glimpses of cool caverns, dark tunnels, long grasses, and deep water. And I find myself thinking about shedding all that is stale and old, and of renewal."

His friends shook their heads.

"I don't see anything except a snake," said Stephen.

"No," said Skye. "Me neither."

"We don't have a wing," said Stephen.

"You have good hearts," said Ardwin, "which is why I brought you. Is there anything you'd like to ask?"

"Who? The snake?" asked Stephen.

"Of course."

"Uh, no," said Stephen. "You, Skye?"

"No. It's just very . . . wonderful to . . . to see him close up like this."

The snake seemed pleased. It raised its head again, looked at her, and bowed ever so slightly. Skye was delighted.

"I never knew that snakes had such winning personalities," she said as they walked back to the garden entrance.

On the way, they passed Conrad idling on a bench near the herbs, toying with a dagger. He tossed it into the earth, drew it out, wiped the blade with a leaf, and threw it in again, point down. He smiled crookedly and said to them, "How *does* the world work? Bugs have many legs, people only two, and snakes none at all. Odd. Very odd. One must open things up, take off the skin, and see how they go. One must see how it all works."

Ardwin felt an undefined threat hanging in the air, but it was nothing he could name. He didn't fear Conrad, though, so he just shook his head and walked on. Skye said, "Idiot!" tossed her hair, and walked past too. But Stephen, glowering, stopped for a moment and said, "Someday we'll have to open *your* head and see how *it* works." The three friends left the garden.

The next afternoon when Ardwin returned with a dish for the snake lord, he cried, "No!" in horror, and dropped the bowl, which shattered on the stones. The corpse of the snake lay before him. It had been decapitated, its white, glistening belly slit open, and its organs torn free. Ants crawled over the dreadful ruin. The head had been set on a small shaved stake cut from an apple tree. More ants were dutifully crawling up and over it, in and out of the gaping mouth. Ardwin bent down and wiped the ants away. He dug a hole with his dagger, put the snake's body and head and the shattered bowl into the cool, dark ground, then covered it all. He thought of words that might comfort a snake. "Dark holes, green water, long grass, and cool nights. May you be renewed, and may all these be yours."

Then he went after Conrad. When he found him in the courtyard he threw down his cloak and, without a word, began to beat him with great buffeting blows of wing and fist. Conrad cried for help. But he bent down too, grabbed a stone, and even as he screamed, smashed it against Ardwin's face. Men dropped their blades, horseshoes, and hammers, women dropped their laundry and herbs, and all came running to pull the two apart. By then Conrad had drawn his knife and was shouting, "He attacked with no reason, like the animal he is! I don't care if he is the prince. I'll kill him!"

Ardwin strained against the arms that held him, trying only to break free and strike Conrad again. Blood poured from his nose and lip. Angrily he exclaimed, "You coward! You are lower than any beast! Animals don't stoop to murder!" Then they were dragged far apart and each sent off, surrounded by a protective knot of men and women.

Ardwin was furious with himself. "I should have understood the menace in his words," he told Stephen and Skye later, while Skye put ice on his swollen lip. "I should have known that Conrad was spying. I was careless. It is an error I will not make again."

Skye said, "Hold still, will you? And be reasonable, Ardwin. How could you have known what Conrad was planning? How could anyone?" Ardwin could tell she was very distressed and furious too.

Stephen was seated on a bench along the wall. Now he glowered and said, "I am going to take that nasty wretch apart, piece by piece."

Ardwin said, "Don't."

"And why not?"

"Because I claim that pleasure for myself."

When the king heard, he shook his head and said, "Ardwin, this has got to stop. You can't go around beating up a minister's son because he killed a snake. What of the slaughterer who kills the animals we eat as food? Would you beat him too? What of our huntsmen? What of the winter boar with the apple in its mouth and the old rooster we ate last night for dinner? I don't care if you don't like Conrad. He is a whiner, and mean-spirited to boot. I agree with you there. But no more of this."

Ardwin said he understood, and he would not do anything like that again.

One evening, under a sky riven with clouds, when he was riding along the lakeshore, he came upon three ragged boys attacking a swan. The two younger ones were about fifteen or so, and the third was more than his own age and big. The boys were laughing and hurling stones at the swan as she sat on her nest out on the water among the reeds. The swan held her neck out, long and low like a snake's, and she was hissing furiously. Ardwin could hear her screaming, *"Go away! Or just come closer! I'll kill you!"* She raised her great wings as if to strike a blow, but would not leave her nest. She was already bleeding from a score of cuts, and several pinions dangled from her wings.

Ardwin leaped from his horse at all three of the boys just as they turned at the sound of his approach. He was on them almost before they knew what hit them. They fell, but rose again angrily, cudgels in their fists, shouting and beating at him. He struck out fiercely in return, and two dropped back. Then his wing beat free of his enveloping cloak and he drew his dagger. They stared, wide-eyed, at this avenging, winged apparition with its bloody, mud-spattered face. "Prince Freak!" they cried, and ran off in terror lest they be punished, maybe even executed, for striking the prince.

Ardwin stood panting on the muddy shore and watched them go. He put up his dagger, lowered his wing, and stooped to the cold water. He washed the mud and blood from his face. Rising, he turned to the swan, who raised her long neck and watched him with black snake eyes. "Strange boy," she said, dipping her head gracefully, "I thank you. You have a swan warrior's strength."

He remembered the power of the swan warriors, and their ferocity against foes. Yes, that was part of him too.

Ardwin sat by the lakeshore. As darkness fell, the swan faded into the haze of evening. When the stars appeared, he finally rode away.

That winter was long and tedious. At first, Ardwin resisted the hunts. Hunting for food was, of course, necessary and honorable, especially when the prey was boar, for they were formidable and dangerous and had been known to attack woodsman and foresters unprovoked. There was merit in thinning their numbers. Although Ardwin knew he would hear and understand the boar's snarls, rants, and death screams, the boredom of the long winter and the promise of excitement drew him in the end.

The first hunt went well. It had been a clean kill, and he returned to the palace enthusiastic about the day's adventure.

He almost died on the second hunt.

When the boar charged at him he drove in his spear so fiercely that the blade passed through its heavily muscled shoulder. Squealing and grunting, spraying froth and blood, the maddened, red-eyed beast worked its way up the spear shaft screaming, *"Kill, kill, kill, kill, kill!"* while slicing at Ardwin with its yellow tusks. Ardwin had danced frantically away, desperately trying to stay at the spear's end, far from those wicked teeth. Then Stephen had leaped from his horse like a diver and cleaved the boar's head from its shoulders, just in time. The hunters drove off the frenzied hounds, lifted the head, hung the boar's body to a pole by its hooves, and praised their winged prince's strength and Stephen's courage.

Stephen and Ardwin celebrated that night with tankards of ale. Ardwin raised his mug and tipsily toasted Stephen, saying, "You are my brother forever! Nothing shall part us!"

Stephen answered, "Brother? Even though I was never a swan!"

"Even better," announced Ardwin, taking a long swallow, his words slurring. "A better brother!" He laughed. "Now say that fast!"

Stephen tried, and collapsed into helpless giggles. "I'll drink to that!" said Ardwin, and he did, finishing his ale and slamming the empty mug down on the table.

"Brilliant!" said Stephen, recovering from his fit and following suit.

"More!" called Ardwin. "More of the same!"

He woke in the morning happy, and with a splitting headache.

Ardwin's eldest brother, Bran, came on some business with their father not long after the second hunt. Elsbeth, Bran's wife, had stayed home, expecting their first child. But Bran arrived, restless as always, it seemed, and apparently relieved to be moving about instead of staying shut in, pacing and waiting.

Ardwin met his brother in the courtyard after Bran's conference with the king. Bran came jogging down the courtyard steps, light on his feet for such a big man, the broad leather belt he wore around his waist creaking like a saddle. Fang and Burrow, his curly-haired wolfhounds, came bounding hugely at his side. Tails wagging, they sniffed curiously at Ardwin's wing before settling patiently on their haunches.

"Little brother." Bran smiled and gripped Ardwin's arm, pulling the wing out, splaying the feathers. His hounds watched, their heads cocked to one side in surprise. He whistled admiringly. "My, but you've grown."

"And you," said Ardwin. "*Big* brother," he said, nodding at Bran's waist. "You've grown too." It was annoying to be patronized. He wasn't little any longer and he disliked being called so. Bran hardly seemed to notice.

Bran let the wing go. "Touché," he said. "Now, come inside and let's eat and talk. It has been too long."

After supper, they sat together, chairs drawn up before the fire. Ardwin looked into the flames and asked, "Do you ever think back to the *Time*?"

"'The *Time*'?" repeated Bran. "Just what '*time*' do you mean, little brother?"

"Why do you do that?" asked Ardwin, annoyed. "You know, when we were swans."

"Ah," Bran answered, looking at Ardwin. "Of course I think back to it. As if I could forget. And when I do, it still makes me furious! That witch's spell creeping over us like numbness, like drowning. First my toes disappeared, then my legs and arms, gone." He shuddered. "Then up it crept, taking my neck, my human tongue, my face. And there I was, neither bird nor boy, my mind flapping about like a creature caught in a snare, no longer itself, nor yet something else. *Ugh.* I'd be happy to forget forever — I wish I could. Thank goodness it gets more distant each day." He lifted his mug. "Cheers!" He took a long swallow.

Ardwin said, "It terrified me too at first. But there were things about it I . . . Don't you miss the flying?"

A log crumpled softly into the coals with a quiet *hiss.*

"No. Are you crazy?" exclaimed Bran, running a hand through his thick brown hair. He shook his head. "I don't miss it. I like it fine where I am, with both feet on the ground and Elsbeth by my side. I don't miss the rain and wind, the cold and dark. I don't miss those muddy shores and icy marshes and snow and hail. I don't miss the stink of rotting reeds and swan turds. I don't miss not being able to talk, or sing, or sit by a fire. I don't miss not being able to hold a sword or a cup or a wife. Why should I? It was a *curse.*"

"Yes, of course. But don't you miss . . . the *wildness*? Having wings? Feeling the ground drop away beneath your feet, and finding villages, castles, towns, forests, lakes, mountains, and seas spread below!" Ardwin closed his eyes, remembering. "Pine smell and ocean salt, marshland and forest. Smoke coiling up from a woodsman's fire, lofts of cloud and precipices of stars, the dark earth tugging below, and us, together, flying in that windy wildness so *free*! Don't you miss knowing what birds and animals say? Bran, I remember the flocks flying, thousands of swans filling the sky, our wings beating, our voices calling with the rest. I felt like I was inside some old saga, each of us a single word in the story. Don't you miss that at all?"

Bran thought about it, and he shrugged. "No, not really. I had to do it and I had no choice. And now it's done, thanks to Rose. Remember, I said to all of you, 'Rose will save us. She said she would and she will.' Every day I kept us together as a flo . . . as a group. Remember how I killed that fox that tried to grab you?" He looked at Ardwin, who nodded back. "I beat it with my win . . . my *arms,* and pecked it with driving blows of my bea . . . my *head,* till it was dead. That was the best thing that happened the entire time, that and Rose saving us. She did it, brave girl. I'm proud of her and eternally grateful. But no, absolutely not. I don't miss it at all."

Ardwin's face fell. "Not even when wild geese call and swans fly?"

Bran sighed and looked into the fire. He tapped his hand on his knee, then turned to Ardwin. *"No,"* he said. "I am glad to be free of it. Those horrid six years took my life from me. I should have been learning to be the next king of this realm, as Father planned. Now I have lost all interest in that. I have my own realm, which is where I'll stay. Let the past go, Ardwin. My only regret is that we didn't skewer that witch, Father's wife, the night we returned and had the chance. I have no yearning for those days, but I've got lots of anger, enough to share. Want some?" He raised his mug and took a long swallow.

Ardwin said, "Maybe I should envy you, Bran. I cannot forget, and I'm not sure I want to. Those memories of when we flew remain the best of times for me. That soar . . ." He never finished his thought. The wing unfolded and hit a cup, which fell over, spilling wine along the table before crashing to the floor. Ardwin muttered in disgust. "You see? It's like that. Especially indoors." He raised the wing, the draft from it making the fire flatten and flare like a living thing. In the semidark of the firelit room, the wing shone white, weird, and immensely out of place. "I still have *this,* but I cannot fly. I alone am still cursed."

"Cursed?" answered Bran smoothly. "Well, you're different, all right. That's true. Why belabor the obvious? It's time, little brother, you moved on. Maybe you're not as alone as you think. Maybe you need not be alone forever."

Ardwin did not respond. *What is he talking about?* he thought. Staring into the fire, he recalled a time, not many years back, when he had been standing in front of the mirror in his chambers. His tunic was off and he found himself staring at the place where the feathers ended and smooth skin began. It was very high up on the arm, just below the shoulder. Then he had lifted his dagger and, without drawing blood, had marked the almost invisible boundary between the human and the bird. He imagined cutting off the wing. He had fantasies after that of having a stump of a shoulder and upper arm, and of wearing his sleeve pinned back like a warrior who'd lost an arm in battle and was now honored in the feast hall for past glories. He could still remember the horrid, imagined wiggling of that awful little stump. And he remembered, too, as the cold edge of the blade pressed against his skin, how much he hated the wing, how much he wanted it gone. And he remembered what he had mouthed at himself in the mirror as he mimed that cutting. "Different," he had said. "You are ugly and different. You are not even human anymore, but a *thing*."

Now their conversation wound down. When Ardwin left, he thought only briefly of what Bran had said: "You need not be alone forever."

As the snow melted and early spring began, Ardwin and Stephen talked again about their journey and decided that they would go to Rose's castle in the borderlands, and then push on farther, into the wilderness of the swans. Ardwin knew he had to see it again. *I am tired of this life,* he'd thought. *I'll miss Skye, but I'll be back. I'll see her again. The world has grown too small for me here. It chafes and pinches. It's time for me to leave.*

Ardwin and his father were having an early supper in the small dining room when the king announced that Ulfius was sending emissaries. "They arrive this evening," he said. "We talk tomorrow."

"Ulfius? Really?" Ardwin said, looking up briefly. He'd heard dark, twisted tales of Ulfius: His queen was dead, and his little daughter had died strangely — abducted, it was said, by a lesser minister angry over some slight. The remains of the man's body had been found beside a northern roadway. Scraps of the girl's clothing lay nearby. She must have been no more than a single gulp for the wild beast that had torn her captor apart. Her mother, the queen, had taken to her bed and died soon after of a broken heart. A son-in-law too had died under odd circumstances. Now strange fires were said to glow in the turrets far into the night, and magicians, alchemists, wizards, and sorcerers, it was whispered, roamed the castle halls.

Emissaries from that realm might be interesting.

On the other hand, rumor had it that Ulfius had gone quite mad, his mind bent and twisted from grief and loss. It seemed likely, then, that bad decisions and dark — perhaps even evil — things would continue to happen there. So why was Father welcoming Ulfius's men?

Well, no matter. Ardwin returned to his dinner and to his plans to leave.

"Ar? Ardwin?" The king paused and put his spoon down. "Ardwin!" he repeated.

"Huh? Yes?" Ardwin answered, distracted. An image had come to his mind of the old sword hanging in the feast hall. It was solid and had seen many battles, having been forged for his grandfather, King Ealdor the Just. He could take it with him when he went north.

"Ulfius's emissaries. We greet them in the morning. You'll be there?" the king said. It was more an order than a question.

Ardwin grunted in reply, his mouth full of food, his mind still on the sword. He chewed and swallowed. Then he said, "Yes, I'll be there. But there's something I've been wanting to talk to you about. I'm thinking of traveling. I am old enough. It is time I was getting about. I want to go see Rose and Conor. And I'd like to have my grandfather's sword."

"That old relic? The one my father named . . . what? Orone, the Hunter? The scabbard is rotted and the blade rusted. Why would you want it?"

Ardwin remembered the heft of that heavy old sword in his small hand when he was a child. Holding it, he had felt the pride of his family, the House of Peredur. With his one arm it had been quite a challenge to lift that blade. Even the servants had complained as they took it down. Now, of course, he could swing it with ease.

"I used to play with it when I was young. I liked it. It was old and heavy and smelled of oil and rust even then."

"Really!" said the king. "I never knew. You *played* with it? Grown men have found that blade a challenge. You must have been determined."

Ardwin smiled. "It drew me. I felt it was already mine. I'll have a new scabbard made and the blade restored. Stephen and I have spoken about traveling together. I am weary of the castle, and that sword will remind me of home." (*When I am far away,* is what Ardwin thought. *No point yet in telling him just how far we plan to go.*)

"It's a heavy, old blade, but take it," nodded the king, pleased that Ardwin was thinking of his connection to the family. He twisted a silver ring around and around on his finger, looked up, and smiled. "Polish it. Have a new belt made. You'll need that." Contentedly he dipped a chunk of bread in his stew.

The old wolfhound, Titus, rose stiffly from beneath the table, stretched, then walked over till his great head was beneath the king's arm. Absentmindedly the king ate his bread, reached down, and scratched the beast behind one shaggy ear. The hound rested his huge gray head against the king's hand. The king chewed, scratched, and considered.

Then, "Yes. But a short trip, Ardwin," he said pleasantly. "Who knows what these emissaries are about, eh? Plans can change, just like that!" He snapped his fingers. "I have a feeling that decisions will need to be made soon," he added. "Certainly a bit of air, some traveling, a good way to clear your head and think about the future. I'll have a company of soldiers ride with you."

Ardwin flushed with anger.

The king noticed and said, "Or they can stay as far back as you like, within reason, of course. Forest ways are dark and treacherous. There are beasts, outlaws, and . . . worse. Believe me, I know," he went on.

"A company of soliders? I hardly think that's necessary," Ardwin said, trying to keep his voice calm.

"I disagree," answered the king. "Around Rose and Conor's lands begins the wild, barren country. Runaways hide there, dangerous men seeking refuge from the law. You will take a company of soldiers. There is no need to discuss this further."

"This is outrageous," exclaimed Ardwin angrily, rising from his seat. "Have you forgotten that I've already gone into your 'wild, barren country' when I was a child? I flew there as a swan. And what harm did I take from it? I have no idea what you are getting at with your talk of the future, but when I travel, I will go where and how I choose! You cannot stop me." He tossed his crumpled napkin onto the table like a gauntlet.

"Ardwin! Enough! Sit down. You will *not* go alone. You will listen to what I say. The emissaries —"

Ardwin laughed aloud. "The emissaries? What have they to do with me? They can wait. They can *rot*, for all I care!" He turned on his heel and left.

Ardwin climbed breathlessly to the top of the tower. The sun was setting and the sky alight. He sat on the turret wall and looked out over forests, the town, and farmlands below.

A carriage pulled by six white horses was coming along the road. Its gold leaf glinted in the last light of the western sky. Ulfius's men. What was this about? Something was going on. He could almost smell it.

The sun sank beneath the horizon as the carriage passed through the gate. Looking down, Ardwin couldn't help but notice that darkness and Ulfius's men had entered the castle together.

Emissaries

The emissaries of King Ulfius!" announced the herald. It was late morning, and light streamed into the great hall. "Lord Guilefort and Count Ringort."

Two men entered. The king sat upon his throne, his ministers and chamberlain beside him, the nobles ranged in rows down the length of the hall, now hung with banners of gold trimmed in scarlet. Ardwin stood among the nobles of first rank.

The emissaries wore burgundy-colored robes of velvet edged with weasel fur. Each also displayed a necklace of rubies. As they passed Ardwin, the taller of the two darted a sidelong glance his way. The man's upper lip curled in distaste. Ardwin stared back and thought, *And hello to you too, lackey of Ulfius.* The tall one's features smoothed as he and the other emissary proceeded to the dais and knelt before the throne.

"Majesty," said Lord Guilefort, rising to his feet. "We bring gifts from great King Ulfius, who sends his most noble greetings."

"We welcome the messengers of the noble King Ulfius," answered King Lugh.

"We have been authorized, Sire, by His Majesty, to speak with you on a matter of great importance, both personal and of state. May we meet, Majesty, to talk at length?"

"Dine with us this night. We shall hear all you would speak."

These two hold no further interest for me, Ardwin thought. He slipped from the hall.

The targets stood beneath the trees. Ardwin hurled a javelin from a long distance, at the edge of his range. It soared up, flexed at the top of its arc, dropped, and struck the target just to the right of dead center.

"Terrific throw!" called Stephen. There had been a break in the long ritual of speech-making and gift-giving, and he had taken his opportunity to leave. Ardwin waved and came to meet him. They sat down on a flat stone, side by side, their boots dangling in the grass. Stephen set the butt of his javelin in the dirt and twined an arm around it, leaning on the upright spear shaft.

"Did they reveal anything more of their purpose?" asked Ardwin, looking up at the sky and clouds.

"No," said Stephen. He yawned long and loud. "Anyway,

it's tonight, when they talk in the council chamber, that they will get down to business."

Ardwin swung himself off the stone and stretched out his wing. "Such a clear day," he said. "A perfect day to fly. I spoke with Father about visiting Rose and Conor. We argued. He wants a troop of soliders to come along, but I won't have it. And I still mean to push on farther to the swan bays."

"Well, I'm game. When do you want to leave? Father will probably want to kill me for attempting such a trip."

"Good!"

"What, that he'll want to kill me?"

"Of course! No, I'm just glad you'll come. We'll have to hunt for food, you know. Or I will, unless you have gained an eye. You're not bad, but . . . spears, not arrows. Bows won't survive the trip well. The cold and wet will slacken the strings and rot the wood." He looked at his friend. "Speaking of rot, let's see how good you've become. I know you've been practicing. Can you match my throw?"

"Make a wager," said Stephen. "Make it worth my while."

"Just match it. You know you can't."

Stephen laughed, spit into his palms, lifted his spear, and drew it back. He paused. "If I do, I go as I choose — on my own terms. Agreed?"

"Terms?" Ardwin looked at him quizzically. "What kind of terms? Bah, what does it matter? You won't match it. You never have! You can choose any terms you like."

"Fool!" said Stephen with a suddenly confident smile, "I have lulled you into complacency with my excellent ploy. I've just never had the proper motivation before." And he hurled his spear.

"So?" said the king. "Prince Bran has advised us that his visit to Lord Ulfius went well, and that we are all in agreement. An alliance between our realms would prove useful to both sides."

The king, his ministers, and the two emissaries sat in the Chamber of Council, a broad room with a large stone fireplace, in which a low fire now burned. A tapestry of gryphons, gyrfalcons, and forests in which knights rode at tourney hung behind the king's chair. Torches burned along the walls, and yellow beeswax candles lit the table. They had finished their meal of venison, hard cheese, herbed bread, honeyed pears, and heavy pudding, and the table, littered with soiled plates, empty wine bottles, greasy platters, nearly empty glasses, and dirty silverware, was being cleared.

Lord Guilefort now rose and faced the king. His yellow-white hair hung down, lank as straw; his smooth-shaven face was lined and serious. "Your Majesty," he said, "King Ulfius is, as you say, in complete accord, and bears you much friendship. Much."

King Lugh raised his eyebrows but said nothing. Something was coming. He could feel it, and he didn't think he was going to like it. He waited as servants finished clearing the table. Fresh candles were lit and more wine brought. At a sign from the king, the serving men departed.

"King Ulfius's daughter, Alisoun," continued Guilefort, "is young, beautiful, and recently widowed. A tragic accident." He lowered his head. Then he looked up and motioned to the second emissary, Count Ringort, a thin-necked, broad-chinned man with brown hair and beard flecked with gray. At the signal, the count rose, bowed, and lifted a small painting, not much bigger than his palm, from its jeweled case.

A velvet cloth of royal purple covered the painted panel. Pearls glistened in its golden frame. The king motioned. The count stepped closer, knelt, held the painting before the king, and removed the cloth.

It was a portrait of a young, smiling woman. Her hair was black, her lips red, her teeth white, small, and even. Her eyes were blue as a summer sky. Her skin was pale as cream, her neck long, elegant, and slender. Pearl earrings dangled from the lobes of her ears. She *was* beautiful. The king leaned forward. Yes. She will do.

"Alisoun, Your Majesty."

"The portrait — how recent is it?"

"A month, Sire."

"Is it a likeness?"

"As is a mirror, Majesty. It is she."

The plan was unfolding as he desired. "The dowry?"

"A great one, Your Majesty, as is only proper and fitting. But there is one . . . *condition.*"

The king stiffened. Ulfius was cunning and dangerous. King Lugh did not like conditions, and never had, but he especially did not like any that would be set by such a man as Ulfius. "Name it."

Count Ringort set the portrait on a stand before the king and returned to the cleared council table. A golden casket rested by his place. The smooth casket, some three feet long, eight inches high, and half a foot wide, was set with a dark red jewel in each corner. Other than that, it was quite plain, with neither inscription nor adornment of any kind. "Within this box lies an object of power created by our Lord Ulfius's most noted magician. This he offers to you. It is not the dowry. It is the *condition.*"

"No riddles," responded the king irritably. "State it in plain speech! The plainer, the better!"

Lord Guilefort nodded. Count Ringort came forward, carrying the golden casket, and knelt before the king. Then, slowly, dramatically, he lifted the lid.

The king leaned forward, and drew a breath.

Inside the box, set snugly in a close-fitting inner case of ruby-red silk, lay a golden arm. A left arm.

"Is that plain enough, Sire?" asked Lord Guilefort.

Awake

Ardwin awoke and lay tossing and turning in the dark. It was no use. He couldn't sleep. The flocks were flying. He could feel them overhead. Spring and fall were always the worst. The desire to be traveling and on the move was almost overpowering. He got up, put on his robe, and walked into the empty hallways. The torches had burned low, but he knew his way so intimately along these corridors, he could wander freely even in pitch-dark. He walked along, his wing out to the side, feathers brushing the wall, and let his feet carry him where they would.

He came as if by chance to the council chamber. He entered.

The room was cold. A chill breeze blew in the open window. A few coals glowed in the darkness like drops of blood. Ardwin bent to the fire and, with two quick strokes of his wing, blew it ablaze. He added kindling and then a small log, thick as his forearm.

The flames rose and danced along the log, which began to hiss with boiling sap. Ardwin turned and saw a gold casket on the table. Dark red jewels glittered at each of its corners. He went to it and ran his hand along the thing, feeling its surface. The lock was simple enough. Press, *here.* Lift, *so.* The catch snapped open with a soft *snick!* He raised the lid, which rose smoothly on oiled hinges. Within the box a golden arm gleamed — and *stirred.*

Ardwin stared in fascinated horror. Subtle gears whined. The fingers of the arm flexed softly, like a dreamer turning in sleep.

"What?" he exclaimed, instinctively stepping back. It was an artificial arm. Yet it moved. He looked again. It was an artificial *left* arm brought, no doubt, by the emissaries. He had already heard rumors of marriage, and gossip about some mysterious *condition.* She was said to be beautiful. A flame leaped in the fireplace — and in his mind! Suddenly he understood! A left arm for a beautiful wife; a left arm for an alliance and a kingdom; a left arm for a left wing.

Ardwin dropped the lid, sealing the arm in its casket. His wing rose in readiness for flight. *My father is going to betray me,* he thought. The certainty of his intuition was searing. He felt like a boar surrounded by hunters. Could he wait for morning to confront the king, or would that already be too late?

It was hard to breathe. The room seemed too small, too tight. He needed space.

He turned and headed down the dim corridors to the cavernous feast hall.

By the light of a last, dimly burning torch stub he dragged a chair beneath the mantel and stepped up onto the chair's arms. Then he leaped onto the mantel shelf, where, standing on tiptoe, with the wing splayed for balance against the wall, he lifted the heavy sword and rotted scabbard from their hook with his fingertips. A single bound and he was back on the chair. A step, and he stood again on the stone floor.

Gripping the Hunter, his grandfather's sword, Ardwin strode purposefully from the hall.

"Stephen," Ardwin whispered.

Stephen groggily opened his eyes. "Hunh?" he grunted. "Ardwin?"

"Shhhhhh," Ardwin said. "If you want to go north to the swans, meet me at the stable in half an hour's time."

"You're joking," Stephen muttered, and turned back over on his side, pulling the covers above his head.

"No. It must be now. I'll explain later. One half hour. Then, there or not, I ride." And Ardwin was gone.

The stables were dark. The horses stirred uneasily at the sound of someone moving about at this early hour, lifting saddle and bridle. They raised their heads and stamped restlessly. "Hush, hush now," Ardwin said, and went from stall to stall letting them smell his hair and wing, letting them breathe him in and hear his voice. He rubbed their necks and noses till they settled. Then he lifted the saddle onto Solo's back. Solo could be sluggish, but he was smart, trustworthy, and surefooted, if not the strongest. Ardwin would ride him.

He could hear soft, booted steps approaching swiftly. He flattened against the stall wall.

"Ard? Ardwin?"

"Here," he whispered back, relaxing now, speaking as loud as he dared. "By Solo."

Stephen entered the stall.

"You made it!" said Ardwin happily. "Come, saddle up. There's no time to lose."

"I . . . I brought," stammered Stephen uneasily. "I promised I would."

"Promised? What do you mean?" said Ardwin, turning toward him, mystified.

A cloaked figure stepped into the stall, then pushed back the traveling hood that concealed its features. Black hair, dark eyes, pale, round face, and firm chin. It was Skye.

"No!" exclaimed Ardwin. "We never said anything about Skye."

"You can speak directly to me, you know," said Skye. "I am standing right here."

"No!" he said, turning toward her. "You can't go! Is that better?"

"I've known of your plan all along, and Stephen promised. I want to go. Why shouldn't I?"

Stephen rubbed his chin uneasily. "I beat your spear toss, Ard," he said. "Remember? We had a bet. Maybe I should have said from the start what my terms were. But I —"

"I don't care," Ardwin said brusquely. Seeing Skye standing there, ready to ride with them, was suddenly unsettling. "Both of you can stay. I'll go alone. Skye makes it too complicated. I have to move fast and there will be all kinds of alarms and her presence will only make it worse. Just stay." He flung the saddle over Solo's back and began tightening the girth. Solo looked back at him, shook his mane, and stamped a hoof. He stamped again. Ardwin saw that he had been tightening the strap too tight, and loosened the belt a notch. Solo shook his mane once more and sniffed the air uneasily, nostrils distended, rolling his dark eyes at the three of them.

"Ard, you can't," said Stephen. "We've talked about this together. And . . . and you promised. We had an agreement."

"I . . . I take it back," Ardwin replied, agitated.

"Ard," said Skye quietly, "we won't let you go alone. If there's danger, let us share it. Please."

Ardwin leaned against Solo and slumped there, his face against the horse's side, breathing in the animal smell. The plan had been so simple: He and Stephen would ride to the north and have an adventure. Then the emissaries had arrived with the arm. Now this.

He lifted his head. "Fine. Saddle up. I'm leaving now and won't wait. If you're ready . . . fine."

They led the horses out with cloths tied over their hooves to muffle the sound, then walked for more than a mile — the less weight, the shallower the prints. Stars glittered. The wind moved the branches of the trees, and a night bird called. At Ardwin's suggestion, they cut and dragged leafy branches behind them, smoothing their tracks, then tossed the branches away, mounted up, and rode into the night. The wind was at their backs, pushing them the way they wanted to go — north. *Yes,* Ardwin remembered, *this is the way swans like to travel. A tailwind can make even the longest and riskiest flight possible.*

It was a good sign.

In the morning the nobles assembled. The ministers stood beside the king, who looked tired, but sat erect and composed. The closed casket lay on a low table beside the portrait, re-covered now and on its stand.

The emissaries entered, approached, and bowed.

"Your offer is generous," said the king, turning his signet ring back and forth on his finger. The emissaries, trained to recognize even unconscious signs of distress, discomfort, and so, of possible weakness, vulnerability, or lies, looked at each other. Guilefort raised his eyebrows, signaling to Ringort. Then they turned their attention back to the king. "We have summoned the prince," the king said, "for he must make the decision. But he is not in his quarters at . . . present. When he returns you shall have our answer. For now, you may take the arm and the portrait and retire to your chambers. The palace grounds and gardens are at your disposal. Our steward shall see to your needs. You are free to go."

The emissaries bowed once more, gathered their offerings, and withdrew.

Ardwin did not answer the king's summons that day, or the next, or the next several after that. As this was not so unusual, the king was not terribly concerned. Ardwin had a place in the woods he sometimes went off to alone, or with Stephen and Skye too, though they were getting too old for such foolishness. He was never gone more than four or five days, a week at most. Surely that's where he was now. When Ardwin returned, the king would sit him down and make him grasp the potential of the offer. There were so many good reasons to accept this *condition*, any one of which might do. *He will be free of his "curse," the kingdoms joined, Ulfius and his armies off my back, and Ardwin married to a beautiful young woman*, thought the king. *What's more, the emissaries said the arm is strong, stronger than any arm of flesh and bone. Wearing it, Ardwin would be able to do anything, maybe even better than a man with two normal arms. Why wouldn't the boy agree?* It all made sense, too much sense to ignore. The arm offered a perfect solution to everything.

On the fifth morning after the meeting with the emissaries, the king was sitting at breakfast over slabs of bacon, eggs, and a newly baked loaf. *Where is he?* he thought. *I have been patient long enough. This waiting is getting on my nerves.*

He called irritably to an attendant, "Go and see if the prince has returned. If so, tell him that I would have a word with him."

The attendant left. The king was wiping the grease from his plate with the last of the loaf, when the man reentered the small dining hall. "He is not in his room, Sire. His bed remains unused."

Outside the open window, wild geese were calling.

The king suddenly remembered his argument with Ardwin.

With a screech of wood on stone he pushed back his chair and hurried out of the room and along the corridor, then down the winding staircase to the great feast hall.

The big room was quiet, cool, and empty. No fire was lit. A chair stood alone, hugely out of place beneath the mantel, and the Hunter no longer hung in its usual place.

The king turned from the hall. His ministers had already warned that Ulfius was not one to take rejection well, and might use it to launch a long-threatened war. *Which may have been his plan all along,* thought the king as he marched back along the corridor. *Ulfius is cunning. He might have foreseen we would refuse the arm. Perhaps that is why he sent it in the first place, to give himself the rationale to strike. Well, the die is cast. I will send men after Ardwin. Maybe they can still find him and bring him back. For now I will gather my other sons for a council of war. Should Ulfius attack, we must be prepared. Then, once my messengers are gone, I will summon those two unctuous emissaries and see if I can buy more time.* The king shook his head. *Damn that boy! Why can't he be reasonable? Things were moving along so well. And now he has given me a very busy morning.*

Farewell, Prince Freak

Way to the north and east lay the borderlands; at their edge stood Rose and Conor's sturdy castle. Out beyond that were the lands the king considered so dangerous. Wild they might be, but there were swans there too, thousands of them. And up there too, there was little chance of being followed. North and west, then, from Rose and Conor's, would take Ardwin through the wild lands extending above Ulfius's realm, and on toward the high mountains and cold seas. Conor and Rose could not know yet of Father's scheme, so he would be safe for a time. But he would have to stay wary. Messengers might come, or Father might send men to entrap him. There was little reason to fear Ulfius, yet. A man like that, so drawn to power, would have little thought of the wastelands. Ardwin would be headed exactly where Ulfius was least likely to look. It would be Father's men he'd have to mislead. Once in the barrens, he'd be safe enough — at least from them.

They stopped at dawn to rest the horses and gather a few hours' sleep. The horses grazed while the three travelers slumbered, exhausted, on the ground. When they rose, they started a small fire, shared a few chunks of hard cheese, and divided a loaf that Ardwin carried in his saddlebag.

"All right, now tell us what happened. And what is the plan?" asked Stephen. He shivered. The morning was cold, and he sat close to the fire. He rubbed his hands together, then held them toward the flames.

"Some of this is conjecture," answered Ardwin, also putting his arm and wing toward the fire, "but I think I'm close to the truth. Ulfius's men brought a proposal of marriage for me. I heard there was some mysterious *condition* attached. Late last night I found an arm in the council room, very elegant and mechanical. Someone amazingly skilled had contrived it. It was a left arm. Chop off a wing, attach the arm, and marry into Ulfius's house. The kingdoms are joined, war averted, and I become what someone else chooses, wingless, but with two arms, of sorts."

"But I thought," ventured Skye, "that the wing . . . well, it *has* been a burden, is what I've heard you say. So maybe this would —"

Ardwin cut her off. "It's *my* burden," he said grimly, poking at the fire with a stick. "Mine. I give it up if *I* choose. It's no one else's to take. And there are things about the arm. Remember the snake? I *know* things because of it. Things I like to know. There are two sides."

Skye nodded. "I see," she said.

"As to the plan, it's simple. Both of you must go south. Stephen can ride Solo while I take Stephen's horse, Raven. The trackers can easily tell their hoofprints apart. If Father sends men after us, they will follow Stephen, thinking he's me."

"That's not what we agreed to at all!" Stephen exclaimed.

"Everything's different now," answered Ardwin, nodding at Skye. "There's no other way."

"We can't just leave you, Ard," said Skye.

"It's how things must be."

Skye and Stephen looked at each other. Then Stephen said, "Well, for now at least we remain companions."

"And I hope our ride together will last for a good long while yet," said Skye. "I want to see your sister. That's where we're going, isn't it?"

Ardwin nodded.

"Rose was an inspiration to me," continued Skye. "She was heroic. What courage! She saved all of you!"

"*All* of us?" Ardwin said. "*Really?*"

"She did her best, didn't she?" said Skye defensively.

Ardwin didn't answer, and there was an awkward silence. Finally he said, "Have I ever told you what happened when we came home?"

Skye shook her head.

"A cold, hard rain was pelting down that night. Father came into the courtyard holding a torch. I remember his hair was whipped by the wind and rain. When the door of the coach opened, I saw my father stare at Rose and the three babies. Then it was as if scales fell from his eyes — I could see the understanding and amazement dawning. He realized who we were. Five of the armed men were *his grown sons.* The woman was Rose Red, and the boy was his youngest. 'My children!' he exclaimed. *'Alive!'*"

"That sounds good to me," said Skye.

"Oh, yes," said Ardwin. "Very. Well, Rose introduced her husband and her children.

"'Come in. Come!' Father insisted.

"The horses were led away, and in we trooped. We swung off our wet cloaks and . . . there I was with my swan's wing."

"Ah," said Skye.

"It shook him deeply. I could see that. He said something like, 'So, what you said that day, Rose, about your brothers turning into swans, was true!' He looked like a man whose world was coming apart. 'But, why?' he asked. 'How?'

"'You are married?' Bran asked.

"'Of course,' he answered. Then Bran said that we'd not met his wife, and we wanted to. So Father summoned the queen. Meanwhile the serving men and women had come in with platters and trays and bowls and trenchers of food and with drink. Torches were lit, and the fire stoked up in the great fireplace. It all looked quite festive."

"I can imagine," said Stephen.

"Maybe you can," said Ardwin. "Maybe you can't. We had lived out in the wild for six years, except for those brief moments during the day when we became human, ate, and rested. Having a roof overhead against the rain and a fire against the cold was still a novelty. The older attendants remembered us as children and seemed happy to see us grown now and safely home. My brothers, all strong young men, had broad shoulders, which were admired by all. They liked that. If they still had their feathers, they would have preened. Everyone admired Rose Red's children too. But they stared at my wing."

"That must have been a lonely moment," said Skye.

"It's past now," said Ardwin. "I'm just telling an old story."

"Please go on," said Stephen.

"The best lies ahead. We had just begun eating when the beautiful, dark-haired queen, Evron, came down. When she saw us, she hissed. Rose stood up, pointed at her, and exclaimed, 'It is *she*!'

"Bran cried, 'Yes, it is!' and drew his sword and ran at her. We all ran. Father stood stunned and confused. Then he cried, 'Hold! Stop!' "

"He really had no idea?" asked Skye.

Ardwin shrugged. "He both knew and didn't know, in my opinion. Bran had grabbed Evron's arm by then, and had his sword at her throat. Evron seemed unfazed. She just looked at him, sneered, and said, 'Boy, you smell of goose down and feathers. You stink of the barnyard.' She had guts, I'll grant her that."

"Maybe she trusted her magic," said Stephen. "Maybe it wasn't guts."

"She had something," said Ardwin. "Whatever it was, it only made Bran more furious. He raised his sword to strike her down. Which is when I ran between them, crying, 'No, Bran! Don't!' "

"Why, Ard?" asked Stephen. "Would you really have minded if Bran had killed her? Conor's mother had already been burned as a witch. Why not destroy Evron too? Wouldn't that have ended it?"

Ardwin looked into the fire and shook his head. "Yes, she should have died, I suppose. Yet something made me stay Bran's hand. I look back to the child I was and I can see I knew it wasn't right. Maybe I hoped she'd take the wing away if she lived; that somehow she could be made to do it. Once she was dead, all my hope for a normal life was ended."

"I'm glad you stopped it," said Skye. "There had been enough sorrow, and enough killing. You were brave to step in like that."

"Thanks." Ardwin still looked into the flames. Then he looked at his friends. "Anyway, Father rushed over and knocked the sword from Bran's hand. Evron said, 'Your children? How nice. I will leave now.'

"'Oh, you will leave, all right!' Bran shouted. 'You'll leave, all right, you witch!'

"I think that's when Father really grasped it. *She* was the one who had bewitched us! Maybe he saw that she had bewitched him too. '*You!*' he cried. He raised his hand to strike her, then stood frozen, unable to move."

"Evron's magic?" asked Skye.

"I don't know. In any case, Evron looked at us: we swan boys still semiwild from our six years of storm and wing; Rose Red, the children, the two kings, the servants with their mouths agape. Her gaze rested on me. I can still see her mysterious, enigmatic smile. 'Birdwing,' she murmured, and curtsied ever so slightly. 'Ardwin Birdwing.' And so she named me. Then she turned and fled up the stairs. We all raced after her. She ran as she flew, up, up onto the roof, and out into the rain. A fistful of stars showed off to the north, where the clouds had momentarily parted. She cried a strange, wild, terrible cry. I will never forget it. It made my hair stand on end. Then down from the dark came a chariot drawn by black swans. She mounted the chariot and flew off into the night."

Ardwin was silent, remembering that cold night, the rain dripping down his neck, the taste of salt on his lip, and the name *Birdwing* clinging to him as tightly as a shirt of nettles.

Mazes

Far to the west and north, Ulfius's realm gaped like a mouth gnawing on the shoulder of King Lugh's lands. There, several months before Ardwin's precipitous flight, Belarius, the inventor, architect, wizard, and lore master, nodded his head and announced to no one at all, "Yes. This is good. It will do nicely."

The old man lifted his torch, which flattened and gave off a dark, oily smoke in the faint, dank breeze. There was a smell of rock dust and clay that made his tongue dry, and he coughed from deep in his lungs. The torch shook. His high forehead, beaked nose, and white hair and beard gleamed in the torchlight; the silver stars embroidered on his dark blue robe glittered. He wiped his dry lips and waited till his coughing fit eased and passed. The rock dust always did that to him, but soon it would settle. He patted the rock wall with a thin, blue-veined hand. Not a seam showed. For all he, or anyone, could tell, he was actually deep underground. Even the air was damp and cool. That was the beauty of it — it felt utterly real. All the cunning twists and turns baffled even him, though he himself had designed this intricate maze. Crazy old Ulfius had challenged him, and once again he, Belarius, had risen to the challenge. There was not a task that wily old madman had set, not one, that he not been able to complete.

Belarius began to roll up the ball of string he held in his hand, enjoying the reassuring feel of the waxed cord running smoothly through his fingers. Ulfius had asked for a dungeon from which no one could escape. And now he had it. It didn't need locks and bars. Once inside, no one would ever exit from it unless the prisoner had a ball of cord to unroll when he entered and to roll up again and follow in order to leave. Simplicity itself.

Belarius stifled a cough. His footsteps echoed as if he really walked deep underground.

Ulfius paid him well, was a patron of his genius, gave him gold, lavish quarters, and rare materials with which to fashion oddities and delights.

And so he'd made other marvels: boats that churned through water without sail or oar; machines, at least models of them, that flew, or might fly, someday, if he could find or create materials light enough to build them; arrows and immense spears with insect brains, which could be directed to their targets. All splendid! Brilliant! Spectacular! The disappearing cloak had worked well too, except for a slight . . . problem, but that had not been his fault, not his fault at all. The unbeatable sword he had wrapped in chains and locked securely away for the time being. Maybe someday he would work more on it. Or maybe he would melt it down forever.

Belarius sighed. He made wondrous things. That was his job. He couldn't control how they might be used. Ulfius's son-in-law had insisted on taking the cloak to spy on others, but his deceit cut both ways. The cloak worked well, as it was meant to. Ulfius had been galloping furiously on his warhorse when suddenly there stood the prince, the cloak gripped in his hand, terror written large on his face. He screamed and turned to run, but it was too late. Ulfius couldn't stop. The fool had waited too long to reveal himself and was trampled into the dust. Now Alisoun, that pretty thing, was a widow. Still, the cloak had worked! That was what was important. That's what he had to remember.

Belarius's hands trembled, making the torch shake and the shadows dance. *Bah,* he said to himself. *Just do your work and worry less. You were born to dream and create! Let others deal with the consequences!*

For he had more ideas, ideas yet untried, that even now were seething up out of his brain. Belarius continued on through the corridors of his dungeon maze, planning, dreaming, building.

In his mind, his latest idea — machine men — took form. It had all started with an arm, one single arm. Ulfius had asked for it, and he had made it. It had worked perfectly too. Now he would build a man, maybe more than one. He would give Ulfius an army of undying iron soldiers. He had Ulfius eating out of his hand, paying him gold to create the very devices bubbling away in his brain, paying him to make his — Belarius's — own dreams real! He smiled, thinking gleefully of the challenges that lay ahead. *That's what draws me,* he thought, suddenly feeling spry as a boy. *Give me materials and give me a challenge and farewell to lonely old age, and farewell too to the past and its mistakes and to . . . and to . . . to all of it. Hang grief and rage and hang mad, old Ulfius too!*

Belarius stopped and stood, puzzled, in the darkness. The torch flared and guttered in the dank, cool breeze. He raised it up and peered forward.

Someone or something had cut the string. The wound-up ball was in his hand, but the cord he had been reeling in and following was gone. He had come quite literally to the end of the line. Beyond him stretched darkness, coiled and empty, blank and signless, and nothing more. There was no way out. It was just as he had designed it to be. He was trapped.

"You're close," came the voice. Then came the high-pitched laughter, maniacal and chilling. "Just a few feet more and you'll be free." The taunting voice almost sang out that last *"and you'll be free."* "Don't you see it yet?"

"Ulfius," said Belarius. "No, I can't see the exit. Show me."

"Show you? Oh, no. That would be no fun. You must find your own way. But I do see a refinement gleaned from observing you, my friend. We must have buckets or spigots for water. Then we could douse any torches on command. Imagine how good it will be if we could add total darkness. You'll do it, yes?"

"Really," said Belarius, trying to hide his irritation. "This has gone far enough. Where's the string?"

"Here," said Ulfius from his hidden vantage. Something whisked through the air; Belarius heard it whisper, saw a faint gleam, and felt the light, spider touch of a length of string dangling over his hand. If Ulfius had tossed it, he could not be more than a few paces away. But where? Belarius held the string and followed it forward, peering here, searching there. All he saw were rock walls and rock floor and a low ceiling of rock. He followed the string at an angle, turned, and now, perpendicular to his previous line of travel, found a slit. He followed the string again, angled himself through, and . . .

And stepped out onto the hillside, where he stood blinking in sunlight under a blue sky, on green grass, the torch still burning in his hand. Ulfius was sitting on a large, smooth, dark stone that had been carved or smoothed further in its center to form a kind of seat, like a natural throne. His big warhorse stood cropping the grass nearby.

"Welcome," exclaimed Ulfius, cheerfully scratching his short, white, unruly beard and looking like a satisfied ghost. He was pale and bony, with blue watery eyes, a gleaming skull showing through thinning hair, and an underslung jaw that gave him an odd, snaggletoothed, crocodilian look. "You made it! How well our maze works! I had to see, you understand. Forgive me. If you, the builder, could not exit, who ever will? I am delighted. A bonus will be added to your hoard."

Sourly Belarius dipped the now unneeded torch, snuffing it in the dirt. Behind him, the rock outer wall of the maze loomed up, ten feet high, twining and twisting along the hillside. He nodded. "It works well. I am . . . pleased. No one can escape. I guarantee it."

"No," said Ulfius. "*I* do. *I* guarantee it. Till now all I had was your word. Now I have *proof.* Come, let us dine and celebrate." He climbed down from the rock. "Peacocks' tongues in honey, sautéed goose livers, boar's flesh in blackberry wine — your favorite, I believe — and broiled salmon too. I know how you like that. And I'll have my own special dish, ribs and brains. Perhaps we can visit the maze again, soon, you and I, together. While we eat, you can tell me what new plans you have been working on. Your mind, my dear wizard, is never asleep. You are always cooking up new masterpieces. Tell me your dreams, and I will make them real. Between us," he added darkly, "we shall remake the world."

Flight

Belarius had once again drunk too much blackberry wine. His head felt heavy, his tongue thick. "More, have more. Drink!" Ulfius had said, handing him the decanter and lifting the goblets. So Belarius drank and, for a time, forgot the mad whirling of his magical mind, the churning of ever-more fantastic ideas, and the pain of the past. He drank and drank. When he awoke, deep in the night, he opened his notebook. He began to fill more pages with delicate, spidery-fine drawings and perfect text, all written backward and upside down so no one would easily decipher his secret revelations and plans.

Now he stood up from his desk, staggered, stumbled, and settled himself gingerly back onto the cushioned chair. His head was still too heavy, his legs still too rubbery and weak. Uneasy, he leaned back, rubbed his face, closed his eyes, and remembered the feeling of being trapped in his own maze and how intensely he had disliked it. But there was something else. All at once he sat straight up: *Ulfius is not eating out of my hand,* he thought, startled. *Instead, Ulfius has* me*! He can confine me in my own maze now, almost anytime he wants. In exchange for crusts of bread and cups of water, I'd have to turn over my brilliant ideas or die. I will be the prisoner of my own ingenuity!*

Belarius did not like what he saw. If his wonderful son, Padraic, still lived, he would have seen through the whole nasty game immediately. "Father," he would have said, "he uses you. He takes your genius and makes it play in the mire. You must leave." And Padraic would have been right. He always was.

Belarius was suddenly wide awake, all dullness gone. Swiftly he began to gather his precious drawings, his charts, models, and instruments. When he had them in a great heap, he looked fondly at these children of his genius. Then he began to smash all his delicate models of flying machines, towers, telescopes, submersibles, machine men, all the pretty things he might have built with Ulfius's unwavering patronage. "Visit the maze again together, is it?" he exclaimed. "Cut my string, will you? Never again! You shall not have them! You shall not have *me*!"

Belarius used his hands to wrench and twist and tear. He lifted heavy, leather-bound, arcane volumes of alchemical lore and used them to smash the various scattered pieces before him to fragments, the fragments to shards, the shards to bits, the bits to powder and dust. When he was done, he stood back and admired his latest creation — *chaos*! Then he leaned over the heavy oaken table and swept the remaining charts to the floor. And he groaned. That had been foolish! It only made more work. Now he would have to bend down and pick them up before he could rip them to pieces.

As he did that, he laughed aloud to think of how furious old Ulfius was going to be. And then he thought of what Ulfius would do when he found out. *I have gold*, he thought. *And I still have my notebooks filled with ideas, drawings, and designs. I will load a few horses with the instruments and the books I need and leave before Ulfius can shut me in, before my magical things can be taken or Ulfius's trap be sprung.*

By the morning, he was gone.

Roses Are Very Red

The three friends traveled by forest roads ever northward toward Rose and Conor's castle. Tall trees stood on either side; the sound of their horses' hoofbeats echoed into the silent woods.

"Four, five days, maybe a week, is my guess," said Stephen to Ardwin. "My father and yours shouldn't expect us back before then. We've gone off before, for even longer than that. But they're likely to start searching by then if they have no word, especially with Skye along. What of your parents, Skye?"

"They will think, 'Never again,'" she answered with a laugh. "They'll want to tie me up until I'm . . . wed, and not let me out till then. They'll fret and moan and fuss. Mother will wring her hands, pace back and forth, and cry, 'Her future! Her future!' Father will go to the king, demanding that he send men to bring me back. Which is exactly why I had to come."

"Will it be any better when you return?" asked Stephen. "Won't they bind you all the tighter?"

She shrugged. "Maybe. My hope is that when I return in one piece, healthy and well, they will see they can trust me. And they'll give me greater freedom."

"Good luck!" Ardwin said, laughing.

"What? Do I detect doubt from our winged prince?" said Skye.

"Doubt, disbelief, incredulity. Still, one never knows."

"No," said Stephen. "One never does. What I mean is, *I* don't. I don't ever know until something actually happens. Until that point, it's *all* possibility."

"That's right," said Ardwin. "Which is why we have to come up with plans that cover enough possibilities to work."

"Have we?" asked Skye.

"I don't know," admitted Ardwin. "We'll see."

"My point exactly," said Stephen triumphantly.

They rode for ten days through dark forests, the occasional small town, and across icy-cold, swift-running rivers. They ate lightly of their supplies, mostly cheese and bread, refilling their saddlebags in the few towns they came upon. They hunted for rabbits, partridge, and pheasants too, and fished when they could. Another ten days would bring them within sight of Rose and Conor's castle. Despite the threat of horsemen galloping after, there were no signs yet that they'd been followed. *So far,* Ardwin thought, *the plan seemed to be working.*

One night, they camped beneath the stars in a little clearing off the roadway. Dark pines rose up, and their fire illuminated the reddish, resinous trunks. Ardwin rested his head on his saddle. His grandfather's old, rusted sword stood upright in its worn scabbard, leaning against a stump and within easy reach. The horses were staked beyond the fire's glow, cropping the grass. Ardwin was lost in thought.

The problem was Skye. He admired the way she defended Rose, even though he didn't completely agree with her, and there was something about the way Skye spoke about feeling trapped at home that made him think they had something important in common. He liked Skye, and that's why everything had become complicated. But he was reluctant to talk about it. He had lived cloaked so long, he did not know how to reveal his heart.

Now, in the back of his mind, an idea was forming, shadowy and exciting. Suppose Stephen went off *alone* on Solo. Then Ardwin and Skye could go to the swans. That was what he really wanted.

Maybe there was some way he could make it happen.

After nearly three weeks of traveling, the only hardship being some days of heavy rain, the travelers came at last to the gate of Conor and Rose's castle.

"Shall we let this wandering rogue and his dangerous-looking companions in?" asked Conor, peering with mock suspicion down over the wall, from where the gatekeeper had summoned him. Conor was of medium height and handsome, with a thin, rugged face. There were lines around his blue eyes and firm jaw and mouth, from laughter and from looking directly into bitter winds. With his tangled red hair he might have been born a Peredur. Now he turned to his young son, who stood beside him. "What do you think, Harry?"

"Yes, yes! See the wing, Father! It's Uncle Ardwin! Hello, Uncle Ardwin!" called the boy excitedly, standing on tiptoe and waving.

Ardwin waved his wing back in greeting. The gate was raised, and the three companions rode within. The castle was very well fortified, with a spare, almost military feeling about it, and without the noisy commercial bustle of so many walled towns farther south. Ardwin liked it. It suited his mood. There was an air of vigilance about the place, and with good reason: Robbers and outlaws could spring out to attack the unprotected. Ardwin suddenly wondered if he was walking into a trap. What if his father had sent messengers ahead?

What if his men were already waiting to lay hands on him and bring him back? *It's not that I don't trust Rose or Conor,* he thought. *We just have unresolved . . . problems, Rose and I. Who knows how things will turn out? As Stephen said, till it happens, can you really know?*

The men who took their horses seemed cordial enough. Then Victor was jumping at him, and Conor clasped his hand, and Rose Red and Harry ran out, and Annie was hugging him, and Skye and Stephen were introduced and welcomed. The cool, disciplined castle atmosphere warmed considerably. It felt light and joyous and very much like home. Actually it was better than home.

"And so, you want to see swans?" asked Conor that night at dinner, raising a slice of roast on his knife.

"That's right," said Ardwin, looking at Stephen and Skye. "I've wanted to go for years. Stephen and I planned it. It's the right time, and Skye . . . well, it worked for her too. She *had* to come along."

Rose smiled. "Adventurous girl."

"You know," Skye said shyly, looking at Rose, "you made such an impression on me when I was young. You were bold and brave and went through so many terrible hardships." She glanced at Ardwin, who avoided her eyes. "You saved your brothers. I wanted to be just like you."

Rose blushed. "Bold? Brave? Please! Father didn't believe

me, so there I was, alone with what I had seen. I had to do *something*, didn't I? But it was a close thing. Too close." She smiled wanly at Skye, wiped her brow with her napkin, then took a long swallow of wine. "Be brave, be bold, my dear, but do not be *too* bold. Do not go looking for trouble. It has a way of finding you on its own, soon enough. More wine, anyone?" she asked, changing the subject.

"Yes, I'd like some," Ardwin said.

Stephen said, "You are being modest, Rose. You persevered despite the terror. Father says that you are a staunch, courageous family, and he is proud to be an adviser to the king."

Rose laughed a short, rueful laugh. "Ah. First bold and brave, now staunch and courageous. How wonderful! And what do you say to that, dear brother?"

Ardwin's laugh was shorter and harsher. He tried to make his words pleasant, but his voice had an edge he could not conceal. "I say that Stephen's father is a noble soul, Stephen is a good egg, and all's well with the world."

"Exactly," said Conor, nodding and taking a long swallow of his wine, so that the raised goblet hid his face. When he put his cup down, he said, also easily and graciously, "All families have their . . . sorrows and . . . problems. But we must learn to do our best and go on despite these things. Try to see the good and stop the bad when you can, eh?"

Rose put her hand on Conor's arm and smiled at him. He covered her hand with his own, and raised his cup again. "To seeing the good and stopping the bad!" he toasted.

They raised their cups and drank to that.

Conor is a good man, Ardwin thought as he set down his empty cup. After all, Conor's mother was the queen who had been burned at the stake for stealing her own grandchildren, while accusing Rose of having murdered them. When the truth was revealed, Conor agreed to the fiery punishment. It could not have been easy. *Young as I was that day,* Ardwin recalled, *I could see the pain clearly on his face. Yet he did what justice demanded. What price did he pay? What price do people pay for their integrity?* Ardwin immediately answered his own question. *A lot,* he thought. *It is always hard-won.*

"Annie and Harry and Vic love having you here, you know. You are almost an older brother to them," said Rose Red as she and Ardwin walked in the orchard a few days later.

Three swans flew overhead. Rose Red followed his gaze. "They draw you?"

"They do. But these last days have helped me forget. That, dear sister, is a testament to what you have here, and to what you — all of you — are."

The children came running between the rows of apple trees. Harry, slender, dark-eyed, with his parents' reddish hair, was in the lead. Victor, broader in build, more like Bran, but fair-haired and energetic, was a close second. Annie, slender like Harry, yet with hair of gold, was skipping at a quick pace. The boys circled, whooping, but it was Annie who leaped boldly onto Ardwin's back. With his arm to one side and his wing to the other, he raced her off among the trees, crying, "Look down, Princess! Look down! From way up here, horses seem tiny as ants!"

She giggled and screamed delightedly, "Those *are* ants, silly!" She clung to his back, exclaiming, "We are so high, Uncle Ardwin!" And then the boys began shouting, "Me! Me too!" each of them also demanding a turn. Ardwin laughed. "You're too heavy!" But they insisted, and at last he sped them each around as well.

That night, with a fire glowing and the geese calling outside against the moon, Ardwin told a story.

"Now, Annie, Harry, Vic," he began.

"Vic*tor,*" called a childish, imperious voice.

"Ah, yes. Vic*tor*. There is a secret you should know."

"A secret?" repeated Annie, leaning in closer.

"What is it?" asked Harry.

"This secret is true of everyone you shall meet or see. Tradesman or serving man, seamstress or soldier, princess, prince, queen, or king, *everyone*, at one time or another, yearns to do something that's never been done. Like *fly*!"

"Oh, but you *can* fly, can't you, Uncle Ardwin?"

"I once could, Annie. All your uncles could. We can't now, not any longer."

"That's why you have a wing!" exclaimed Harry. "Because you could fly."

"Yes."

"That makes you special, Uncle Ardwin," exclaimed Victor proudly. "It makes you better than anyone, better than our other uncles. You still have your wing, but they lost theirs."

"Thank you, Victor. Not better, though — just . . . different. To go on: Long ago there was a man who wished he could fly. In the fall and spring, when the swans flew over the mountains, he said, 'I can do that!'

"Then he lifted his elbows, flapped his arms, and jumped. All that ever happened was that he fell down, bumped his nose, and bruised his knees." Ardwin mimed it, and the children laughed and giggled. "But he wasn't the kind of person to give up. Instead he got up, brushed himself off, straightened himself out, looked up again, and said, 'If I just work hard, I will do it!' And once again, he tried to fly.

"This went on for years. In time he was bumped and bruised, I can tell you. Still, he persisted. One day he suddenly caught the knack of it, the way a baby learns to walk. He flapped his arms, lifted off the ground, and flew away over the mountains with the wild swans.

"The people watched him flying back and forth every spring and fall. 'Look!' they'd say. 'There he goes!'

"One day he flew away, and was never seen again. He had become a swan himself, and could no longer be distinguished from all the other wild swans he flew with."

Victor jumped up and began to race around the room, arms outstretched, making a flying shadow on the walls. "I'm a swan!"

Harry said very seriously, "It's not true. He couldn't become a swan."

"He did," said Ardwin, just as seriously. "That's just what he became."

"Oh," said Harry. "Oh."

"Again!" cried Annie.

"Another time, maybe."

"Well done!" exclaimed Rose Red, clapping her hands. "Time for bed, everyone." Dutifully the children said their good nights and Rose and Conor led them off. Rose paused at the doorway. "Stay, would you, Ard?" she asked. "I'll be back soon."

Skye yawned ostentatiously, covered her mouth with her hand, and said, "Oh my, but I'm tired."

Stephen rubbed the back of his neck, yawned, and said, "Me too." They left together.

When Rose returned, Ardwin was standing at the window, gazing into the night. One of Rose's cats, a large gray-and-black tom, was rubbing against his ankle, its tail raised in the air. It marched around him like a miniature lion, with dignified, golden-eyed presence. Ardwin reached down and scratched behind its ear. The cat wandered away and leaped up on the window seat, where he curled up to watch the moon.

"Pouncy," said Rose happily, walking to where the cat lay gazing up into the night. "He was the tiniest kitten. Now just look at him! What a monster! Sir Pounce, we call him. And you're such a hard worker too, aren't you, you good cat." She stroked the cat's head and scratched under his chin. Pounce half closed his eyes and began to purr. "The mice are nearly gone from the castle. What would we do without you?"

Ardwin smiled. There was something about the cat, an *I-like-it-here, I-like-being-with-you, but-I-do-have-my-own-life* kind of attitude that Ardwin found refreshing. It radiated from Pounce, filling the room with wildness. He rarely felt anything like this around his father's dogs. It reminded him of his old, winged life. Then he remembered Harry's skepticism. "Harry is so serious," he said, watching Rose and Pounce.

Rose straightened and said, "He's a lot like you were at his age."

Pounce jumped down from the window seat and walked off to explore the darker corners of the room.

"Me?" said Ardwin, surprised. "I was the youngest! He's your eldest."

"Nothing to do with it," said Rose. "He's brave, sensitive, and serious. And while he's eldest, remember, I didn't see him for nearly two years. Victor, I lost for a year. Annie was only hidden from her birth until the hour of my execution."

"The forester's wife was kind, wasn't she?"

"Yes, she was," said Rose. "But they were not hers to be kind to. Nor were they the queen's."

"You mean Conor's mother."

"Yes — Her Royal Savage Devouring Madness," said Rose with bitter anger. "The Hag of Horror herself!"

"She's dead, Rose," said Ardwin, surprised at her sudden heat. "She's been dead these last seven, almost eight, years."

"Not dead enough. She haunts my dreams still. Two of a kind, they were, she and Evron, whom Father married. Both of them witches, both walking around without human hearts in their breasts. May they rot!" She rubbed her hands together as if they stung, or burned, then paced by the window in silence. "Come, sit here by me," she said at last, and settled herself on the window seat. She smiled and with one hand patted the place beside her.

"Meow," he said.

She laughed and brightened and patted the seat again. When he sat, she said, "Now, good Sir Pense — for that is what I shall name you in your cat guise because you think so much — I must tell you something."

"Meow," said Ardwin, making purring noises.

"All right," said Rose. "Have it your way. As I was putting the boys to bed, Harry said, 'I want to be like Uncle Ardwin.'

'You mean brave and kind and good at telling stories?' I asked. 'No,' he said. 'I want a wing.' And Victor chimed in, 'Me too!' "

"It is not a wish to encourage," said Ardwin, immediately dropping his friendly cat persona. "Don't."

"But why? Because of wings, you have seen the world whole, not in bits and pieces like the rest of us. It must be beautiful. You understand beasts and birds in their own secret tongues. What I wouldn't give —!"

Ardwin interrupted her. "Because of *a wing* I have been called freak and cripple and witch's spawn and devil's child," he said hotly. "People have hidden their eyes or spat between twisted fingers to ward off my curse. Because of a wing I have smashed cups and plates when I most wished to impress or to appear mature and dignified. I once started a fire reaching for bread and almost burned the castle down. In moments of excited conversation I have knocked friends in the teeth or nose, and almost taken out someone's eye. In case you haven't noticed, I have only one hand and a useless wing. . . ."

"All right. It's true. All that has been bad, maybe worse than bad. But you *flew*, while I remained terribly earthbound."

"Terribly?" he grunted. "Has it really been that bad?"

"Compared with you and the others, definitely. You soared while I stumbled, with burning, stinging hands. My children were stolen and where was I? Bound to a stake, unable to speak! Now I raise them here, on this solid ground, and of that I make no complaint. None at all," she added almost hastily. "Solid ground is a pleasant place, the right place to raise one's crops. Still . . ." She looked at him and, seeing his somber face, suddenly paused. "But how is all with you, Ard? How is everything at home?"

Ardwin was thinking about her odd envy of him. *She doesn't understand,* he thought. *Why should I reveal myself? She* failed *me!* Yet, he needed her for his plan to go off alone or with Skye to work. He would have to be skillful and wary.

"Your question covers a lot of ground," he answered evasively. "But if you must know, everything is . . . fine. Just fine. I wanted to see you and the children, and see swans again, and mountains, and the sea."

She sighed. "You have so many untried paths before you. You'll end up someplace different from any of us."

"I start out different! Or haven't you noticed?" he blurted. Already he was revealing too much.

"I didn't mean that."

He could feel some dam of restraint crumbling within. "I did! Can't you see what I am? I'm a cripple, a freak." He raised his wing. "Look! Will you finally just look and *see*!" The air swirled up in the wing's draft, making the flames leap in the fireplace. "With one wing I can't fly, and I can't live like others do. It's a no-man's-land I inhabit." He lowered the wing, making the fire sway and flare again. "Father wants me to marry, but I won't let him take it. He doesn't have the right! No one does."

"Take what?" exclaimed Rose, confused.

"Rose," he said, in a cold, strained voice, "can't you see that I am cursed? The *wing*! What else have I been talking about! He wants to take the wing and give me an arm of gold in its place, then have me marry Ulfius's daughter. I won't let him do it!"

Rose paled. She stood up and began pacing. She rubbed her hands together. "Cursed?" She stopped. "I . . . I tried to *save* you," she said, "all of you! Those wretched shirts! That is where the real curse lay, little brother! Not to be able to cry out when there was need, to speak the truth, or laugh or murmur words of comfort or love. Six bitter years! And all you still see is how *I* failed *you.* You are still young and selfish! Can you even begin to imagine what I risked for you? What of my children? What of my failure as a mother?"

She began pacing again and rubbing her hands. Then again she stopped.

"To remain silent when my babes were stolen, maybe killed, or see you all, whom I had vowed to save, lost forever. That was my choice. I made it, and still I wonder why. Skye thinks I was bold and brave. But I am also Father's daughter, too proud, driven, or simply willful to turn back with any task undone. When the fire drew close, I still knit, even as beyond the flames I saw the gleaming teeth and red lips of my monstrous mother-in-law. I saw Conor's terror too, for me, for the loss of our children. But my mind was ablaze, flame-hardened to a point, charred and stern. I was thinking only, *Just a bit more. I can do it. The task is nearly done. Hurry! Hurry! Finish the last shirt, the littlest. Finish the left sleeve, and save them all!*

"I am Rose-All-Too-Red, marked by blood and flames. See!" She held her hands out to him. There were patches of skin rubbed bloody and raw.

"My hands bled then too. I was about to be lit red by flames." She sat down, breathing hard, one hand at her heart, the other clenched in a fist. "And the last little shirt, the left sleeve —" She couldn't finish. Her voice choked off, and she burst into tears.

Ardwin was stunned by her outburst, and his own anger stuck in his throat. He managed to say, "We saw the torch being set to the wood. In a minute *all* the shirts would have gone up in flames. We could not wait. Six years came down to one instant too few."

They sat watching the fire in silence together, listening to its crackling, remembering other flames, Rose still rubbing her hands. Spots of blood appeared on her knuckles and fingertips. She wiped her eyes and left red streaks across her brow and cheeks.

Ardwin drew a cloth from his pocket and wiped away her tears and the streaks of blood. "Shhhh," he said almost brusquely, for the enormity of what he could not say now burned like a fire in his chest: *You should have spoken and saved your children. I would have been happy as a swan.* "All right, all right," he said. "Yes, you were innocent."

Rose Red turned on him angrily. "Innocent? I wish I were! I was blameless of the crime, but *innocent*? Hardly."

Ardwin was startled. "What do you mean?"

"I *chose* to keep my vow of silence. I chose my brothers over my children!" Rose shivered and began rubbing her hands again.

This was too much for Ardwin. He stood up swiftly, stepping back from her. The wing was unfolding in fury, tossing back its covering cloak. If he stood too close, and it lashed out on its own, he might break her neck. He gritted his teeth, holding down the wing with sheer will. Using all the energy that might have gone into a blow, he exclaimed loudly, "So, it's *I* who don't see? What do *you* see if you can't see *this*?" The wing flashed out, white and stark between them. "All you had to do was finish my shirt! Why did you save the others and fail *me*?" It burst out of him, sudden and savage. He gulped for air and turned away, and looked from the window into the darkness and saw nothing to hold to, nothing to guide him. He had said it, and it was raw and small and petty and stupid as ever. But it was out in the open at last.

And then from somewhere, perhaps from the wing itself, words arose, and he turned to her again and surprised himself completely by revealing them too. "And yet, I loved the swan life," he admitted quietly, and all the anger seemed to rush from him. "I . . . I relished the gifts the wing gave me. When I was young and alone at night, and it rustled and moved, I did not hate it, but loved it, ugly and strange and odd and crippled as it made me. I loved its stiff, silky feel and its wild, oily smell, and the memories of flying and of blue water and endless white mountains and animal voices that lived among its feathers."

They looked at each other, exhausted, like two fighters who, circling each other, find themselves evenly matched.

"Only later," he said, "as I grew older and more alone, did I come to hate it." The wing folded again, and he was calm, as if he had flown a great distance and come to safe harbor. He could feel the feathers settling into place down to the tip of the great flight feathers, the veins and barbs connecting and smoothing as if he preened. The storm had blown away.

He sat down and said, "And if we hadn't been turned into swans, you would never have met Conor."

"And then . . . ?"

"No Harry, Victor, or Annie. We're all of us strangely tied together in this. It's beyond me — beyond all of us, maybe."

"Yes," she said. She sighed and shook her head. "The children are the balm and they are the blessing. But the darkness still whispers that some things should not be risked."

They sat again in silence, no longer alone, each taking comfort from the presence of the other.

Then, because she was a queen and knew the arts of statecraft, having been bred to the office, she took a deep breath and said, "Now, what is this of Father and the wing?"

"Ah, so we come back to that, do we?" He paused, then explained to her fully about the arm and Ulfius, and the odd proposal of marriage. Ardwin said, "I wouldn't have had much hope for Father's long-term health. There are slow-acting poisons that work invisibly. Ulfius could easily kill him and claim both realms."

Rose thought for a moment, then said, "Yet by your refusal, you might cast us into war."

"Exactly."

She pursed her lips. "Father is not easily frightened. War would not be his first choice, but he will fight if he has to. He always has."

He looked at her appraisingly and nodded.

She said, "Ard, why not stay here for a time? There are things we have only touched on. Maybe we could work them out."

"I'm glad I came and that we spoke. I think that that is enough for now," he answered. "I don't want to force you and Conor to take a stand against Father, against our brothers too, who owe him allegiance. If Ulfius seeks war, you will need to stand together. I had been meaning to leave the castle and Father, anyway. My childhood home was the sky, Rose. I lived in it. I can't return to it, but I can travel beneath it. Tomorrow or the next day, I will go."

"What will you do?" she asked practically, more like a mother than a sister. "If you go to the swans, well and good. But you can't just stay there. What would you eat? How long could Stephen and Skye stay in that barren waste? You are not a swan anymore."

"I . . . we will take supplies. And I won't stay long, at most maybe a few weeks. As to where I will go afterward, I don't know. Maybe the time has truly come for me to give up the wing and be a man, a crippled man, but one who will do what's right for the kingdom. An alliance with Ulfius might save lives. I am not as stupid or selfish as I appear."

"All right," said Rose. "I understand. But know this — for Harry, Annie, and Victor you are splendid, just as you are. To them, your wing is a mark of wonder. No, don't shrug it off. Children see truly." She paused, looking down. "Oh, look!" she exclaimed, and pointed.

Pounce was walking proudly from the darkness, a mouse dangling from his jaws. The mouse gave a single high-pitched, pitiful *squeak!*

"Help!" is what Ardwin heard. He jumped up, the wing instinctively raised in sympathy for the desperate plight of the terrified little creature. He yelled, "Drop it, Pounce!" and

ran at the startled cat, waving his wing. Shocked, Pounce dropped the mouse, then raced off and hid beneath a chair.

Ardwin went to where Pounce was hidden, lowered the wing, and spoke quietly. After a moment, Pounce came out and looked up oddly at Ardwin, then looked around for his mouse, but it was gone. Ardwin knelt down and began stroking and calming the big cat. Pounce rolled over in a friendly way, exposing his belly, then suddenly grabbed Ardwin's hand with needled paws, gave it a quick, hard bite, and ran off.

"All right. We're even," said Ardwin. He grimaced and shook his hand, flinging off a few drops of blood.

"Are you all right? He can be rough."

"Just a scratch. I'll live."

"So will the mouse," sighed Rose. "And all its countless progeny."

The Truth

"What is it?" asked Conor. "Are you all right?"

Stephen too swiveled in his saddle to look at Ardwin.

They had been riding across a meadow and were nearing the forest's edge, when Ardwin had suddenly stiffened and groaned, his face pasty white.

"This way," he gasped, and rode into the forest beneath the trees, Conor and Stephen following, mystified.

They found the fox in a snare, its hindquarters and spine crushed beneath a great stone. The fox looked up at them with yellow cat-eyes and snarled feebly. With each in-breath, its belly was sucked up horribly, almost to its backbone, and its ribs showed like a skeleton's.

Ardwin dismounted. The fox growled and panted. Ardwin nodded, saying, "Yes. Yes, I will," and drew the Hunter from its sheath. Conor's armorer had restored, sharpened, and polished the blade, and made a new scabbard for it. Now the old, once-rusted blade gleamed. "I wish your story had a better ending," Ardwin said quietly. Then he whispered to his sword, "Be merciful," raised it, and did as the fox asked.

They dug a hole for the slight, mangled body, then rolled the large stone, the one that had killed it, onto the grave mound. Conor stood up, wiped his hands on his cloak, then swung himself back up in the saddle. "So you still understand animals. I heard all of you could do that, once."

Ardwin got back up in the saddle too, leaned forward, and patted Solo's neck. "Most people can, with an animal they know and love. Sometimes for me, though, it just happens, especially with wild creatures."

"I have enough trouble understanding other people," Stephen said with a grin.

Ardwin nodded. "I find it hard enough understanding myself."

"There's the truth," said Conor.

That night Conor found Ardwin walking along the rampart, looking out over the darkened lands and forest below. The moon was high, silvering the trees.

Conor said, "There you are. Listen, Ardwin, I have men — rangers, hunters, craftsmen, merchants, and such — who watch for me, and report. They serve as my eyes and ears."

"Yes?"

"One has just brought news that riders are headed our way. They are still several days off, but are riding hard, and they wear your father's livery. I thought you might want to know before they arrived."

"I appreciate that. Thanks." Ardwin paused. Then he said, "I have a favor to ask."

"I thought you might. Ask away."

"Tell them, when they arrive, Conor, that Stephen planned to circle north alone before returning, but that Skye and I took the long, southern road together. Tell them that that's what you understood of our plans. I've been meaning to talk to Rose about this, but now . . . would you tell her?"

"Of course," Conor said. He rubbed his chin thoughtfully. "Skye and you, together, eh?" he repeated, with a little smile.

Ardwin felt himself blushing. "It's not what you think."

"Well, we'll tell them whatever you want, don't worry. And we'll keep our mouths shut too, about whatever it is we may know that you *don't* want us to say. But, listen, Ardwin, just so you know, that northern route that 'Stephen' is going to take . . ."

"What about it?"

"It can be rough and dangerous. Sudden storms, real blizzards, can spring up there and trap a man and horse in a very short time. There are dangerous creatures living in those wilds, things you won't see elsewhere. And odd people sometimes take refuge in that wilderness." He paused. "Strange things and strange people. I'm not a worrywart, but do let 'Stephen' know."

Ardwin smiled. "Thanks, Conor. I will tell him. Thanks for everything. I'm saying as little as possible so you won't have to lie straight out, all right? I just hope that you and Rose won't get caught in my battle," he added.

Conor put a strong, sinewy hand on Ardwin's winged shoulder and said, "Don't worry. We've faced bitter things together before. We'll manage."

Looking into his brother-in-law's honest face, Ardwin relaxed. "Good."

Clouds were covering the moon, and the wind was coming up, making the trees down below toss and sway. There was moisture in the air too, the smell of rain. Thunder growled and rumbled, and there was the faint flash of lightning.

"I'd better go down before the storm hits," said Ardwin. "I have to find Stephen — the real one — and Skye, and give them the news."

When Ardwin found Stephen and Skye, they were sitting on a bench under a stone arch beside the rose garden, out of the pouring rain.

"We must leave tomorrow," he said. "Conor says there are men on our trail."

"We're ready. We've been waiting," Stephen said, and Skye nodded.

Ardwin said, "I just hope we haven't waited too long."

Nothing but the Truth

The next morning Ardwin was seated restlessly on Solo in the courtyard. He was anxious to be on his way. The rain had stopped before dawn, and the sky was clear. The air felt fresh, newly washed, and clean.

Stephen was on Raven, his great black horse, and Skye sat easily on Thornbush, her bold little mare. The horses were loaded with supplies: dried meats, breads, hard cheeses — all of which would keep well. Annie was teary-eyed, and held Rose's hand tightly.

Harry said, "I want to go with Uncle Ardwin." He had a wooden sword tied to his waist and a cloak over his shoulders.

"You can't, Harry. Not this time. Maybe another," said Conor.

Harry drew his cloak more tightly around himself and turned away, looking up at the sky.

Victor crossed his arms and said angrily, "I don't want Uncle Ardwin to go!"

"Victor!" said Rose.

"I don't!" he added, kicking a stone.

Conor nodded. A soldier came forward and handed Ardwin a long, narrow package wrapped in linen.

"What's this?" Ardwin asked.

"Open it."

It was a spear with a fluted head, and spiral designs engraved on the faces of the blade. Ardwin hefted the spear. It fit his hand and the weight was right. "Conor, thank you!"

"Annie, would you take this to Uncle Ardwin?" From behind her back, Rose brought forth a squat, squarish package.

Annie took it, holding it carefully before her. "Here, Uncle Ardwin. It's a . . ."

"A cake!" laughed the boys, dancing crazily around. "A cake!"

"A cake?" said Ardwin. "Hmmm." He began to smile, and for a moment, his impatience to be going vanished. "Let's see." He dismounted and took the package. "Hmmm. Feels" — he shook the cloth-wrapped package — "not cakelike, anyway."

"Open it," said Annie.

"Open it!" exclaimed the boys.

Ardwin nodded and unwrapped the gift. It was a light, sturdy, leather helmet with iron bands running from the point of the crown to the rim. In the front, the iron rim narrowed, crossed over itself, and bent upward, making a small raised V like two thin horns or wings.

He held it up, admiring it. "You're right!" he exclaimed. "It *is* a cake!"

The children screamed rapturously at this stupidity. "NO! It's not a cake! It's a helmet! Put it on!"

Ardwin set it on his shoulder.

"NO!" they screamed. "On your head!"

"Oh," said Ardwin, laughing despite himself. He put the helmet on, and it fit very well.

"Thank you for this bounty," he said to Rose, and he bowed graciously.

As he bowed, Rose draped a beautiful, thick, dark blue cloak over his back. "A last gift. In case it gets cold on . . . on the southern road."

"Travel well, brother-in-law," said Conor. "Be strong. Be safe."

Ardwin nodded.

"And now," said Rose as an attendant came forward, "road gifts for Stephen and Skye, as well." They were each given warm cloaks too.

Rose raised her arms and said, "A traveler's blessing on you all: May your road be smooth, your skies clear, your winds fair, and true companions always at your side." She turned to her brother. "A special blessing, Chieftain, on *your* road." She dabbed at her eyes and smiled. "You look grand, you know."

If he could have seen himself at that moment he would have known that it was true. The new spear, the helmet on his head, the blue cloak across his shoulders, and the white wing ruffling in the breeze made him a sight out of some old legend come to life, a broad-shouldered, winged youth ready for any adventure.

He remounted Solo, who raised a front leg and pawed impatiently at the stones. When Ardwin said good-bye, the children began to cry. "Wait," he said, and dismounted again. He pulled three feathers from his wing and knelt before the children. To each he gave a feather, saying solemnly, "Hold to this as a keepsake between us, Princess and Chieftains." He saluted them, mounted up, waved his wing, and rode away. Stephen and Skye called out their farewells, waving and riding with him.

The three camped that night in the woods off from the road. Skye sat cross-legged, watching the flames. Stephen crouched forward, twirling a stick, burning the tip till it burst aflame, then blowing it out so it glowed in the darkness. There was the smell of wood smoke and pines. The air was cool and a wind gusted, making the fire crouch down, then flame up. Ardwin cleared his throat and said, "I don't know if we are followed. But . . ."

Stephen tossed the stick into the fire, watched it burn, and said, "Would your father really bring you back as a prisoner against your will? Would he take your wing by force?"

Skye lifted her head and tossed her hair back. "Ard, it's hard to imagine he would be so cruel. He's never actually betrayed you, has he?"

"All those years we were gone, he never believed we were swans," Ardwin said. "Rose went off alone because he would have brought her back to our stepmother, Evron."

"Yes, but he *meant* no harm. It wasn't deliberate."

"It was a failure," said Ardwin. "We . . . I lost faith. He was supposed to be our protector. He was all we had, yet when danger threatened — one brought to us *by* and *through* him — he hid us away rather than face the truth of his marriage to a witch. It was not enough. I will not chance it again."

Skye turned to Ardwin. "This is not the adventure I dreamed of," she said. "I do not know when I . . . when *we* will see you again. Do you realize that?" She shook her head unhappily.

Ardwin took a breath. *She cares about me!* Still, he was afraid to come out and speak his secret plan. It was too embarrassingly obvious. He'd be asking Skye to go off with him. *They'll see right through me,* he thought. *They'll see what I really want.*

What he said was, "The wing is pulling me. I *want* to do

this. I've wanted to go for so long." He could almost taste the happiness that lay ahead.

"We could go with you," insisted Skye. "They'll never find us there."

Speak, fool! Here's your chance. Say, "Why don't you come with me, Skye, and Stephen on Solo could be our decoy and lead them away. What a great idea!" But the words stuck in his throat. He shook his head. "No," he said. "No. If Father is sending men, they'd track us easily. My mind is made up, so don't make this any harder. I will miss you both."

He paused and looked up. His friends' faces were fading into the darkness. He set a short log among the coals then fanned it aflame with a few strong sweeps of his wing. The fire flared quite suddenly and Ardwin swiftly turned away, his face burning from the intense and sudden heat. "OW!" Stephen and Skye both yelled. The flames died down again. There was a rank smell. The three friends looked at one another, rubbed their eyebrows, and burst into laughter. Each of them, brightly lit by the now glowing fire, could see that all their eyebrows and some of their hair, too, had been singed. Ardwin even had a few charred feathers.

Ardwin blushed. "Oops," he said. "Overdid it. Sorry."

Skye leaned over and kissed Ardwin's cheek. "Travel safely," she said. "I will think of you. And now I have a remembrance." She touched her singed eyebrows. "Mementos."

Ardwin said huskily, "Thanks, both of you." He lay back

from the fire where it was darker, not wanting to be seen, feeling that spot on his cheek where Skye's lips had touched him.

He awoke deep in the night. The stars shimmered; the trees bent and rustled in the breeze. He rose quietly so as not to disturb the others, put another log on the coals, fanned it softly aflame, then looked around. Where were Stephen and Skye? He didn't even see their blankets. Odd. He walked softly away from the fire. Farther off among the trees he saw a mound. He went closer.

And found Stephen and Skye asleep beneath one blanket, their naked shoulders exposed, wrapped in each other's arms.

Mad Ulfius

Ulfius sat on his throne, a small table set before him. He reached forward, lifted a rib from a silver plate, and gnawed it, then tossed the bone to the floor. Two hounds leaped up and began to fight over it. Ulfius tossed another bone, hitting one of the hounds on the flank. With a yelp the dog dropped its tail between its legs and scurried to the far side of the hall.

"So, the freak is gone, eh?" he said.

Lord Guilefort licked his lips and nodded. "Yes, Sire," he answered. "We stayed for several weeks, but he never returned. So we took the arm and left. Lugh insists that the boy will be back and that then the terms of marriage will be accepted." He shrugged. "He may have been telling the truth or just bargaining for time. In any case he wanted us to leave the arm. But Count Ringort and I felt you would want the arm until such time as we had proof of their intentions."

"And commitment," added Ringort.

"Good. Good," nodded Ulfius, wiping his greasy fingers on his filthy robe. "You may go."

"Sire," said the two emissaries, as if with one voice. Then they bowed smoothly and withdrew.

"Captain!" called Ulfius when the courtiers had left.

"Yes, Your Majesty."

"Take a few men skilled with a bow — just a few — trail the winged monstrosity, and kill him. Do you understand?"

The captain's eye twitched and a vein pulsed in his neck. "Yes, Sire," said the captain. "As you command."

"Of course as I command," smiled Ulfius. "Am I not king? Is my word not law? Are not all things to go as *I* wish? And, Captain, when you kill him, bring me the wing, with a bit of shoulder attached. I want to know that the job has been properly done."

The captain bowed, turned, and left. The mad king hardly noticed. He was watching a fly settle on his plate. The fly washed its face. Then it rose, circled, and landed on the last uneaten rib. Ulfius's eyes narrowed. He raised his hand and, with a swift and cunning blow, mashed the fly and flicked it away. He laughed to his hounds and said, "No one denies me. Whoever opposes me, pays. Now I will have war. My foes will be ground into the dirt and I'll take what I want." He lifted the rib and ate. Then he tossed the bone and watched his hounds fight all over again.

Late in the night Ulfius awoke and cried aloud, "Light! Bring light!" His men came running, torches lit. Ulfius cried hoarsely, "Go to my throne room! Find a dead fly. Bury it with full honors. Once it lived — now it is dead."

When his astonished men left, Ulfius lay in his bed, tears streaming down his cheeks.

Of Spears and Toast

Raven was big, much bigger than Solo. Ardwin felt high up riding him, high up and distant from everything, especially the past. Stephen and Skye should have had the decency to wait. Well, from now on they could do what they wanted. *As long as they lead the trackers away, what difference is it to me, whatever they do?* he thought. *I am free of attachments and deceptions. Free of Father and his fears and schemes. Free of Rose and her guilt! Free of Skye and Stephen and their betrayal! Free of it all, at last!*

Yes. Before him lay only happiness! No more human tangles and lies to trap him. He would be among swans, and they would understand him. They knew what was important. They knew about water, wind, and skies. This was not like before. He was finally going where he chose. At last.

So why this knot in his chest, and why this weight pressing

on his shoulders? *It will pass,* he told himself. *And the good news is that the wing seems to be waking up the farther north I go.* Indeed, over the last several miles it had almost begun pulling him forward, as if it remembered the trees, the rocks, the scents, and very breezes of this place. Soon he would forget all about Stephen and Skye. All he had to do was keep going.

When he was back among the swans, everything would be all right. He would be home. Some of them might even remember him. He'd show the wing openly, and find acceptance at last. The wing and its intuitions would be wide-awake there. He'd build a shelter and stay for a while, living on fish, seaweed, and seal meat as he sorted things out. He would grow strong and fit and be very happy. Everything was going to be just fine.

It was early morning, and a chill wind blew. The fire was dead, but a thin coil of smoke rose from the ashes. Stephen opened his eyes to the gray day. "Skye," he murmured. A crow called. Skye rolled to him, smiled, then gave a little gasp.

"What? What is it?"

She pointed over his shoulder behind him. "Look."

Stephen looked. Solo and Thornbush were tied where they'd left them. But his own horse, great black Raven, was gone.

"We should have told him," Stephen said. "He always

thought he was so good at hiding his feelings, but I knew how he felt about you."

"We should have waited. A few more days, whatever it took." Skye sighed. "He must have felt so angry, so . . . betrayed to just ride off like that. But he must know too that we love him. I hope he does."

"He was going to go, anyway. His mind was set. You know how he is. Now we have to do what we can to protect him," said Stephen.

"Yes," she agreed. "We'll do everything we can." She looked at Stephen, and she smiled. "And who would I rather ride a long and difficult road beside, than you?"

"No one, I hope," said Stephen, and kissed her. "The time has come to earn our pay."

They had a quick meal, then broke camp, saddled Solo and Thornbush, and started south.

The western sky was aflame and darkness was gathering among the trees when Ardwin came to an old, ramshackle, two-story inn. Swallows darted in and out from under the dark, green, ivy-covered eaves. It had been a long day. It was time for rest and food.

The wooden sign creaking over the door proclaimed that this was THE RACK. Underlining the inn's name was the gilded image of a spear. Ardwin's stomach rumbled. He hadn't eaten all day. In part, he'd been trying to make his meager supplies last as long as possible. Then again, he hadn't had much of an appetite till now.

He tied Raven to the hitching post, patted the horse's neck, and entered the inn, carrying his spear and saddlebags.

"Spears on the rack," said the innkeeper, a short, round, red-complexioned, balding man, hardly glancing up from the ledger spread on the counter before him.

"What?"

"Swords, daggers, and such are all right," said the innkeeper, looking up now and pointing to a wooden spear rack of dark, well-oiled wood that hung on the wall nearby. "But spears go on the rack. They're not to be taken to the rooms. We had a nasty accident once. Several years back, you understand. And ever since, I always insist, with no exceptions, 'spears on the rack.' You'll get it back safe and sound when you leave. Haven't lost a spear yet. They all get their own back when they want it. Isn't that right?" he asked a stout woman who went bustling past into the tavern room, a tray laden with jugs of ale balanced on her strong arms.

"That's right, dear," she answered as she moved swiftly past. "Safe and sound as babes in a nursery. That's how you are with your spears. Quite *rotund* about them. Quite *combustible*."

"You see," said the innkeeper with a toothy smile. "Spears on the rack. And no need to tip the establishment. It's a service of the house." He bowed graciously to Ardwin.

Ardwin gave him the spear.

"Nice," said the innkeeper, taking it. "Well made. Of the highest quality. Excellent balance," he added, hefting it in his hand. "And I do like the contouring of the head and blades. Good forging too." He tapped the head with an expert finger and put his ear to the metal. "Has a *ring* to it," he said, looking up at Ardwin with a smile on his face. "A kind of metallurgical *splendor.* Conor's livery? With some personal touches?"

"You're right," nodded Ardwin, impressed. "How did you know?"

"It's nothing," said the innkeeper. "I have a way with spears. They speak to me, if you will. I can tell where they're from, sometimes where they've been, and sometimes even" — and now he leaned in close to Ardwin — "sometimes I can almost tell where they're going. I like spears. Always have. Ever since I was a little boy. And this one is a beauty. So it's the place of honor for her."

He put Ardwin's spear on the topmost rung of the rack.

Then Ardwin asked, "What did your wife, if that was indeed she, mean by *rotund* and *combustible*? I have never heard those words used in quite that way before."

"Oh, it was she all right," said the innkeeper with a grin. Then he leaned in close to him again and very conspiratorially admitted, "As to her meaning, lad, I have no idea at all. She likes words, and likes to use them. But often her sense of them seems to shoot right past me, if you know what I mean." He winked.

"Ah." Ardwin nodded. "Yes. I see. Well, for now I'd like a room and dinner and breakfast in the morning, if you please."

"Very good, sir. A pleasure meeting a spearman of your caliber. Sign in the registry, if you will. My name is Bluestone, Samuel Bluestone, at your service. And you are . . . ?"

"Ardwin . . . Birdwing, at yours."

"Birdwing? Birdwing?" repeated Mr. Bluestone, as if searching through stacks of ledgers his mind. "Hmmm. I don't remember hearing such a name in these parts before. Unusual. 'Birdwing.' And you are from . . . ?"

"The south."

"How very fitting and birdlike, if you get my drift. South to north. North to south. Migrations and all. Ah, well. Excuse my poor sense of humor. A pleasure to meet you, Mr. Birdwing. Welcome to our humble inn. Leonore's and mine."

"Meet Mr. Birdwing, my dear," he called to his wife, who now rushed through, moving in the opposite direction from her first foray, carrying a tray of empty jugs. "How very *daring* to meet you!" she called. "How very *figurative* and *mellow*!" And then she was gone again.

"Now let me have my helper show you to your room. Actually," added Mr. Bluestone, scratching his nose ruefully, "I don't have a helper at this exact time, if the truth be known, which it now is. So, if you don't mind, you'll just have to help yourself. Go up these stairs and down the hallway to the sixth room on the left. Nice and quiet it is, with a view of the mountains."

"Thank you, Mr. Bluestone. It sounds perfect." Ardwin shouldered his saddlebags and headed up the stairs and down the hall to his room. Inside there was a little wooden table, sturdy and simple, and a bed of similarly practical design. A woolen throw rug with stripes of reddish brown, cream, and blue lay on the stone floor. There was a small fireplace and a stack of firewood beside it. Several iron candlesticks, with half-burned beeswax candles in them, stood on the shelf over the fireplace. The walls had been freshly plastered and white-washed. Tan curtains of rough cloth covered the windows, and when Ardwin pulled them back and looked out through the leaded glass panes, he could make out, in the gathering evening, a rocky stream below. And there before him, far to the north, stood immense snowcapped mountains gleaming in the last light of day. It *was* perfect.

When Ardwin entered the crowded, low-ceilinged tavern after taking Raven to the stable and making sure the horse had fresh water and grain, he found the noise almost deafening. The clatter of silverware, the sounds of voices in conversation, the calls for beer and ale, and the tumult of pewter mugs and plates banging down onto wooden tabletops was like an assault. Mrs. Bluestone was hurrying in and out with trays of beer and ale and an occasional plate of food, calling out, "Here it is, almost *taciturn,* if I do say so myself!" Or, "Just try the venison. So *pernicious* that it is *awful*! And the ale, why, it's *awful,* too!"

Her pronouncements were a mystery, although no one seemed to notice. But Ardwin thought he almost had the sense of the last. If you substituted *delicious* for *pernicious,* and *awesome* for *awful,* it all worked. He nodded politely and said, "Hmm. Yes. Venison, please. Pernicious. And a pint of the awful ale, of course."

The crowd was drinking and talking and laughing, and he kept his cloak draped and pinned over his wing so that he blended in easily enough, enjoying the local atmosphere and the strange relief of being where no one knew him, his wing, or his story.

Soon Mrs. Bluestone rushed back like a perspiring whirlwind, and dropped a tankard of ale before him. *Bang!* Beside it she set a plate loaded with venison and roast potatoes. Ardwin's mouth watered and his stomach grumbled at the sight of the full plate before him.

"Eat hearty, lad!" she cried as she whisked away. "It's *terrible*!"

By that he assumed she meant *terrific* and so he took a sip of ale and it *was* terrific. Encouraged, he sliced off a piece of the roast venison and stuffed it into his mouth and nearly gagged. She was right. It *was* awful! It was salty as the sea and so doused with pepper that his eyes watered at once and he began to sneeze uncontrollably. He took a great gulp of the thoroughly admirable ale to wash it down and sat eyeing his plate in dismay. Gingerly, he tried the potatoes. But they too had been so salted that his throat nearly closed and he gulped for air like a drowning man. He took another great gulp of ale.

"Isn't it *abominable*!" cried Mrs. Bluestone as she whirled past with more ale for the next table. "My favorite meal. Venison and potatoes. Most people don't use enough salt. That's the secret of success. Use salt, I say! And plenty of it! Then your venison and potatoes will be properly *terrorized*!" By that, he thought she might mean *tenderized*. But *terrorized* was closer to the truth. So he just nodded and smiled in agreement and croaked from between dry lips, "More ale, please! Two tankards!"

And wiping the venison on his napkin to remove, at least, some of its crust of salt, he floated it in his mouth on a sea of ale.

As he tried to eat he noticed three men drinking at a table in a nearby corner. Their clothes were various shades of dusty gray and green. Though the inn was noisy and their voices were low and raspy as if they were dusty, too, he caught words like *tracking, spy, money,* and *king* in their mutterings. He made sure that his wing was covered. He put so much attention on their raspy talk that he hardly noticed what he ate. He shoveled food into his mouth, grimacing at the horrid saltiness, gulping ale to wash it down, trying to look like he was not listening, but straining to hear anything that might suggest they were following him. He ate and listened, but still could not be sure.

Mrs. Bluestone was quite pleased when she returned to his table. "All *groan*! My word!" she exclaimed. "Why, you are a terrible *marble*!"

"Marble?" he croaked hoarsely, his mouth and lips puckered, his throat parched by the terrible saltiness. His stomach had begun to ache.

"Truly *marbleous*! You have *divined* the whole platter. Good for you!"

"Ah, yes," he croaked again. "Divined. Marbleous."

"Would the young gentleman like more?"

He shook his head swiftly, desperately. "Ale," he whispered, his throat closing with the effort. "More ale."

While Mrs. Bluestone took the plates away, the three dusty men rose and left.

At breakfast Ardwin looked around carefully, but there was no sign of the men from dinner. Though he was relieved, he decided he would leave immediately after eating. No point in taking chances. He ordered a meal of oatmeal, toast, and bacon — it seemed the safest of his breakfast choices. When the oatmeal came it was heavily salted, burnt, and crusted; the bacon was nearly black, and shattered at the first bite. He settled for toast with butter. "Lots of butter, please, Mrs. Bluestone," he added. "Hmmm. Excellent," he exclaimed, chewing, when it came. "More toast, please! And more butter!" He ate until he was full.

Ardwin went to retrieve his spear. As he paid his bill, Mr. Bluestone leaned over the counter, looked around as if to confirm that no one stood nearby, and said, "She's an awful cook. We all know it, but no one has the heart to tell her. Nice customers, we have. And the beer and ale are both very good, thank goodness. Should have warned you. Took a bit off the bill by way of compensation. She insists on being the cook. Loves it. Says it's highly *regurgitable.*" He shook his head.

"So true!" Ardwin said, keeping a straight face. "I do appreciate that very much, Mr. Bluestone."

"Ah, well," added Mr. Bluestone. "It's not every day we get company like this. We'll miss her." He reached up and gently took the spear down from the rack. "She's a real lady. Highest quality. It was an honor to board her with the local riffraff. Wait," he said slowly, mysteriously, as he held the spear in his hand, extending it to Ardwin. He stopped and stood perfectly still. A tremor went through his body. His eyelids drooped and closed.

Suddenly he yelled, "Damned spies! Let him go!" He swung the spear fiercely back and forth as if fighting invisible foes. Ardwin ducked beneath the flashing blade. "Blood!" the entranced Bluestone whispered dramatically, eerily. "Dark blood, white snow, and teeth! The wizard!" Then he moaned, "Winds and buffeting wings! Blood, claws, and beaks! Oh, oh, *Her.* Yes, yes." He grew quiet, stood still, the spear still gripped in his hand, his eyes still closed. Then he murmured, "Blood and *it* and *Her.* No, not just *Her.* Not just the *Ever One,* but another — and *wings.*"

Very slowly Mr. Bluestone opened his eyes and stood blinking as if dazed by the light of day. He seemed to be trying to get his bearings. Sweat beaded on his brow. He looked down at his arm, the spear extended in the fist at the end of it, and seemed confused. He let his arm drop to his side, and blushed. "Oh, I'm afraid I . . . Did I say something? I . . . It's like a dream, it comes on so. Did I . . . ? Are you all right, sir?"

Ardwin stood up from behind Mr. Bluestone's counter, where he had been crouching in safety.

"Pay it no mind, please," begged Mr. Bluestone, looking all around, embarrassed and relieved to see no other guests present. "It was one of my fits. I hope I said nothing displeasing or disturbing?"

Ardwin stammered, "I don't know. I . . . but what did you see?"

"I . . . I can't remember!" exclaimed Mr. Bluestone in dismay, wiping his brow with his apron and handing Ardwin the spear. "I can never recall. It's all a blur. Snow, I think . . . blood?

Someone. Something. A bird? Oh, I'm sorry. It's no use. It is gone."

"Well," said Ardwin, looking at his spear now in his own hand. "It was a bit of a shock."

"My apologies," said Mr. Bluestone. "Come back again, sir, and I'll set it right. Free ale for as long as you stay. I meant no harm, and hopefully no harm was given. Please do return. And bring her again, do. That's a well-bred spear, if you get my drift. And she's going places. Samuel Bluestone, and that's me, can almost always tell."

"Thank you, Mr. Bluestone. Very . . . reassuring, no doubt," said Ardwin without much conviction. Then he said, "Right now what I could use are supplies. Could I purchase some from you? That would be a help. Bread, dried meat, cheese, apples too, if you have any."

"Yes, yes, of course," answered Mr. Bluestone, seemingly happy to be of some use and to leave his spear prophesying behind. "Come. We'll set you up with all you need. On the house," he added generously.

He led Ardwin to a storeroom beneath the inn. It was cool there, like a root cellar. Ardwin filled a sack with supplies. "Thank you," he said. "This should do nicely." He hefted his sack and slung it over his shoulder.

They had just stepped outside and Mr. Bluestone was closing the heavy wooden door behind them, when Ardwin heard a sad, grunting, pitiful moaning. *Unnhhh hunnnh unnnhhh.*

Unnhhh hunnnh unnnhhh. He shuddered. His hair stood on end. The wing unfolded as if preparing to fly. Quickly he pulled his cloak up higher, hiding it from view.

"What is that?" he asked almost harshly. "Tell me! What have you got trapped here?"

Let It Go

In response to Ardwin's question, Mr. Bluestone looked down unhappily and seemed uncomfortable, almost ashamed. "I don't know what to do with her," he admitted. "Four men brought her here in chains just days ago. Three of them were so big, they were like bears themselves. They had caught her to sell for bearbaiting. You know, bets and dogs. They'd already sold her cubs. They beat her with spear shafts to make her dance. It . . . sickened me. Spears were not made for *that*." He shook his head angrily. "And Leonore, my good-hearted soul, wouldn't have it. 'Samuel, dear,' she says, 'you must buy her. I don't care what it costs. Her cries *broach* my heart.' So I did. I don't like keeping her caged, but if she is only chained and collared, why, she strikes out at anyone who gets close! Now all she does is sit and moan. She hasn't eaten. Would you like to see her?"

"Yes. At once! Lead me to her."

They went along a narrow path and around a corner of the ramshackle building off behind the kitchen. As they stepped around the corner Ardwin had a clear view of the snow-capped mountains. The stable was to the right. And there, dead ahead, in a rusted, wheeled cage, not much bigger than its own body, sat a great she-bear. Her dark eyes ran as if with tears, and two wet lines darkened the fur along her round face and muzzle. She was slumped forward, sitting forlornly, one paw resting on the bars. A few brown apples and a crumbling, soggy loaf of bread lay uneaten between her feet. There was a bucket of water beside her. There was a strong odor, a stench of confinement, feces, and urine.

Ardwin held the wing firmly beneath the cloak and walked closer.

She was not a pretty sight. There was a ring of worn fur around her neck where she had been too tightly collared, and ragged, bare patches ran along her back and heels. Her pelt seemed to sag, hanging loosely from her bones. One ear was torn, either from a spear or by dogs, or it might have been just a memento of her life in the wild. Her black nose was dry and cracked. She looked up when he came close and tentatively sniffed the air, taking several quick, short breaths. In response, the wing moved, fanning the air beneath the cloak. She sniffed again. For an instant those dull brown eyes showed interest, became flecked with gold. Her head swayed from side to side. Her body began to rock. *Unnnnh hunnnnnh,* she moaned. *Unnnnh hunnnnnh.* "Death! Cubs! Death! Cubs!" is what Ardwin heard.

Ardwin took some coins from his pouch. "She is in a bad way. Take this money, Mr. Bluestone, and let her go!" he said hoarsely.

"I will, sir. I will do it," exclaimed the innkeeper, slapping his fist onto his open palm. "It's been in my mind to do that very thing! You've given me the push I needed. I'll get some men to drag the cage into the bushes, open the door, and let her out. Just the thing," he said.

Ardwin nodded with relief. The grief pouring from the bear was overwhelming. Silently he wished her health and peace. But the bear's eyes had lapsed again into a dull sadness, and she seemed beyond his reach. She sat lethargically now, head lowered, staring at the bare, damp earth and at the grass growing outside her cage.

Ardwin turned back to the innkeeper and said, "Mr. Bluestone, let's not wait. I can't leave her like this. Let's set her free right now!"

"Now's as good a time as any," said Mr. Bluestone agreeably. "Yes! Why not!" Two of his tavern men were walking from the stable. "Here, lads!" he called. "Give us a hand!"

The four of them began pushing the cage. The bear hardly seemed to notice.

The wheels of the cage creaked and groaned and rumbled

as it dipped and swayed along the rough ground behind the inn. Ardwin was working hard, pushing with his one hand, and trying also to keep the wing cloaked at the same time. So far the others were busy enough not to have seen it.

"Far enough," gasped Mr. Bluestone as he straightened up and mopped his brow.

The two tavern men nodded in agreement, shaking out their hands from the pressure of the iron bars they'd been pushing against.

"If you're ready, I'll draw the bolt," Ardwin said.

"Go ahead," said Mr. Bluestone. "Help yourself."

"Wait," said one of the men. "There's work to do! I want to get to it! I'm off to the stable."

"Me too!" said the other, rapidly heading off as well.

Ardwin and Mr. Bluestone watched as the two scurried away. "I've never seen those two so anxious to be working," said Mr. Bluestone calmly. "It's a miracle." Then he added, "Our Mrs. Bear nearly took off a man's leg the day she arrived. I think that may have something to do with it."

"I see. Well, how about you? Ready?"

"She looks harmless enough," said Mr. Bluestone. "But I'll just step back a bit farther. No sense in taking unnecessary chances." He strolled back about fifty paces toward the stable and the inn. "All right," he called, cupping his hands around his mouth. "Pull away!"

Ardwin stepped up to the cage and said quietly, "I'm going

to set you free. We mean you no harm. Go now and wander freely back into your wild. Get healthy and strong. Find your cubs, if you can. A traveler's blessing on you."

He pulled the iron bolt. With a rusty, grating *creeeaak!* the cage door swung open.

Ardwin backed slowly away.

The bear rose up onto all fours and shambled to the open door. She dropped her front paws onto the earth in front of the cage and moaned miserably, sad and low.

That is the voice of pure grief, Ardwin thought.

Then she stepped from the cage, turned, and looked at him. She looked and looked, her eyes growing brighter, her head and neck straighter. He felt as if she was fixing his image in her mind. Then she started off through the fields, moving steadily toward the distant forest and mountains.

Mr. Bluestone came forward, and together, he and Ardwin watched as the bear got smaller and smaller in the distance. Not once did she look back.

Ardwin and the innkeeper walked to the stable. Then they said their good-byes and parted, Mr. Bluestone returning to The Rack and Ardwin going to the stable, where he tied his provisions to Raven's saddle, mounted up, and rode toward the mountains that had called to him from his dreams.

Swan Home

That night Ardwin camped in open country. The road was steep, the land rugged, the overhanging sky, vast and wide. The shrub-covered hills were set with rocky outcroppings of pale, yellowish stone. Up ahead still rose the tall mountains, not yet any closer after the day's long ride. A good deal farther north and to the west, he knew that the coast cut deeply in, forming a large open bay. It was there that the swans gathered in their great flocks. Tremors of happiness ran through his wing as he thought about it, making his whole body shiver with anticipation. He remembered that bay from when he and his brothers had flown there above Ulfius's lands. What had borders meant to them then? Nothing at all. The mountains, he recalled, had been high and steep, but he remembered seeing a pass twisting between the massive peaks. With a little luck he'd find it now and be able to cut through to the sea.

It was getting cold. He unpacked his helmet and put it on. The wing, buried under the two cloaks, kept him warm enough so that he slept all right, if somewhat fitfully. On he went the next day at the same steady pace, creeping toward the mountains, which seemed to remain as distant as ever.

The next night he camped where the road, such as it now was (it seemed not well used, and was overgrown), veered east. He wondered how much longer he could stay on it. If it didn't start threading its way back west or north, he would have to leave it and set out across untracked wilderness. He could wait, maybe, a day or two more. But then he would have to decide.

That night the stars seemed cold, bright, and very close, and the wind had a bitter edge. Ardwin was restless and uneasy and lay listening for the sound of hoofbeats. Raven felt it. He snorted, tossing his head and pulling at his rope. "Shhhh. Shhhhh," Ardwin said softly. "It's all right. Be easy, Raven."

But he himself was not. The whispering men at the inn and the pitiful moans of the caged bear echoed in the shadows. He got up, put another branch on the fire, and wrapped his cloaks tighter, stretching the wing out full-length and splaying the feathers to cover his body. The ground was cold and hard. He slept poorly, his dreams filled with cages, traps, chains, whispers, lies, and horrid moans.

When he woke in the morning his right side was stiff and sore. There was a coating of frost on the grass. Breath rose like steam from Raven's nostrils. But many swans were flying north and west, and that was exhilarating. His wing quivered, pointed, trembled. He rose, boots crunching on the frosted grass, and started a fire with dry, twisted branches. After a quick meal of hard cheese, a slice of dried meat warmed on his dagger point over a blaze of twigs, and one small, wrinkled apple, he saddled up, fitted his helmet to block the wind, and set off eagerly.

It was midmorning, the road still veering east, when the wing suddenly lifted, rousing itself like a body throwing off sleep. A commanding voice from somewhere deep within him cried, *Run! Hide! Get off the road! Now!*

Startled, he spurred Raven into the juniper scrub, branches snapping and breaking around him as he rode forward, then reined up, heart pounding, behind a tall outcropping of stone. Hoofbeats were approaching from the very direction he had just come. Three riders wearing silver and scarlet, his father's livery, swept past on panting horses. When the sound of their hoofbeats faded, he rode cautiously back onto the dusty roadway. It had not been the three men from the inn — at least he did not think so — but how could he be sure? Maybe those three had recognized him and notified these riders. Maybe Stephen and Skye had already been caught and had revealed his plans. (How much did they care about him and his well-being, anyway?) Maybe Rose and Conor had been persuaded to tell what they knew.

He peered along the roadway. A cloud of dust still hovered there, marking the trail of the three men who had ridden so swiftly past. He crossed the road, determined to head into the northern emptiness that showed on his maps as an uncharted blank. His eye caught a movement in the east. One rider, tiny in the distance, was riding slowly back, looking down along the edges of the rough road, as if seeking signs they might have missed in their haste. Then the two others appeared trailing farther behind.

Ardwin saw that the time had come. He dug his heels into Raven's sides. The big horse exploded into a gallop; the riders saw him and charged off the road and toward him at a steep angle, seeking to cut him off, coming at him on his right. He veered left to avoid them and to keep them strung in a line behind. His hope lay in Raven's strength, and in the fact that Raven was nearly fresh, while their horses, given the pace at which they had passed, must be nearly winded.

Winded as they were, they were fast, and if he had been on Solo, he doubted he could have escaped. But with Raven . . . He leaned down low on Raven's neck and pressed in his heels again. "Go, Raven!" he urged. "Run!" Raven lay back his ears, stretched out, and poured himself over the ground, breathing hard, his great heart beating, beating, his hooves pounding the dry soil. The shouts grew fainter as the pursuers dropped farther behind. "Go, Raven! Run, boy!" Ardwin cried. And Raven, hearing, ran.

Ardwin and Raven rode across a high, bare plateau. The snowcapped mountains rose tall and sheer, dominating the land, blocking the sky. For six days they had been riding steadily across what seemed like an endless plain. Now the mountains loomed close. If the riders were still after him, he estimated they must be at least half a day behind. Raven was strong, stronger than he had known, and had been able to maintain a steady, long-strided, blistering pace. Someday he would have to thank Stephen — but he didn't want to think too much about Stephen or Skye just yet. Let them stay where they belonged, in the past.

He could see a glacier looming far ahead, shimmering like a wall of glass. Snow was falling, and a bitter wind gusted and moaned, making the going hard. But it was good too, for soon windblown snow would bury his tracks and he would be lost to all pursuit.

As they got closer, Ardwin could feel the intense, biting cold billowing from the glacier. Raven snorted nervously. Ardwin looked back and saw a slim, gray shape — a wolf — padding stealthily among the ice-coated boulders.

"All right," he said. "I see it." He patted the horse's neck reassuringly.

The glacier would soon block their forward path, anyway, so now Ardwin turned Raven's head and they set off over the snow-covered ground, heading west. The wolf did not worry him yet. Raven was fast. But wolves hunted in packs. He would be watchful.

That night he kept his fire bright, and saw a pair of yellow eyes glinting just beyond the flickering light. Raven raised his head and whickered nervously. Later Ardwin slept fitfully. Several times he rose and dragged more branches onto the flames. In the morning the wolf was gone, but its paw prints remained clearly impressed in the snow all around where he'd slept.

He continued west, and eventually found the pass. Though it started as a gradual slope, it soon turned steep and grew treacherously slippery as well. Soon, in many places, Raven slid back before he was able to dig in his hooves and push on higher. Ardwin dismounted and sometimes led, sometimes pulled, their way forward.

It was slow, exhausting work. The way up was extreme. After many hours, Ardwin found himself wedged into a narrow V of rock. The cold wind blew a fine rain of icy particles into his face and neck. He let the rock hold him and caught his breath, gathering strength. Below he could see the mountain dropping down into cloud and mist.

And still the sheer slope led up.

"Come on, Raven," he said, pushing off from the rock, back into the full force of the wind. They started slowly, painfully, upward again, Raven advancing only because of his great courage, strength, and trust in the man before him. But

Ardwin was now pushing himself on as much as he was urging Raven upward, drawn by a vision of happiness, which could only come closer step by exhausted step, and his strength was nearing its limit. His legs shook. A crust of ice had formed over the snow and as he sank into it, the edges cut him painfully. Raven's legs too were cut. Each time he sank through the icy crust, he left a trail of blood.

Ardwin now tried easing their way by breaking trail, first swinging his spear, then, when the arc of that got too tiring to bear, drawing the Hunter and using its blade to clear their immediate path. Finally, too exhausted for such efforts, he just pushed drearily through the deep, rime-crusted snow with his own body and legs, half floundering his way ever forward on sheer determination. "I will get there," he repeated to himself through gritted teeth. "I will get there."

When they at last reached the crest, Ardwin's fingers were stiff and numb and his face masked with ice. But when he saw the ocean bays glittering far below, white with thousands of swans, he shouted for joy. It was just as he had remembered. And he was almost there! It was warmer on the coastal side too. He could feel moist breezes rising. The snow and ice began melting, dripping from him.

Ardwin remembered an old swan named Strongwing he had spoken with years ago. He had gone off from his brothers (they hardly ever consorted with the other swans) and struck up a conversation with Strongwing, who had been pleasantly surprised. "None of the other young swans show much interest," he'd said. They had talked about flying, a love they shared. "Never try those passes in a storm," Strongwing had advised at one point, motioning with his head toward the mountains that rose just behind them — the very ones that Ardwin was now trying to cross. "Treacherous. The winds will dash you against the rocks. The heavily falling snow will cake your wings, and you won't have enough lift to rise above the peaks. Many swans have died there."

The memory of the old swan filled Ardwin with hope. Perhaps Strongwing was still alive, and they might talk again.

Ardwin dug a den in the snow using the Hunter as a spade. At the den's entrance he built a small fire of twigs that he had carried with him. Crouched over the flames, he cooked a slice of nearly frozen meat. He ate greedily while it was still too hot, burning his fingertips and tongue, which he had to douse with snow. With stiff fingers he laid out wisps of hay for Raven and gave him a brown, shriveled apple, almost frozen solid inside. He crawled into his shelter, curled up, and slept, shivering and shaking with cold and anticipation, praying as he dozed that no storm would bury him.

It was late afternoon when Ardwin entered his shelter. Luckily, no storm descended during the night, and Raven was still there when he woke in the morning. Raven had been weary too, and there was no place, really, for him to go. There was no food nearby, and Ardwin was the only living thing in sight, the only companion in that vast, frozen emptiness.

When Ardwin crawled from his meager shelter, he could already feel the warmer air rising from the sea. It was just the encouragement he needed. Now, with little delay, he and Raven started on the treacherous downward path. The physical exertion needed to go down was less than it had been to go up, but the descent was exhausting and perilous nonetheless. The deep snow was wetter on this side of the mountain, and many times they slid and slipped downward, sometimes spinning slowly out of control beside the edge of a sheer drop of thousands of feet. Black rocks reached up like teeth through the snow to gnash them, or hovered massively above, jutting from the cliff face, threatening to fall and crush them to a pulp.

When they were finally safely below the snow line, Ardwin's relief was overwhelming. The narrow ravine through which they had been descending had become green with vegetation. It was like the coming of spring after a lifetime of winter. When they stopped there for a time, Raven bent his head and began cropping the moss and grasses; Ardwin, exhausted by the ordeal of their descent, flopped down and stretched out on the ground.

An hour later, when he sat up and rubbed his eyes, he was relieved to see that even here, where there was grass for him to graze on, Raven hadn't strayed far. Clearly he had been well trained. A mild breeze was blowing, moist and salty, tasting of the sea. Ardwin stood up and yawned, swung back up onto Raven's broad back, and they continued on the rest of the way down the mountain.

Down and down they went, the slope becoming ever gentler, until at last the blue sea surged before them, and the snowcapped mountain loomed behind.

Ardwin patted Raven on his solid shoulder and exclaimed, "It's beautiful!"

Swans circled, rose up in great whirling flocks, or floated on the glittering water of the blue bay like immense flotillas of white-sailed ships. Thousands of elegant swans, many followed by fuzzy, yellowish cygnets, paddled along the shore. Out in the deep water of the mountain-ringed bay, the ridged back of a whale broke the surface. The great beast exhaled, venting a plume of white spray that caught the light like a rainbow. Harbor seals raised their spotted heads, looked at Ardwin with black eyes, then sleekly dove. Nothing had changed. *Maybe,* he thought hopefully, *some things, the best things, never do.*

He got down off Raven, raised his wing to the sky, and shouted for triumph and joy.

The Wild

Ardwin rode along the pebbled beach to the edge of the sea, and began to plan. He would unpack his food and gear, build a shelter of driftwood and stones, and see what wind and sky, sea and swans had to tell him. He would try to find the old swan, Strongwing, or any swans that might remember him from before.

Ardwin got down off Raven, enjoying the crunching sound of his boots on the sea-worn pebbles, and walked to the water's edge, letting the waves wash to his heels. Six times in all he had come here: one for each swan year. He had played tag on these very shores, among these waves, with other young swans, and he had flown over these very mountains and bays. He remembered the touch of this wind, and he let it lift his feathers now, feeling welcomed. He inhaled the wild, salt air, remembering the smell of these waters, these stones and shores.

Memories welled up. After they had left the robbers' shack and migrated here, he and his brothers often had gone off alone and hid, so as not to be seen turning into human form. His brothers wept, raged, and moaned at each transformation. Then, once back in human shape, they set quickly to work, spearing and grilling fish, then gobbling the pieces that Bran shared out evenly, like treasure, among them. Almost as soon as they finished their meal it would begin again: *the Change.* They writhed and moaned and cursed as it came upon them, transforming them into hissing swans with feathered skins, dull beaks, and sad, human eyes. Ardwin alone had not been gripped by anguish. *Perhaps I was too young to remember much of my human life,* he thought now. *I had few attachments. There was not much I dreaded losing once Mother was gone.*

He bent down, removed his helmet, took a palmful of water, and poured it over his head and neck. "Ahhh!" he exclaimed with a shout. It was cold! But it cleared his head. Raven snorted and reared, hearing Ardwin's yell. Ardwin, laughing, went to him, grabbed the reins, and patted Raven's nose with a cold, wet hand. "It's all right," he said. "See? It's just cold, really cold!" The cold water trickled down his neck and back. He sighed happily. The swans lifted their necks at his cry and seemed to be watching him intently. He waved at them.

He led Raven back from the beach toward a hill that sloped up into the valley he had just descended, unpacked his gear, and spent the rest of the day dragging heavy driftwood logs and branches together. Sometimes he hitched Raven to the heaviest logs and had him pull. He formed a rough shelter, plugging the spaces between the logs with stones and seaweed, then lugged all his gear and food inside. It was crude shelter at best. The driftwood ceiling, covered with seaweed for insulation, was very low, too low for him to stand fully upright, and he would need to keep a fire going to make the cold nights even begin to be manageable. Even then it would be smoky and uncomfortable inside. But he could do it. He *would* do it. He had food enough for several days if he was frugal, and the sea was full of fish. He had hooks and line and his spear. One seal should last a long time, too. Yes, it was all going to work.

He was right about the nights: They were cold. His rude shelter was drafty, and even with a seaweed and driftwood fire going, there wasn't much heat. But fish oil burned well, and that helped. And night was good for thinking. So he lay in the semidark, watched the flickering of flames and the curling of greasy smoke, and thought.

If I go back, I'll either have to give up the wing or fight to keep it. He remembered how settled Bran appeared, how content to have a wife and lands and a realm of his own, how done and finished. How *whole.* What might it be like to be so happy, so *ordinary*? With two arms, even if one was artificial, he might find out.

"But if I don't go back, if I keep the wing, where will I go? What will I do? Can I just wander the earth alone, talking with wild animals, doing . . . what? Being *what*? I am a prince of a realm with some power. Can I just become a wayfarer? And how could I ever be happy hiding among my brothers or behind my sister's skirts to save my wing?"

There were no answers.

Lying in the close, smoky darkness of his little hut by the sea, he thought about Conrad and the others who whispered about him or called him names. "With the wing I am living proof that old and very strange powers still haunt the world. That's what frightens them. I see that now."

He sat up. "Enough! I am done preparing. Tomorrow I will go out and talk with any swan who will listen. I will never be more ready. It is time."

When Ardwin awoke, the sun was shining through the cracks in his hut. His little seaweed and driftwood fire still smoldered weakly. He rose, stepped out into the clear day, and stretched. Swans were flying, rising from the sea, and descending back to it. They floated beyond the breakers, making the surface of the wide bay white. The sun felt so good after many days of gray weather. Raven fortunately seemed to be still managing well enough on seaweed and the scrubby shore plants.

Ardwin grilled a fish he'd caught the day before, ate, and cleaned up. His nerves were taut. Through all the difficulties of coming here, he had never, not once, felt that it might be for nothing, that he might be rejected. But now there was a small and nagging doubt. He set off along the beach and walked to a sheltered stretch of bay where thousands of swans drifted easily on the calmer water. There were nestlings there too, and many swan mothers, like a living carpet of swans bobbing before him.

Ardwin cleared his throat loudly, then, "Hello!" he called. He raised his wing high so it was clearly visible. "My name is Ardwin. I used to live among you, years ago. I came six times when I . . . I was a swan. See?" He waved the wing. "I mean no harm. There is nothing to fear. I've only come back to talk. Has anyone seen Strongwing? He knows me."

Harsh, hissing cries began rippling through the flocks. A crowd of swans ran along the water and rose up into the air with a great beating of wings, sounding like the sails of many ships unfurling all at once. Those with young paddled out into deeper, rougher water and sat there hissing, anxiously tossing on the waves.

"Don't be afraid!" Ardwin called. He raised his wing again, hoping it would be taken as a badge or token of recognition. This was not a good start. "I was here before. I am a friend! I am more even than that. I was one of you!"

"Afraid? Who's afraid!" gruffly shouted a male swan, a cob, near the shore. The cob waddled out of the sea onto the beach, while its mate, the pen, out on the ocean, screamed, "Kill it! Drive it away! It is man and it is *strange.* It smells odd, and odd means danger. We have cygnets. Drive the thing away! It's not normal! Protect the young! Protect the cygnets!"

"I mean no harm," said Ardwin again, trying to keep calm. "Be easy, I pray. Truly, I was one of you. I flew here with my five brothers — maybe some of you remember us? I just want to stay a while and talk. Please understand you have nothing to fear from me."

"He says he was a swan and one of us," wickedly laughed a young cob, eyeing Ardwin as if sizing him up for a fight. "Hey, *Thing*!" he shouted. "You don't *look* like one of us!"

"Go away," hissed another young swan warrior, waddling closer, spreading its wings and lowering its head like a snake about to strike. "You're not wanted here. See? We've been watching you. You're not right. You're not normal. You're strange, you freak! Now get going while you still can!"

It was no idle threat. When angered, the male swans could be deadly. Ardwin remembered when Swan-Bran had bludgeoned and pecked a fox to death. Now other pens had taken up the hysterical scream for their mates. "Kill it! Drive the thing away!" Shouts of "Protect the nestlings! Save the cygnets!" rose from the marshes and the sea, and fell harsh as stones hurled from the sky. Soon, Ardwin knew, the males would rouse themselves to a warrior's fury. Many of them were already gliding down from overhead or marching up staunchly, shoulder to shoulder, onto the land. They flapped their broad white wings, making a sound loud as cannons, and cried, "Death to intruders!" When they got their courage and purpose in line, then, red-eyed and maddened, they would mob him, beating him with their wings and pecking him with their beaks until he was as dead as Bran's fox.

Ardwin backed from the beach and water. Farther down the beach Raven lifted his head and began to hoof the sand uneasily.

"Wait!" exclaimed Ardwin. "Please! Is Strongwing here? He would be very old now, but I think he would recognize me even as I am now, and vouch for me too."

"Strongwing?" said an old swan waddling slowly forward. Her wings were tattered and ragged; one eye was rheumy and blind. Her white feathers had a yellowish tinge. "He was my mate."

"Was? Did you two have a falling out? Or, did he . . . die?"

"My, my, but you're polite," answered the old swan. "Die? No, he didn't 'die.' He was murdered, horribly. Shot with an arrow, right through the eye as we flew low over southern lands."

"Oh, no!" exclaimed Ardwin, sickened. "I'm sorry. I'm so sorry." He knew who had fired the arrow: Conrad, practicing for their competition. Illegally killing old Strongwing had simply been part of his preparation.

"Talk is cheap," said the old pen. "People don't want to talk, anyway. What they want is to hunt and trap us. What they want is our eggs to eat and our flesh to roast. And this wing, how did you get it? Did you kill a swan and cut it off? Is it a hunter's trick to bring us in close so you can kill more of us? Where's the strap holding it on? Come on, show us! Tell the truth."

"Yes, talk!" shouted a young swan. "Or we'll make you talk! At him, lads!"

The situation was turning nightmarish and ugly. "Wait, please. Listen," said Ardwin, desperately trying to keep them, and himself, calm. "You can talk with me without need for threats. See, I understand you and can answer. I really *was* a swan. Here, just see!" He pulled off his cloak and his shirt, exposing his body. He turned around so they could see him back and front. "The wing is *me*! No straps. I'm not like any of the other humans you've encountered. Isn't that clear? A spell was cast on my brothers and me, and we were turned into swans. I still have a wing. I have returned because I felt so happy here, so *accepted*. I loved to fly. I talked with Strongwing about that. Now I just want to talk with you and —"

"Say," said one young swan. "He *can* talk to us. That's true. And look, it *is* a real wing."

"Yes. But what good is it? You can't fly with only one. What an odd thing it is!" said another, sniffing at Ardwin, then turning away as if detecting some foul scent.

"He smells, all right, but it's only of fish," said another young cob.

"Fish?" said the first swan, turning back with sudden

interest. "Hmm. Maybe he has food. Food is good. Why not let him stay?"

"I'll talk to anyone or anything for food," said yet another swan, lifting a black leg and scratching the side of its head. He peered at Ardwin with beady, glittering eyes. "Give me a fish, boy, and I'll talk with you. You have fish?"

"What else do you have to eat?" exclaimed a tough young swan that pushed himself through the gathering crowd. He fluffed his feathers, squatted down, wiggled his tail, produced a long green dropping on the sand, and said, "Ah, that's better. I've got room now. You have bread? Cheese? I like those. We get all that in the south. You're from the south, right? Give us that southern food and we'll tell you things that'll make your feathers stand on end. Anything you want to know, we'll tell. Just feed us. Isn't that right, lads?"

"Yeah, that's right. Just feed us!" called some of the other young adults. They shoved one another and chortled.

A matronly swan raised her narrow head on a long, elegant neck. Seaweed was draped on her head, looking like a kind of crown. "How uncouth," she said, addressing her fellow swans, "to even think of taking food from such an oddity! Its food may be poisoned. Mark my words! It will trick us. It wants our eggs. I can sense it. It wants nestlings to roast. Young birds will disappear. You will look for friends, but they will be missing. Do not let this foul thing stay among us! There will be murders! I know humans. I have migrated among them for many years and I say this: Drive it away! For it is trouble! Just look at it! A wing bound to a human body! And how did it get it? Enchantment! Disgusting!"

"Please," said Ardwin. "All I want to do is stay, think, and talk."

A tough old cob spoke up gruffly. Twisting a ruffled head all around, he looked Ardwin up and down. "Luxury," he announced. "That's what I say. Talk and think? Who has the time? We feed our young. We patrol our borders. We drive our enemies — wolves and foxes and even eagles — away. We're workers. We're doers! Talk and think! Bah!"

"I mean no harm," Ardwin said, pleading.

"People never mean harm," put in a young swan warrior. "No. People always say, 'We *love* swans! We adore them. We love their purity and beauty. We love to watch them glide serenely across the still pond at twilight. Oh, stay among us, beauteous swans.' Then, *wham!* The traps. The arrows. The nets. The eggs start going. The nestlings disappear. We've heard too much of that sweet talk before."

"Let's drive him off or kill him."

"Just kill him."

"Let's see what kind of food he has."

"Let him alone."

"Save the cygnets!"

"Destroy the menace!"

"Play it safe!"

"Drive him down the beach."

"Send him away."

"Remember the fish! The cheese! The bread!"

The many conflicting voices of the swans rose in a dizzying clamor. Ardwin backed away sadly. "I'm going now," he said. "Back to where I've built a shelter. I have food there. I have fish and I will gladly share it with you. If you want to talk I'll be there, far from the nestlings. Good-bye."

Still the clamor rose. The swans hardly noticed that Ardwin was leaving. They were busily flapping their wings and arguing. Feathers and soft bits of down were flying. Squawking and honking, they dropped long, green droppings in their excitement, fouling the beach and water's edge. The young warrior swans, liking the chaos and hubbub, were ruffling their feathers, pushing with their shoulders against one another, daring one another to stand up for their words, daring one another to march down the beach, talk with the thing, and eat all his food.

Ardwin trudged away disheartened. This was hardly the wonderful, restorative, kindly, welcoming conversation he had hoped for.

As he walked on, troubled and dazed, he passed a big boulder.

The boulder opened one eye, and a deep, gravelly voice

said, "Ahoy, matey. Don't take it so hard. They never listen, not to anyone."

"What!" Ardwin jumped back in surprise, his hand on the hilt of his sword. The boulder moved! And it spoke! What kind of evil magic was this? Then he realized it wasn't a boulder at all but a big walrus, its thick skin roughly scarred from many battles. Long, whitish lines — tusk marks, most likely, the record of past encounters with other walruses — ran along its sides. Where its right flipper should have been was a horribly tangled mass of puckered white scar. It looked like the flipper had been torn away.

The walrus grinned, and its tusks gleamed in the sun. "They don't listen to anyone, not even one another. All that lovely plumage and those elegant necks, but for all that beauty they're narrow-minded and suspicious. Though the gulls, I have to tell you, shipmate, are even worse. Not a brain among them." He fanned himself with his one good flipper, clearly enjoying himself. "Nice day, isn't it? Savor life's pleasures when you can. That's what this taught me." He motioned with his cannonball of a head toward his scar.

Ardwin couldn't help staring at the ugly mass.

"Aye," said the walrus, nodding toward his side. "A great white shark took it. The gulls screeched and circled, waiting for me to belly up and die. Fish, gulls, and seals too sipped the sea, red with my blood. But I didn't die. The shark did. Good riddance!"

The walrus puffed out its cheeks with pride, its stiff bristles sticking straight out as it huffed and blew.

"I'm a gentle soul, shipmate. But get my back up and put me in a fight and watch out! When the shark ripped off my flipper, it hurt. Oh, it hurt! But I didn't let that stop me. I turned on it and stabbed it through the heart. It sank, dead. The problem was, I was stuck to it! I couldn't pull my tusk out. So, down we went, live meat and dead tangled together, into the dark and the cold. At last, I wrenched myself free. The shark disappeared into the gloom below." The walrus closed his eyes like a cat, relishing his memories. Then he opened them again. "But I rose back up into the light and air. Not many walruses can tell such a tale!" he exclaimed. "Name's Ivnuk, by the way.

"Now listen, matey, if you've come here to experience the beauty and harmony of nature, you've come to the wrong place. Wait! No need to go running off. Maybe there is no right place. Nature, your nature and mine, is everywhere. But it's an awful mess. The harmony is shot through with lots of muck and blood. My advice? Open your eyes wide, and keep 'em that way. That's how you want to see the world — truthfully! Right?" He turned away. "I'll be shipping off now. Good-bye!"

"Wait," exclaimed Ardwin. He held up his wing.

"Nice," said Ivnuk. "Very nice. And unusual. I wish I could get something to grow in this clotted mess of nothing where *my* flipper used to be," he said, nodding toward his side. "Of course, I've learned to compensate. It hardly slows me down anymore. How'd you lose your flipper? And how'd you grow one back?"

"I didn't lose it," said Ardwin. He explained.

"That's very handy," said Ivnuk admiringly when Ardwin finished. "I still wish I could grow something to replace what I lost."

"Let me ask you a question."

"Ask away," answered Ivnuk, nodding his bald, round head with interest.

"Let's suppose, just suppose," said Ardwin, "you could be whole again. Not just grow *something* on your side, but have a flipper, a flipper made of ivory or gold — something like that. It would fit perfectly. It might even be stronger than the flesh-and-blood one you lost. But to get it, you'd have to give up something — let's say . . . your tusks. What would you do?"

"That's a hard choice. Tusks are useful," said Ivnuk, scratching beneath his chin with a hind flipper. "I can rake the sea bottom for clams with them. I can use them to help pull myself up onto slippery ice floes. And I can fight. Nothing is better than tusks! I'm used to having one flipper. My remaining one has grown very strong. Then again, with two, I'd have even more freedom and strength. I could really travel. I could dive deep. *Interesting.* Gold, you say? Ivory? Hmmm. The ladies might like that. It might attract their sweet attention."

Ivnuk puffed out his chest and fanned himself with his flipper, considering. Then he said, "But without tusks, what kind of fighter would I be? I'd be nothing more than a big seal. Ugh. Who wants that? How manly is a bull walrus with no tusks?" He shuddered. "No, that tears it. I'd stay as I am."

"Oh," said Ardwin, disappointed yet relieved at the same time. Then he asked, "But what if instead of the ivory or gold one, you could have your own real flipper back? What then?"

"Would I have the scar?"

"No. That would be gone. You'd be just as you were. Though you'd have a very strong left flipper."

Ivnuk's head sank down between his shoulders. His mustache of stiff whiskers blew and rippled. He looked at Ardwin. "But no tusks."

Ardwin shook his head. "No tusks." Then he added, "What if it only took *one* tusk to get the flipper?"

Ivnuk sighed and said, "It was already hard. This is rough water, rough going." He thought silently. Then he looked up. "Forget it," he said decisively. "Nice chat. But I keep both my tusks. I'd rather be a cripple, which is what I am, than lose either of them. Though others might choose differently."

He sniffed the air. "The sea is calling," he said. "Thanks for the chat. You never know how things will come out once you start, do you? Well now, once more, good-bye . . . what did you say your name was?"

"I didn't. But it's Ardwin."

"Good-bye, Ardwin. Don't let the swans get under your skin. And do stay wary. They can be mean."

The walrus nodded its ugly cannonball of a head with those great bristly whiskers and long ivory tusks. It hunched up its maimed heap of a body, humped itself like some huge caterpillar down to the sea, and launched itself with a mighty splash. And there, for all its girth, once back in its own element, it breasted the waves as gracefully and elegantly and lightly as a swan. Then, with a splash of its flukes, down it sank and was gone, leaving a dozen gulls circling and screeching over the spot.

Ardwin went back to his hut, put his head in his hands, and wondered what madness had ever drawn him here.

A few of the younger swans flew over in the evening. Surly and aggressive, they ate his food, made rude comments, mentioned offhandedly how, in the south, they had attacked men who had angered them and beat them severely. They left slimy droppings around his fire, then flew off, laughing.

"That's it," said Ardwin aloud, when they had gone. Disgusted with how badly things had turned out, he began grabbing pots and lengths of rope with his hand, scooping up assorted bits of gear with his wing. "I will leave tomorrow. Why did I ever think there would be answers among the swans? I must be a fool."

In the morning he walked along the shore, gathering driftwood to make a last breakfast fire. As he did, the heads of the swans floating on the waves rose as one and turned to watch him. They pivoted and twisted, keeping him steadily in sight. It was unnerving when they began paddling in toward shore.

A pen shouted, "The cygnets need room and we don't need you! This is our home! Go back wherever it is you belong! We don't want you! We've had enough of your skulking and spying!"

Before Ardwin could tell them he was already on his way, another swan shouted, "That's right! You're not wanted. We fight to protect our own. We're not pigeons, sparrows, or parakeets. We're swans! See? We're big and we're tough, and we mean business. Better get going if you know what's good for you. And we do mean *now*!"

With that, as if at some kind of prearranged signal, hundreds of swan warriors swam to the shore and waddled onto the beach, where they began ruffling their feathers, and shaking and looping their heads. They hissed like snakes and growled like dogs, rousing themselves to a fighting fury. Low at first, then more and more loudly, they began to chant:

"Swans! Swans! We are swans!
We hate foes and kill them dead.
We are the fighters all must dread!"

They began marching shoulder to shoulder in rows, toward Ardwin, chanting their battle cry as they came. Their black eyes took on a reddish tinge. They spread their wings and lowered their beaks, coming forward like a white wave rising from the sea.

A hard wing buffeted his shoulder. A swan warrior had dropped from the sky, swooping down at him. More, many, many more, were mobbing, circling overhead. In self-defense, Ardwin drew the Hunter and waved it aloft. Frightened now, angry, and sick at heart, he shouted, "Leave me be! I came to you as a friend! I would not hurt you. But if you attack me, I warn you, I will fight back. I will saddle my horse and gather my gear and leave."

Ardwin backed cautiously up the beach, watching for more surprise attacks. But though the swans still came steadily forward, they allowed him to get safely to his hut. Twisting their necks, hissing and flapping their wings, they settled, hundreds deep, in a great half circle around him, where they squatted down, watching him through red, narrowed eyes as, with shaking hands, he quickly loaded his saddlebags and saddled Raven, who, nostrils dilated and eyes wide, was angrily pawing the sand.

"Steady," Ardwin said, but his voice shook. Never before had he felt so much raw anger directed at him. Even Conrad had cloaked his hostility behind civil speech. Raven shook his head and chomped on his bit, in no mood to be soothed.

The swans hissed nastily, "Steady *yourself.* We mean business. And here we *come*!"

Ardwin did the wisest thing possible in the circumstances: He leaped onto Raven's back and galloped from the beach toward the slope of the mountain. Behind him, a mob of furious swans was already smashing the roof of his hut with their wings and beaks, while others hurled themselves bodily against the logs in full-fledged madness.

Angry swans rose up with a great loud flapping of wings and circled above Ardwin as he rode away. "Go, freak!" they cried. "Keep your wing and your ugly life."

"Ugly!" Ardwin cried out in frustration and rage. "*You* are the ugly ones! Your beauty is all on the outside! Inside, you have the brains of gulls and the hearts of crows!"

"Gulls, is it! Crows!" shrieked the swans, beside themselves with rage.

Gripping the Hunter, Ardwin rode into the valley toward the ravine that led up the mountain. He heard a loud *whoosh* just over his head and he ducked. A wing tip slapped his helmet, but he only held his sword up, and did not strike. He rode steadily on, while enraged cries of, "Chase the freak! Drive it away!" sounded from above, behind, and around him. Wing beats slapped his shoulders and helmet. He turned and, fiercely brandishing the Hunter, forced his attackers to break off their attacks and veer away. As he rode on farther, the calls gradually died down and the attacks ceased. But still he heard wing beats above. He looked up and saw dozens of swans circling overhead.

The way back up was long and difficult. Raven was slick with sweat, steaming and reeking in the cold damp air when Ardwin reined him in. He looked back from that great height, down to the glittering sea below. So many swans were swimming there, it looked as if a white island were floating on the water. He was so high that most of the flying swans were beneath him now; only a few stragglers still circled above. He sheathed his sword and slid down off Raven's back. The horse stood, head lowered, panting out clouds of steaming breath, while Ardwin threw himself onto the snowy ground.

After a time, Ardwin rose, dried his eyes, and looked down at the bay of swans for the final time. Then he mounted Raven and rode on, going ever higher, making the difficult ascent to the crest of the pass, back into snow, ice, and wind. When he reached the top he did not stop but, driven and careless, without aim or purpose, he began the slippery, treacherous descent back down the dangerous way he had come.

As Ardwin rode on, a heavy snow began to fall, whirling down thick and wet. It fell steadily, fell and fell. The storm he had feared days before had finally come.

The snow rose past Raven's hocks, then to his knees, then to his belly. By then they were no longer riding, but swimming and sliding down the mountain.

The dark gray, snow-filled sky and steep, snow-covered earth merged into one vast, smothering whiteness. Ardwin could not see ten feet in any direction. The weight of the snow piled on his head and arms made every movement dreamlike, heavy and slow. Raven's black head was mounded with wet snow and his mane seemed braided with thick white feathers. It was as if Raven had been transformed into a swan. And still the big flakes fell, drowning them both, horse and rider, in yet more snow. Raven, big and strong as he was, foundered and fell in the drifts. Heavy, wet snow caked Ardwin's head and cloaks. He shivered and shook. Raven began to panic and buck as he slithered downward. "Easy," said Ardwin, sliding off and floundering forward to grip the reins, trying to hold the big horse steady. "Easy." Slowly they continued doggedly on, step by torturous step, descending deeper and deeper into the cold, wet gloom as night swiftly fell.

Near an outcropping of stone, they stopped, man and horse both utterly exhausted. Here, Ardwin thought, they might at least find shelter from the wind. He dismounted and dug a rude den in the snow with his hands and sword and made a small fire in the shelter of the rock. Using the last of his wood, he roasted a few scraps of dried meat and melted snow to drink. To Raven he gave the last of his bread and a handful of grain. He drew his cloaks over him, spread his wing, leaned back against the stony outcropping, and shivered, watching his meager fire burn down. He thought of the crippled fox he had killed at its own request. *Unless morning brings better weather,* he thought, *this could be the end of my own brief, strange tale.*

When he awoke, the wind was moaning and gray morning was brightening the east. *The day might bring some relief yet,* he thought. There would at least be light. He shook with cold and drew his cloaks and wing more tightly around himself. He had had a terrifying dream. In it something big had leaped on Raven and torn out his throat. Raven's dying screams still rang in his ears. That's what had wakened him. He shivered at the awful dream-memory, then suddenly stiffened and lay very still.

For something big was chewing and growling, very close nearby. Cautiously Ardwin lifted his head and looked. Raven lay a few yards away. One round eye was open, staring blankly. Raven's lips were drawn back, showing his teeth and gums in a horrid grin. Crouched upon him, one huge paw resting across the big horse's broken back, was a pale-furred snow lion, its glistening teeth red with Raven's blood.

Raven, the good, brave, powerful horse, was dead. It had not been a dream.

Ardwin's wing awoke and whispered, *Be still. Do not move.* But Ardwin inched his hand forward till it gripped his sword.

The lion looked up and, yellow eyes ablaze, *ROARED!*

The sound was deafening, numbing, beyond all possible sounds. It was a vise squeezing the air from Ardwin's lungs and hope from his heart. It grabbed him and shook him; it reverberated and rang, piercing into the marrow of his bones. His arm became weak as a child's, and the Hunter nearly slipped from his nerveless grasp.

Now I must die, he thought.

But the wing whispered, *No! You shall not!* and Ardwin rallied, as if casting off an evil spell. His strength returned.

"*MEAT!*" the lion roared. "*You are meat! My meat!*" And it rose to its feet, drooling horse blood and saliva onto the reddened snow.

Ardwin answered boldly, "You are mistaken. I am not meat! I am your master."

The beast laughed and snarled triumphantly, "*Meat-boy, food-thing. You are mine!*"

Even as it spoke, Ardwin was sliding the spear back, bracing it firmly against the rocks, steadying it there by pressing the wing tightly against the polished shaft.

The lion gathered its legs beneath it for the spring. Ardwin drew the Hunter and leaped to his feet, the great sword held forward, the rock-braced spear leveled. The lion sprang. The sword flashed, cutting into the beast's neck, its blood spurting onto the snow, and the spear, held against the rocks, caught it mid-chest, the force of its own leap impaling it. Roaring in agony, in shock and rage, biting madly at the bitter thing that pierced it, the snow lion rose on its hind legs, its claws ripping the air inches from Ardwin's chest, its breath foul on his face.

For an endless moment the spear held. Then, with a terrific *CRACK!* its shaft snapped. The lion lunged forward, its massive paws slamming into Ardwin's chest like hammers. A dagger of a claw caught in the links of his mail shirt, and as the lion tugged it free, the claw tore a red furrow across Ardwin's chest.

Then the beast's weight fell upon him, and there was only blackness.

Relief

Skye and Stephen veered from the trail and rode down a thickly wooded slope toward the stream that flowed in a narrow gully below. They splashed from the bank into the water and continued downstream. After little more than a mile they came up out of the water and continued on along the rock shelf by the riverside. The stream widened and deepened here and ran rapidly on, foaming over many smooth boulders. As they rode, they left a trail of wet hoofprints that quickly dried, vanishing in the warmth of the sun.

In this way, using hard ground and streams for cover, they had stayed ahead of the trackers, whetting the appetites of their pursuers, giving them just enough to keep them hopeful. It was risky. They hardly slept, and while Solo was steady and dependable, he was nothing like Raven, Stephen thought. If it should come to an out-and-out chase, Solo would soon labor. But Thornbush was fleet, and Skye, at least, might escape.

Stephen put the worry from his mind. So far, all was good. He looked at Skye as they ambled side by side, and smiled. "I'm glad things have worked out so that we could be together. It will be different when we return. We can always leave again on our own, of course, if being home isn't to our liking. We're getting good at this. I know I'd be ready, if you were."

Skye laughed. "One step at a time! I don't plan to return home for some time yet. I'm feeling like Ardwin these days. The call to go and just keep going is definitely on me."

"Good," said Stephen. "Castle life feels so closed in when I think about it now. But it can have a way of taking over — food on hand and conveniences like hot baths can be very tempting! But thanks to Ardwin, we have had a life outside those old walls."

"Stephen, have you ever wondered," Skye asked, "what it must be like for him, really?"

"Yes. I once asked him straight out what it was like to have a wing."

"Really? What did he say?"

"He grabbed my left arm, twisted it around to my back, and stuck it into my belt. He said, 'Now try and put on your pants and belt your buckle. Try and belt on your sword too, lace your shoes, and button your tunic. Get a mail shirt on and secure it. Heft a bow, swing an ax, swim and row, or just carry a plate of food and a cup of water at the same time. Try doing all those simple, ordinary things. That should give you a taste of the first half.' 'I begin to see,' I said, and tried to unbend my arm and tug it free. 'And . . . the second half?' I asked. 'Ah, well,' he answered, 'the second half is much more complex. More subtle.' This surprised me, because he always seemed straightforward."

"Yes," said Skye, "but if you asked me . . . No, first go on, then I'll tell you."

"All right. 'That,' he said, 'would be for you to have something else where your arm was, something that was *not* an arm; something without fingers or wrist, something that flares and flashes out and feels and weighs and smells different from your arm, from *any* arm. And this *thing* will also have a will and mind of its own. It will want to do what it can't. It can't lift or hold or throw or catch or be useful in any practical way. Your wing will not be able to *do* anything much at all. It will only yearn and dream to return to its proper element, the sky. But it is stranded here and knows it, and it doesn't like that trapped, abandoned feeling. So it will show its unhappiness, and your own hidden feelings too to the world. Rage, fear, joy, whatever. *Flap flap flap!* It will flap it all out. Which is to say nothing of the dreams and voices and intuitions that you're not certain you can — or should — trust and follow. It *knows* things, and will bring what it knows into your heart and mind, whether you want it to or not.

"'So, one side, your right side, is ready for action. Of course, one arm and one hand, attempting to do the work of two, will be frustrated, at a disadvantage. And your other side, your left, has no practical, earthly use at all. It's like being split down the middle. How's that for starters?'"

"My gosh. What did you say?"

"What could I say? I said, 'I think that will do nicely by way of explanation; very thorough, thank you. Now please be a friend, and help me get my arm out of my belt. My trousers are about to fall.' He laughed, and we went on. Of course I made a joke too. You know me."

"What kind of joke?" She looked at him. She did not always appreciate his humor.

"Oh, I said . . . all right, please don't look at me like that, Skye. It was dumb. I admit it. I said, 'So, tell me — how do you undress a girl, then, with only one hand?' He blushed and answered, 'With permission, fool! Only with permission! Don't you know *anything*?' And that was that. He didn't mention the cruel jokes and other kinds of nasty business I've seen him have to put up with. Conrad and his friends, for example. Ardwin has been alone, on a hard road."

"Yes," said Skye. "That's what I was going to say. I think it must be very lonely to have a wing. I am afraid we have only made him lonelier."

"No, Skye," said Stephen. "We did not make him anything. We have only been truthful, at least with ourselves.

Something was growing between us. It took both of us by surprise, and he . . ." He paused, his head cocked curiously to one side, looking at Skye.

Skye had reined Thornbush to a stop. She had an odd expression on her face, withdrawn and distant.

"Are you all right?" he asked. "We'll work it out. It's all right, Skye. Trust —"

"Stephen," she interrupted, "do you hear . . . hoofbeats?"

He swung around in the saddle. Then, "Ride!" he yelled. "Ride, Skye! They are coming!"

She didn't hesitate, but took off at once, galloping fast. Stephen on Solo was close behind. A dozen riders were coming after them, riding hard. They were already splashing through the stream and clambering onto the rocky shore.

As they raced along the riverside, Stephen called to Skye and veered to the right, charging up a small embankment and onto grass and dirt, off from the river shelf. Solo's breathing was already labored, and Stephen hoped that he might have more purchase off the rocks and last longer. Thornbush was small, but fast. Already Skye had outflanked him and was racing alongside.

Stephen looked back; the riders were gaining. He could not escape, though Skye might. He thought of fighting, but these were his own king's men and he knew what they came for. And if he started fighting, it would be he and Skye who would have the worst of it, outnumbered as they were. They had come to the end of the road. It would still take a good three weeks to return to the castle. They had bought Ardwin all the time they could.

Solo stumbled and almost tripped, his breath coming in gasps.

"This is it!" Stephen shouted to Skye. "I will face them here. Ride on!"

Skye reined in Thornbush alongside him as he slowed. "We'll meet them together. We did our best. It was a good chase."

In a moment, the riders stormed up, circling around them. "Hold!" called the leader. "We mean no harm. Draw no weapons and no harm shall come. The king orders that you return. But where is the prince?" he asked, puzzled. "We tracked his horse."

"We don't know," said Stephen, reaching down and patting Solo, who stood breathing hard, flecked with foam, his head low. "We rode with him to his sister's castle. Then we parted, weeks ago. We will not go anywhere just now. The horses are tired. Solo needs rest."

"So I see. They traded mounts," said the leader, turning to the rider alongside him. "I'm glad we sent those three to follow the other tracks. That clearly was the prince's trail, despite what Conor's queen said. I did not trust her exactly. With luck they will have caught him by now." He turned back to Stephen. "Yes, poor Solo looks winded. Fair enough." He nodded and motioned to his men. "We camp here and leave in the morning." Then he turned to Stephen and Skye. "Do you have food?"

Stephen and Skye looked at each other. "We are down to hard crusts and the rinds of cheese," said Skye.

The leader swung down off his horse. "We'll make a fire and you shall eat well tonight. Welcome back to civilization," he said. "Your parents will be relieved. Believe me, everyone has been worried."

"And the king?" asked Stephen, dismounting.

The leader took off his gloves, stretched his arms, pulled off his helmet, and rubbed his head. "Ahhh." He sighed. "That's better. What a ride you led us! As to the king," he said, scratching his bearded chin reflectively, "I do not think he will have you drawn and quartered; at least not immediately. Cheer up, lad. Who knows — you might only be beheaded."

Stephen was sliding the bridle over Solo's head. "Thanks," he said. He bent down, loosening the sweat-darkened saddle girth. "That's certainly good news. Did you hear that, Skye? Only beheaded."

Skye was lifting the saddle off Thornbush's back. She set the saddle down and brushed a strand of hair from her face and straightened. "What a relief," she said drily. "Now I can hardly wait to get home."

Then the leader said, "Come. Rest a bit, then eat with us

and don't worry overmuch. Clearly you've done what you can for your friend, the prince. Surely deep down the king knows and respects it."

Stephen said, "Perhaps. But how 'deep down'? That's the nub of the problem."

"Come now," repeated the leader quite kindly. "It's still a long journey back. Who knows what will be when we arrive?"

The Wizard

"Aha," a voice murmured. "He wakes, at last."

Ardwin opened his eyes. He was lying on a bed, half beneath a robe of fur. His bare right shoulder and chest were wrapped in a wad of soggy grasses tied over with a cloth bandage. His wing lay exposed, above the robe. He was groggy and seemed to hurt everywhere. He had had a bad dream, a very bad dream. Where was he? What had happened? Where was Raven?

A small fire blazed in a stone fireplace. The blaze lit a ruddy-cheeked, elderly face. Ardwin saw long, gray-white hair and bushy eyebrows, a high forehead, a jutting beak of a nose, and a white beard. But the eyes peering down at him were youthful, clear, and bright. A fur cloak was draped over the man's shoulders. Beneath the cloak Ardwin saw a dark blue robe covered with silver stars. The man smiled and said,

"Be easy. Rest. But good for you! You live! It was touch and go, I have to tell you. You are strong and very lucky. A bit deeper and that claw would have torn your heart wide open. Then, good night."

Groggily Ardwin muttered, "Raven, my horse?"

"Dead," said the man. "And so is the lion."

"So, it was not a dream," murmured Ardwin.

"No," said the man. "You should be proud. Not many grown warriors have killed a snow lion unaided. It takes courage, not to mention considerable strength and skill."

"Who are you?"

"My name is Belarius."

"Where am I?"

"In my little fortress. Which is lucky for you. If the lion hadn't killed you, the storm would have. The beast must have been prowling nearby. He has tried before to make me his prey, but despite the nuisance, I let him stay to drive off unwanted visitors. Now you have deprived me of my door warden."

Ardwin raised his head as if to apologize.

"Rest easy," said Belarius again with a smile. "I forgive you. In any case, my . . . servant found you and carried you back here, where I tended your wound as best I could. You have lost much blood, but will recover. My potions will see to that. After you rest you must eat and regain your strength. You were attacked five days ago and have been feverish, ill, and only semiconscious since. We shall speak again later." He lifted a cup to Ardwin's lips. "Drink," said Belarius.

The liquid was warm, bitter, yet soothing. Ardwin drank it all, then lay back, closed his eyes, and slept.

When Ardwin awoke, the room was dark except for a few oil lamps and a glowing fire. A raven's head, a hawk-wing fan, and a dried hawk's claw with a pebble in the talons hung from the roof beam. On a table nearby lay a great thick book, its wooden covers held closed with an ornate silver clasp. Charts and maps and what looked like plans for strange towers and engines and other odd devices were jumbled all around, half opened on the table and floor. Black charts with white dots and lines on them, star charts marked with constellations, hung on the wall above his bed. Along the wall to his left, a stone stair mounted a circular tower.

Ardwin could hear a voice repeating words low and rhythmically, like a chant. He lifted his head gingerly and looked. Belarius sat beside the fire, his face and body illuminated by the flames. The arms of the chair he sat in were carved into serpents' heads; the reddish flickering light made the snakes' eyes glow and their tongues slither. A black iron pot hung above the flames. The old man was reading from a big book spread heavily across his knees, crooning as if to a child. But it was not to a child he was speaking, but to the bubbling potion simmering above the fire.

He finished his chant or spell, closed the book with a dusty *snap*, and looked to where Ardwin lay. "Just adding some good words to the brew," he said, and smiled. "I'm glad to see you awake. You have slept a full day since we spoke. Here is more of my healing drink for you. . . . What *is* your name?"

"Ardwin."

Belarius paused, his brow wrinkling. "Yes, that is what I thought. The wing proclaimed it. You are Ardwin, prince of the House of Peredur, are you not?"

Ardwin nodded.

"Well, Prince Ardwin," continued Belarius, "I have made a brew to help you heal and to restore your strength. And I have some food for you too." He set the book on the table, stood up, and carried a bowl of stew and a cup of the healing drink to Ardwin. "Drink. And eat some of this. It will help with the weakness."

Ardwin sniffed the steam rising from the bowl and discovered that he was famished, and he willingly ate and drank all that Belarius set before him. When he was done scraping out his bowl, Belarius said, "Now, if you can sit up, let's take a look at your wound."

Ardwin put down his bowl and very cautiously sat. As he moved, the skin pulled and he grimaced with pain, fearing too that the edges of the now healing wound might tear open.

"Hmmm," muttered Belarius with concern. "Is it bearable?"

Ardwin took a breath and nodded.

Belarius unwound the bandage and removed the dried, stiffened grasses. The raw, torn edges of the wound had closed well, but it still showed as an angry, throbbing gash. Belarius looked and considered, as Ardwin watched anxiously. At last the wizard nodded. "The worst is over. There seems to be no infection, and it is healing. It is the best we could hope for."

He rose, walked across the room, and poked among bundles of dried herbs and grasses hanging in the corner from a wooden beam. He picked one and put it in the cauldron hanging over the fire. When the grasses were long and slick, he fished them out with iron tongs, shook them in the air to cool, and bound them across Ardwin's chest. "There," he said. "It will do for now. Not too hot?"

Ardwin shook his head.

"Good. Be patient. Soon you will be up and about. My potions dramatically speed healing."

"Who are you?"

"Belarius."

"Yes, that I know. But who or what are you?"

"Ah, well, I am just as you see. A dabbler in herbs, potions, devices, an observer of the stars and skies, a master meddler in the magic of human affairs and dreams; in short, an alchemist, inventor, herbalist, architect, scholar of ancient lore, or, as you would say, a wizard. A wizard on the run," he added.

"The run? From what or whom?"

"From your neighbor, Ulfius, the Crazed." Then he added, "Perhaps like you?" And he glanced at Ardwin out of the corner of his eye.

Ardwin was impressed by this shrewdness. "Yes, in part," he said. "Ulfius did set a trap, but I escaped. But why do *you* run? Surely he did not try to trap *you*?"

"Try? Alas, no. He simply did it," said Belarius. "More or less. That madman is quite brilliant in his own demented way. The story is long, dull, and not especially pretty. When you are well enough to sit at my table and eat a meal, I will tell it. You already know the important part, anyway: I escaped! We are allies against Ulfius, you and I. We are both misfits too, things fallen out of legend, a wizard and an enchanted prince. But, my winged Prince, what you do not know is that you not only escaped from Ulfius, but from *me.* And now, though you ran very far, almost to the ends of the earth, fate, it seems, has brought you to my very door. Don't you find that somewhat *odd*?"

"What do you mean, 'escaped from' *you*?" asked Ardwin, confused and distressed by this turn in the conversation. "I do not know you! I have never even seen you before!"

"No," said Belarius, "you haven't. But you have seen my handiwork. It was I who made the arm."

Secrets and a Tale

Now Ardwin lay in bed thinking, *I planned my escape carefully and switched horses to throw off pursuers. I overcame obstacles and got to the swans and was driven out and lost. Raven was slain and I was almost killed, and yet, after all that, here I am, back with the arm! Well, with its maker, at any rate.* It seemed more than odd. It seemed uncanny. He could not avoid the disconcerting thought that he had been led here. *Belarius is not just some kindly old uncle of a hermit*, he thought. *If he was one of Ulfius's wizards, he must be cunning, powerful, and dangerous.* Evron, the Enchantress, had already ruined his life. What would a wizard do? Belarius had treated him well so far. But what does *anyone* know of wizards and magic folk? *The sooner I am out of here and on my way again*, thought Ardwin, *the better*.

Belarius entered the room and said, "Dinner awaits. It is

time you stood, walked, and ate something substantial. My potions work wonders," he added proudly. "I've cut your healing to days, instead of many weeks. Get up. You'll see."

Ardwin slid his legs from under the covers and rose. He took a dizzy step and said, "I remember this, but my legs don't. Give me a minute." He walked forward, began to stumble, and reached for the wall. As Belarius stepped forward to steady him, the wing flashed out, hit the wizard on the side of the head, and knocked off his hat.

"I'm sorry!" exclaimed Ardwin, embarrassed and concerned. How would the wizard respond? "Are you all right?"

Belarius picked up his tall hat and rubbed the side of his head. "Full of surprises, I see," he muttered. "Yes, yes, I'm all right. I'll be more aware of your range in the future. We'll work on the coordination as you heal and, with training, make improvements. You must learn to use your wing's wildness to your advantage."

"Better walk here, by my right side," said Ardwin, relieved that Belarius had taken it so calmly. "That way, there will be fewer . . . accidents."

Belarius nodded. "There are your clothes," he said, pointing to the corner. "Your cloaks too are on the hook, if you are cold."

Ardwin went to the clothing, and Belarius helped him on with his tunic. The rip in his leather shirt had been neatly sewn. As he raised his arm and wing to dress, the wound pulled, and he flinched, but the pain stayed within manageable limits and the wound remained closed. He headed toward his cloaks.

"Wait," said Belarius. "This is warmer, yet will let you move freely." He held up a vest of thick, pale, tawny fur. "Your lion's parting gift," said the wizard. "Come. Try it on."

Ardwin slipped his arm and then the wing through. "It fits," he said, looking down and admiring the vest, which was warm and comfortable. "Thank you."

Belarius nodded, took a torch from an iron ring and, with Ardwin following, led the way into the hall and down a short flight of stairs, which Ardwin descended slowly, using the wall for support. They walked along a windowed corridor. It was dark, and he couldn't see much outside except moonlight gleaming on the snow. They came to a long, rectangular, torch-lit room, where a fire burned brightly. Two places had been set at the table. There were flowers in a vase and fresh fruit, not just wrinkled, barrel-stored apples, in a bowl. *He is a wizard!* thought Ardwin. *How could anyone grow such things in deep snow and bitter cold?*

Belarius drew back a heavy wooden chair for Ardwin, who sat down cautiously.

"Trinculo, my lazybones," called Belarius, clapping his hands twice, "bring the meal."

There was a heavy, grating, metallic sound from the kitchen, as if a portcullis were being raised, or a suit of armor were stirring a pot. A stiff, slow, toneless voice answered, "Ye-es, Mas-ter." Heavy, shuffling footsteps drew closer.

Around the corner came a man walking stiffly and slowly, encased in a weird, flat, blocklike suit of armor, and wearing an apron. The outlandish figure came closer, closer. *Screech!* went its metal foot on the flagstones, *creak* went its legs. *Rumble rumble rumble* echoed hollowly from within. The armor gleamed golden bronze in the torchlight.

An old, arthritic man should not be wearing such heavy armor, thought Ardwin with pity. He thought less of Belarius, who would make an old man in armor serve his meals. The apron was surely some final indignity. The armored figure turned, and Ardwin saw red glowing glass eyes shining in the smooth, almost visorless helmet. The serving man stopped and bowed slightly. *Rumble rumble rumble, creeeeaaaak!* "Din-ner, Mas-ter," it groaned hollowly.

"Fine, Trinculo," said Belarius cheerfully, as if unaware of his old servant's suffering. "Serve our guest first. You may address him as Prince Ardwin, or Master Ardwin."

"Yes, Mas-ter," came the stiff, expressionless, hollow, slow voice. *Rumble rumble rumble, creeeeaaaak!* Trinculo stopped obediently before Ardwin and bowed stiffly.

"Roast, Mas-ter Ard-win?" came the voice.

Maybe the man within the armor has been horribly wounded or disfigured and that is why he is dressed as he is, thought Ardwin. He was covered in bronze plate down to his fingers and toes. His two arms looked very much like the arm, though less ornately finished, more utilitarian, and built on a more massive scale. Had the man's arms been torn off and then restored by Belarius in this way, awful as it was?

"Uh, yes, thank you, Trinculo," said Ardwin.

The armored figure held the platter with one massive hand and, with the other, delicately lifted a slab of meat and set it on Ardwin's plate. "Car-rots, Mas-ter Ard-win?"

"Uh, yes, Trinculo. Thank you."

"Wine, Mas-ter Ard-win?"

Trinculo held the platter and serving utensils on one flat palm and slowly bent down, lifted the decanter, and poured red wine into Ardwin's goblet. Then he bowed stiffly and slowly turned and rumbled and creaked to the other end of the table, where he repeated this performance for Belarius.

Then he stood attentively at Belarius's elbow. "You may rest, Trinculo," said the wizard.

At once the glowing eyes dimmed, and the hulking, armored figure went limp, locked into its limbs. No more sounds came from within its armored trunk. Belarius nodded pleasantly to Ardwin and began to cut his roast and eat. "Come," he said, his mouth already full, chewing. "Begin. We don't stand on ceremony here. Eat!"

Ardwin took a forkful of food, then stopped, his fork raised halfway to his mouth, leaned across the table, and whispered, "Wha . . . what is he? Is he all . . . right?"

"Quite," said Belarius, taking a sip of wine. "He is an automaton, a mechanical man. I made him. There is no one within that shell, nothing but gears and counterbalances and cunning little magnets and, oh, bits of this and slices of that."

"You *made* him . . . it?" repeated Ardwin, correcting himself. His fork remained poised in the air.

"First I made Trinculo and then Stephano, my two rustics. They built *this.*" Belarius motioned grandly, taking in the room as well as the whole surrounding fortress, with one sweep. "It would have taken me and a crew of workmen years. I made a hut, built them, and set them to work. In a little more than a month I had a warm, solid, and most important, impregnable home. Do you like it?"

"What I've seen of it," said Ardwin, putting down his fork and looking at Trinculo with new interest. "Why does he, uh, it, wear an apron?"

Belarius leaned in closer and whispered, "He insists. He feels he must dress appropriately for his work."

"Ah," said Ardwin. "And you, you worked for Ulfius? Was this before or after he trapped you?"

"Before," said Belarius. "I left after he trapped me. I escaped." He took a sip of wine and, with his other hand and his head, encouraged Ardwin to resume eating. "The arm was my last finished project. It was a marvel. Of course I didn't know *you* when I fashioned it," he added. "From its construction I first conceived of building my men. You like Trinculo?"

"Yes. He is amazing. Though at first, I thought he was an overworked, arthritic old man encased in iron." Ardwin chewed, then took another slice of the roast. Once more he was impressed. The food was very good.

"Arthritic old man!" laughed Belarius. He leaned forward again. "Your arthritic old man has a little secret. Watch. Trinculo!" he called.

Rumble rumble, creaaak. "Yes, Mas-ter."

"Take this." The iron hand reached out and took the bone Belarius presented. "That shield hanging on the wall, the one with the green gryphon painted on it."

The head and glowing eyes swiveled. "Yes, Mas-ter."

"Strike the eye," ordered Belarius. "Half strength. *Now!*"

The iron arm drew slowly back, then suddenly whipped forward, becoming a blur moving faster than any eye could see. Something white whirled through the air with a keen, whining *whirrrrr*. Then *clang!* The shield jumped, and a small cloud of dust rose. When the dust settled, Ardwin saw that the shield was pinned to the wall. His jaw dropped.

"You see!" exclaimed Belarius triumphantly. "Go look."

Ardwin rose and walked to the shield. The bone had pierced the iron shield through the gryphon's eye, then penetrated nearly two inches into the stone wall behind. "It's unbelievable!" exclaimed Ardwin, astonished. "The aim! The strength! To do that . . . why it's —"

"And that was only half strength," interrupted Belarius

proudly. "Trinculo and Stephano are good workmen and cooks, as well as excellent domestics and stable hands. But they are also powerful bodyguards and warriors, should the need ever arise, and could probably rout a small army unaided if I ordered them to. Axes and swords cannot easily stop them. Lances and javelins, even armor-piercing crossbow bolts, would have a hard time penetrating their clockwork vitals. They are not just for show. I have enemies, and need protection. The arm, you should know, would have made you powerful too. Not at that level, of course. It was, after all, only a first attempt. But you would have been very strong."

Ardwin's eyes narrowed. He walked to his chair and sat back down. "I would have been cut in two," he said.

"Ah, yes. There is that. Though some people might have thought the sacrifice worth it. *Some* people will do anything for power. Ulfius is one such. Hmmm. Speaking of Ulfius, perhaps this is a good place to start my tale. It is not particularly flattering to yours truly. No matter. I have always felt that in telling tales, no matter how fantastic, you must speak the truth. Just a minute."

Belarius instructed Trinculo to refill their glasses. "Bring my pipe and tobacco too," he said. When he had done so, the wizard took a sip of the wine and smiled appreciatively. Then he lit his pipe, blew a cloud of smoke, and began. "Ulfius gave me riches, challenging me with tasks no other could manage. He lured me and played me, I see it now," he added, blowing a ring of smoke, "for a fool. My own genius trapped me." Belarius drew on his pipe reflectively and exhaled more smoke. "So I destroyed everything I had made, and left. Now I stay here, where storms, winds, barren lands, and iron men protect me from prying eyes. That is my tale, more or less complete.

"Now, how did *you* get here? You weren't looking for me, were you?" He puffed on his pipe, making the bowl glow red, and looked at Ardwin through the coil of smoke rising between them.

"No. I didn't even know you existed. I was still running."

"Still?"

"I found your arm and saw my danger," said Ardwin. Suddenly the wing flapped at the memory of that flight. As it did, it struck the handle of a fork sticking over the table edge and sent it flying. Belarius ducked. Sparks flew from his pipe. The fork spun over his head and clattered on the flagstones.

"Sorry."

"Go on," said Belarius, straightening again, looking into the bowl of his pipe and reaching for his wine. "You missed. No harm done."

Ardwin lowered the wing carefully. Then he recounted what he knew of the arm and the marriage plan, concluding, "I didn't wait, but left before the trap could be sprung."

The wizard nodded, listening to his explanation. When Ardwin was done, Belarius tapped the bowl of his pipe on the heel of his hand, knocking out the ashes, and set the pipe down on the wooden table. He plucked a grape from a bunch in the bowl before him, dropped it in his mouth, and chewed. "Alisoun would be a dainty dish," he said. He drank the remainder of his wine. "Lips like cherries. Skin like cream. And mad old Ulfius as an ally." Then he said, almost ruefully, "Another of my devices lies at root here too, I'm afraid."

"What do you mean?"

"It's what widowed Alisoun," Belarius said, and he frowned.

"Something you made, one of your marvels, killed her husband? It was that uncontrollable and dangerous?"

"Bah! No! Certainly not!" exclaimed Belarius, eyebrows bristling, eyes flashing with sudden fire. "No more dangerous than an ax or fire or . . . or *sword* in the hands of a fool! What is not dangerous, then, eh? Tell me that! A fool uses things foolishly. Is that my fault? Can *that* be laid at my door?"

As if in answer, the wing leaped forward and swept a cup to the floor.

The wizard's bristling eyebrows settled. The fire died in his eyes. He smoothed his beard and seemed almost amused. "Well," he said. "Well, well. No, no," he said to Ardwin, who had risen from his chair. "Let it lie. Trinculo!" he called. "Clean up our mess!"

At once, Trinculo set to work, gathering the shards and mopping up.

Ardwin sat down and said, "I'm sorry again. The wing —"

Belarius waved him off. "A natural response, given my silly outburst. Where were we?"

"You were talking about your inventions in the hands of fools."

"Ah, yes. Well, enough of that for now, I daresay. Just go on with your tale."

So Ardwin told Belarius about Evron and his brothers and sister and the enchantment, and of their return, and of his life at home. "If I am to relinquish the wing, it must be my own choice, not anyone else's," he concluded. "I wanted to return to the swans. I had dreamed and planned of doing so for a long time! So, when I left, I went over the mountains to the sea. It was a difficult journey and treacherous, but I made it. I found them," he said with some pride.

"You know how powerful my arm would have made you?"

"I can guess," said Ardwin. "But it would have made little difference to me, even if I had known. My mind was made up."

"I see. And so you stayed with the swans?"

"Not exactly," answered Ardwin, remembering. He paused, lifted his glass, and drank. "I lingered too long, and they drove me away." He sighed and shook his head. "I was naive to think they would accept me. I was confused by childhood memories. Things had seemed so good, then. But I am a freak, and I don't fit in, either among humans or swans. I can't fly anymore, and that is where a swan's real life lies." He paused. "They are beautiful when they fly, and are courageous navigators. But they can be just as shallow and dangerous and cruel as . . . I had expected much more. When I saw all that, I no longer wanted to be part of their world. Then, when they attacked me, I ran and got lost in a storm, and, well" — he shrugged — "you know the rest." He sipped his wine again, unhappy with the memories.

"You were lucky," said Belarius gravely. "Trinculo noticed the vultures circling, so I sent him to investigate. He came back with you, near death. Now, with proper food and rest, your strength will return. Despite attacking silverware, smashed crockery, and a head wound — no, no, I am joking. A slight bruise only! — I am glad of your company. These are small prices to pay to make the acquaintance of such an interesting — even enchanted — guest." Belarius raised his glass to Ardwin, and made a small, courteous bow.

That night Belarius had a nightmare. He was running through a maze, colliding with walls, stumbling in darkness. The maze became a web with a great spider at its core. The web trembled, and the spider, dripping poison from its jaws, began to slide toward him. He looked up and screamed. The spider had his own face.

Belarius awoke in darkness. With trembling hands he lit a candle, then lay in his bed listening to the wind. Ulfius had made a mistake worse than he knew, trapping him in his own maze like that. It was not the first time he had been lost in tangles of his own devising. Padraic, his own wonderful son, had been no fool, yet the magic sword, the sword Belarius had made that sliced through all defenses, had one day gone awry and pierced the boy's throat. He had warned Padraic not to fool overlong with it. *It is dangerous. I told him that,* Belarius tried to console himself. "*Use it for short periods only,*" *is what I said,* "*or it will learn the weaknesses of your defenses and attacks. If it feels your strength flagging, it may turn on you and seek its own advantage. It has no heart! Listen to me! It is not to be trusted.*" *Oh, Padraic! You were strong and smart and brave! Why, why,* why *would you not listen?*

Belarius wept in the darkness for his dead son and his old and all-too-true nightmare. Wizards' mazes could be lethal. Marvels could turn deadly, and when they did, it was often their creators and those nearest them who suffered first.

Now this winged youth, hurt, lost, and running from another of his magical devices, had killed his door warden, entered his fortress, and found him.

Belarius was a wizard, and wizards know that behind the oddly tangled tapestry of visible events lurk invisible forces. So he knew that what seemed to be mere chance was actually only a first, weak manifestation of a greater mystery.

Lying in the darkness beside his flickering candle, Belarius steadied his mind and set patiently to work, untangling the as-yet hidden web that held the greater pattern in place.

Horse and Guests

The next day Ardwin headed outside for the first time since the lion's attack. Though the air was cold, the sun was bright and the sky clear. He sat on a bench and leaned against the sun-warmed stone of Belarius's house and tower, relishing the life that was still miraculously his. He could see a trail winding off among the trees and down the mountain. He was on the heights, he now understood, still high up on a level ridge of the mountain, well above the plain.

Belarius approached. "Come," said the wizard. He led Ardwin to a stone stable behind the house. "One of my little . . . experiments is in here."

"A weapon?" asked Ardwin. "A spear with a brain? Some new machine man?"

"No," said Belarius. "You'll never guess. Just come and see."

It was semidark in the stable. Two horses craned their necks over their stalls and looked at Belarius and Ardwin. Their brown eyes followed Ardwin warily, eyeing the brightness of his wing in the dim light. Belarius petted their noses and scratched their heads. "The brown is named Dust, and the gray, Ashes," he said by way of introduction. Dust and Ashes stamped uneasily, their nostrils flaring at the sight of Ardwin's wing.

"Are they the experiment?"

"No. Follow me," Belarius said mysteriously, crooking his finger. He led Ardwin deeper into the darkness of the stone-vaulted stable. There was a scuffling noise, and then a small, compact, muscular little horse briskly trotted out to meet them. It wasn't a pony. It wasn't exactly a horse. It was a kind of wild horse that Ardwin had never seen. Its head seemed oddly big for its body. It was bristle-maned, lion-colored, and gray-bellied. Its step was springy, its black eyes seemingly filled to the brim with intelligence and sly humor.

"Hello," said Belarius. "I've brought you someone."

The little horse marched up to Ardwin. It looked him up and down, and cocked its head to one side, examining the wing with curiosity. Then it looked Ardwin in the eye and boldly neighed, "Tell me about yourself. You're quite the odd duck, aren't you?"

Ardwin laughed aloud in delighted surprise. "My name is Ardwin. I was a swan. Who are you?"

The little horse's eyes opened wider. "Well, well, he walks, he understands, and he talks too! Thank you, Belarius! A live one, at last!" Then, addressing Ardwin, he said, "Dust and Ashes are not the most agile conversationalists. I thought Belarius was the only human I'd ever be able to speak with — you *are* human, aren't you?" Before Ardwin could answer, the little horse went on. "But to answer your question, Horse is my name and horse is my game. That is, I am *Horse*, and I am *a* horse. The ur-horse, the original horse, if you will," he added quite grandly. "The wild, primal, undomesticated, before-humans-ever-got-hold-of-us sort of horse is what I am. Before the wind was taken out of our sails and the smarts bred from our brains. I am the horse that put the horsiness in horses." He bowed his head. "Pleased to meet you.

"Now, Ardwin, tell me about this wing. And what do you mean when you say you were a swan? Are you one of Belarius's accidents? Did he hatch you from an egg? Did he try to make you human and botch the job? He's good at botching things."

Belarius interrupted, saying, "I don't need to hear any more of this. I'll leave you two to get acquainted. I have things to do. Things to *botch*. Be nice," he cautioned Horse. "No tricks."

"Who, me?" answered Horse.

When Belarius returned several hours later, Ardwin and Horse were outside in the sunlight walking together. Horse was nodding his head at what Ardwin was saying, then looked up and said, "Hey, Belarius! This winged person told me such a story, full of treachery, magic, and enchantment! Best of all, he swears it's all true."

"It is, Horse. Would you like to be part of that story?" asked Belarius. "You could go with him back into the tale."

"I do want to see the world!" answered Horse. "But I want to be in my own tale, not someone else's."

"If you go, you'll make it yours, or I don't know you. By the way, Ardwin killed the snow lion, alone and single-handed — literally — all by himself."

"He *did*?" said Horse. He stepped back and looked Ardwin up and down. "A lion-killer. Interesting. Snow lions are big. You might do as a traveling companion." Then he said rapidly in one long breath, "No saddle. No stirrups. No reins. Jaw-rope only. Keep it simple. Those are my rules. Equal partnership. I stay as long as I choose. I leave when I decide. Take it or leave it."

"Wait, wait," protested Ardwin. "Let's see. I can ride without saddle or stirrups. My spear's already broken short. If I keep it that way, I won't need a footrest." He paused and considered. "All right," he said. "I agree. Only I don't know yet where we are going, or when."

"When? Why, when you're ready, all healed and well," said Belarius. "Where? Where you choose. Now, lunch is served. Good-bye, Horse."

Without a word, Horse turned and raced off, galloping

and bounding over the cold, wet ground where the snow was nearly all melted and only isolated patches remained.

"So you created Horse by breeding back to ancient stock?" asked Ardwin as they ate.

"Essentially," said Belarius, nodding. "Trinculo, bring more bread, will you?"

"Yes, Mas-ter."

"Though I had to speed things up. Fortunately," said Belarius, taking a half loaf of bread from the basket that Trinculo now set before him and breaking off a good-size chunk, "I had several old books that indicated how it might be done. An interesting challenge, and one I had wanted to explore for some time. Up here I finally had the chance. Trinculo, more wine, too, please, and tell Stephano he can serve the pudding."

Trinculo bowed stiffly, then shuffled off to the kitchen. *Rumble rumble rumble, creeaaak.*

"Yes," said Belarius, returning to his conversation with Ardwin. "There are old types up here, herds long isolated by the glacier. I bred them back, and got Horse. He is quite a bundle of energy, isn't he, quite an interesting little handful. And smart! He already had a proclivity for language. I simply worked on it a bit more. It was in the breed from the start, that's clear. It seems that horses became duller as we humans took over and began ordering them about."

"I can believe it," said Ardwin, taking the remaining half loaf, setting it beneath his wing, and breaking off a piece with his hand. Putting the rest in the basket, he said, "Who wants to be ordered around all the time?" He dipped his bread in the last of his soup, then said, "I wouldn't. It would make anyone dull, don't —"

"Mas-ter," interrupted Trinculo, his red eyes glowing, his head turning at an angle toward the outer wall. "In-trud-ers."

"What?" exclaimed Belarius irritably. "Well, you know what to do. Drive them off. Go!"

Trinculo removed his apron and hung it neatly on a hook by the kitchen doorway. Then he and the other iron man, Stephano, marched from the room and down the corridor, their heavy, clanking footsteps becoming distant and faint. Ardwin heard a groan as the heavy outer door opened and closed.

"I was followed at one point," he said. "Maybe . . ."

"Or maybe Ulfius has again sent spies after me," said Belarius. "No matter. They can do nothing. Come. This will provide our after-lunch entertainment. We shall watch."

He rose from the table. Ardwin put the rest of his bread into his mouth and followed Belarius from the dining room to the windowed corridor. The wizard stopped there and pointed. Ardwin saw Trinculo and Stephano emerging from the courtyard. Arrows struck them, bouncing off harmlessly. A spear hit Trinculo in the head and glanced away, rocking him backward. He strode forward, stripped a sword from a man's grasp, and bent the iron blade as if it were soft clay. Three men in dusty gray and green clothing ran. Stephano lifted a boulder and flung it after them. It struck at their heels, sending up a shower of dirt and rock. The men threw up their hands and ran faster, disappearing below the ridge. Stephano and Trinculo watched, red eyes glaring. They gnashed their bronze jaws. They lifted great rocks and hurled them down, shattering them to bits. They kicked boulders with their iron feet, smashing them to pebbles. They ripped up bushes, tossing them high so that branches and dirt fell on their shoulders and heads. Then slowly, stiffly they turned, settled themselves, seemed to heave mechanical sighs, and reentered the courtyard. Ardwin heard the door groan open and shut. Iron footsteps echoed down the corridor, coming closer.

Belarius looked at him, one eyebrow arched as if to say, *You see!* and led him back to the table.

"We'll have dessert now," Belarius said when they were seated again and the two machine men clanked into the dining room. "And wipe off the dirt and leaves from your head and shoulders before you return."

"Yes, Mas-ter," said Trinculo obediently.

"Yes, Bel-ar-ius," said Stephano. "Would you like more wine?"

"No. No, thank you. And you, Ardwin?" asked Belarius.

Ardwin shook his head. He was looking at Stephano and Trinculo with new eyes. He had already seen a demonstration of strength and skill when Trinculo had thrown the bone. The ferocity he had just witnessed was something else entirely. Anyone having to face these two seemingly arthritic old serving men would find the experience terrifying. "That . . . that was astonishing!" is what he said. "Your men are formidable."

"Yes," said Belarius with a pleased smile. "As I meant them to be."

The machine men bowed stiffly and walked toward the kitchen. Stephano passed through the doorway, but Trinculo paused, took down his apron, and put it back on before he left the room.

When they returned, each carrying a tray of small cakes, their metal surfaces gleamed. There was not a trace of dirt left.

Advice

Ardwin's wound had healed. The pain was gone, and his strength, as Belarius had predicted, was back to normal, but he had been with Belarius several months and now he was ready to leave. He was no longer content to wander the halls or sit idly in the sun, or even to explore the mountain ridge by riding upon Horse. He had begun having dreams, uneasy ones, of traveling, of being out on the road and on the move. When he awoke, the restlessness and the frustrating sense of needing to be somewhere — but *where*? — remained, haunting him. Then, one night, Evron came to him in a dream. She glided out of a dark wood, her blood red lips curved in that odd, knowing smile, her long hair hanging down, black as a raven's wing. The sun was rising behind her, outlining her with a reddish glow. "Birdwing," she murmured eerily, her breath rising like steam, "why not have what you really want?" He awoke shivering with cold. Even her dream presence had been chilling.

Then he thought, *Yes. That's it! Why not find Evron and make her remove the curse? Rather than go home, cut off the wing, and put on a metal arm, why not find Evron and get my* own *arm back? Why not be really whole again?"*

Over the next days he quietly began to gather his things and prepare. He took out his saddlebags, sword, shield, and helmet, mail shirt, leather jerkin, brown cloak, blue cloak, cooking pots, and broken spear, spread them out on the bed and floor of his room, and inspected each item carefully. He oiled and polished the armor, sewed up small rips and tears in leather or cloth. He had not made a new shaft for the spear, but had simply smoothed off the broken end and made a harness so he could wear it beneath his wing, the blade sticking down so that the point emerged from behind the long, primary feathers.

Belarius had been training him to let the wing unfold only when needed, and he was getting better at it. Fewer broken plates and bloody noses would be nice. More significantly, with a spear attached, an uncontrolled wing could be deadly. There had been a few mistakes. Some loaves and apples had been shredded, a candlestick broken, and a roast neatly skewered. Which was not too bad, all considered. Belarius was an innovative and surprisingly spry teacher. The old wizard had taken to springing out at him, a heavy wooden pot lid raised like a club to strike him. *Whang!* Without conscious thought, the wing and spear could now block the falling blow, the spear's point embedding itself in the lid. Yes, he was learning. The spear and wing in combination were going to make a fine weapon.

That evening he sought Belarius, and found the old wizard atop the turret of the tower, beneath a star-studded sky, bent to the eyepiece of a telescope.

"Take a look," said Belarius, stepping back and, with his hand, motioning Ardwin forward.

As Ardwin bent to the lens, Belarius said, "Look from the corner of your eye, not from the center. You can see better when you don't look directly."

Ardwin looked. He saw glowing smudges, little spiraling clouds of gold and silver, and more sparkling stars than he'd ever imagined. Then he straightened and looked up. The river of stars still sparkled, but the smudges and whorled clouds of light were gone. He bent to the scope, looked, and there they were again. "What are those clouds like tiny fingerprints, glowing in the darkness?"

"Sometimes there are so many stars together, they look like a splash of spilt milk or, as you say, a glowing fingerprint. Each star is actually a world. The 'fingerprints' as you call them, are clouds of worlds, and are not tiny at all but unimaginably huge, as well as immensely distant. So my old books say."

"Strange," said Ardwin. "So many worlds. And so far." He looked into the eyepiece again. Then he asked, "Are they all like ours? Do people like us live there?"

The wizard shrugged. "Like us? But what are *we* like? You are winged. I am a wizard. Ulfius is a madman. And let's not forget your stepmother, whatever she may be. Who knows?"

Ardwin nodded. The wizard was right. What were we like? How could there be one answer, when there were Conrad, Ulfius, and Evron; Marjorie, Rose, and Conor, Harry, Annie, Victor? He thought to himself that leaving the mountaintop was going to be like leaving one world and going to another.

Ardwin said, "It is time. In the morning, I will go."

Belarius pursed his lips, and his brow wrinkled. "Yes," he said. "I thought so. Well, you know best. Where will you go?"

"To the east. I had a dream that I will find Evron there. I want her to take back her curse. I want my own two hands again. That is my wish."

"And why east?"

"In the dream I have seen her against a rising sun."

"I see. Well, that is bold. In dreams, the east is the direction of new beginnings. But be careful, young Prince. Witches and wishes can be equally dangerous. I wish you luck and happiness, but I'm not sure I wish you success, for what then? How do you plan to make her take back her 'curse,' as you call it? Do you think a sword will frighten her into submission? And then there is the little problem of *where* to find her."

Ardwin began to interrupt, but the wizard raised his hand, saying, "Yes, I know. 'East.' Well, you may search toward the east all you want, but I think it is more likely that *she* will find *you.* She may have something of her own in mind. Your dream may be a call."

"There *are* problems," admitted Ardwin, "and risks. Still, it must be done," he added. "For now, I will trust that. And no, it is not much of a plan, I admit. But I think that if I start, if I am decisive and take the first steps, then the rest will get clearer as I travel on." He paused. Then he said, "I am restless. I have to go. If you have any ideas, they would definitely be appreciated."

"Ah," said the wizard, nodding and raising his eyebrows. He looked carefully at Ardwin, then said, "Yes, sometimes hard things must be undertaken, and who knows how they will work out? A plan, any plan, only goes so far, and then . . . well, if your mind is made up, you'd better tell Horse. He's rather cautious and doesn't like surprises. For now, I will think of what you ask. If there is any help I can offer, I will."

"Thank you," said Ardwin. "I'll tell Horse."

In the morning, Ardwin put on his vest, armor, and helmet, and belted on the Hunter and his short spear. Then, accompanied by Belarius and the two iron men, who carried the rest of his gear, he went to the stable and called, "Horse! Horse! It's time."

But when the little horse came trotting up and saw that pile of gear and Ardwin fully dressed in his lion-fur vest, armor, helmet, cloaks, and a sword and spear, he let out a wild, whinnying cry, backed warily away, and raced off. Ardwin ran clumsily after him, calling, "Horse! Horse! Come back!"

Belarius nearly fell over, convulsed with laughter. Even Dust and Ashes began to whinny and prance.

At last Horse calmed down and returned, casually shrugging off his anxiety as if it all had been a big joke. "You should see yourself," he said to Ardwin. "What a sight you make in that gear! I had to run just to let you know."

"Not nervous, were you?"

"Listen!" exclaimed Horse testily. "I'm a herd animal. I *expect* companionship. We take care of each other, see?" Dust and Ashes nodded. Horse continued, "Together, we make one big creature with lots of ears and eyes, hooves and teeth. We weren't meant to wander on our own. It makes us vulnerable to predators. So, if I'm nervous, it's my *intelligence* at work. Nervous horses are smart horses, and they're fast horses. Nervous horses are horses that *live* longer. Get it?"

"Yes, I do," said Ardwin tactfully. "You are a horse setting out on a journey, and that makes you unique. You are a bold wanderer, a genuine individualist. I'm proud to travel with you."

"All right, then," said Horse. "That's better. Just don't

lay it on too thick. You might make me suspicious of your motives."

"Here," said Belarius. "Now that that's settled, I have something for you." He handed Ardwin a leather strand on which a great sharp tooth dangled. "Let this remind you of what you have done and what you yet may do. You have already faced terrible danger and come through, thanks to luck, skill, strength, and courage. May you do so again, and always. Let this tooth be your sign."

Touched, Ardwin took the necklace and slipped the thong over his head. The lion's tooth hung above his scar. "Thank you, Master Belarius," he said humbly. "I hope our paths will cross again, and soon. For now I have nothing to give you but my thanks, and that I give with all my heart. It is hardly enough. When we meet again, I shall do better. You have my pledge on that."

"Graciously offered," said the old wizard, moved by Ardwin's courteous words. "I accept your gift of thanks and will remember you."

Ardwin raised his hand and silently held the tooth for a moment, then set to work. The saddlebags were already packed with cooking gear and other necessities. Now Ardwin slung them over Horse's back and adjusted them, shifting a few items between the two bags until he was satisfied that they were equally balanced. Next he tied on his bedroll, roping it to the saddlebag straps. He made sure that the Hunter was securely belted, and that his spear's straps were cinched tight (the last thing he needed was to have the spear slip out as he rode). At last, he took a handful of mane and swung himself up onto Horse's back.

"Ooof," said Horse. "That's a heavy load for a free spirit like me. Give me a minute to let it settle." He stood swishing his tail and mouthing at the jaw-rope. "All right," he said. "There's a price, it seems, that must be paid for every adventure. Now that my payment has started — let our adventure begin!

"Good-bye, Belarius. Good-bye too, old Dust and Ashes! I'm off, but I'll be back to tell the tale."

"Yes! Come back to us, you brave, bold, strange little horse," whinnied Dust.

"Return and tell your tale," neighed Ashes. "We want to hear it all."

Belarius put his hand on Horse's neck and said gently, "See that you do return safely, Horse. We'll be waiting. Good luck, Ardwin. I do have one bit of advice. I read the stars last night. Go down the mountain and to the east. The stars say if you do, you will meet Evron, and maybe more than once."

"Do they say what will happen?"

"No," said Belarius. "They do not. They only say that there will be danger and trouble, which is what we expect, but also opportunity. That is the good news. They say you should be wary. They say to watch your back and trust your intuitions. There will be choices and dilemmas, and yet there is reason for hope.

"Evron has power. Your wing proves it. There are many kinds of wizards. Some can be very cruel. Be careful. You are alone."

"What do you mean *alone*!" snorted Horse.

"I meant alone, without an army," said Belarius. "Well, now, ride on, both of you, and may all go safely till journey's end."

"Good-bye, Master Belarius!" said Ardwin. "May you be safe from Ulfius and his schemes. I'll take good care of Horse, or try to." ("Ha!" snorted Horse. "I think it will be me taking care of *you*!") "Good-bye, Trinculo and Stephano."

The machine men bowed stiffly and answered with their hollow voices, "Good-bye, Prince Ard-win. Safe jour-neys."

Then, almost reluctantly, feeling suddenly how hard it was to leave the safety of Belarius's protected mountaintop and the friendship and support the old wizard had given and the kindness he had shown, Ardwin rode off along the trail and headed down the mountain. He turned and looked back, waving his wing until Belarius, the two iron men, and Dust and Ashes too had become no more than specks in the distance.

Ardwin sighed as Belarius disappeared from view. Here had been someone, one of the few, for whom his wing had been no problem at all. Going back as he was into the dusty old world of schemes and deceptions, he wondered if he would ever meet with such kindness again. Suddenly he realized that the wing was a kind of touchstone. Those who were put off by it should not be trusted. Conrad types and such. Others would easily stand the test, and for them it would pose no difficulty at all. *Why haven't I seen that before?* he wondered. Still, it heartened him to see it now as he and Horse headed down the rocky trail. He felt that it was a good sign.

Belarius watched Horse and Ardwin go and thought, *The stars also told me that your fate hangs on the edge of a knife, young Prince. One wrong move and . . . But why burden you with knowledge of that?* He sighed. *Maybe I should have said more. As it is, I may have helped set in motion the very events that will lead you straight to Evron. Danger and opportunity, indeed! I have become quite the meddling old fool!*

She is scary, that one. Full of the old, dark magic. She may be the last of that kind. I, and those like me, are of another order. The world that is coming will not be the world that has been. We are smarter, brighter, and lesser. They call me a wizard, and yes, I am. But my powers are not like hers. I could never have transformed those boys into swans and given Ardwin a wing. No, my powers are born of concentration, focus, application, hard work, and genius. But she dwells in the old magic like a fish in water. Like a root pushing into the depths of the earth. Who knows her purposes? Of what she plans or may do?

He looked down along the trail. Ardwin and Horse had already disappeared. "Good-bye, Ardwin," he said aloud. "I will miss you. Be courageous and be safe, if it is possible to be both. Good luck to you, lad, very good luck." Then he added, "For I'm afraid you are going to need it."

Downstream

As Ardwin and Horse went lower down the mountain, the day turned cloudy and it began to rain, a steady, cold, unrelenting downpour. That night they camped beneath the overhang of a boulder, which almost kept the rain off, unless the wind turned. Then it blew straight in on them. Creating a windblock of stones and crouching behind it, Ardwin managed, after numerous unsuccessful starts, to build a small fire beneath the shelter of the boulder. Horse, having gotten bored with watching Ardwin's dismal efforts, wandered out into the rain, where he grazed nearby, unmindful of the weather.

Ardwin lifted his wing out into the cold, flaring the feathers in a good stretch, then settled it back beneath his cloaks. He wore both cloaks over his lion vest, leather jerkin, and coat of mail, for warmth. The fire hissed as the wind turned and blew cold mist and rain under the overhang. He drew his cloaks to his chin. Even with the fire going, by morning everything would be cold and sopping wet.

Far to the south, Ardwin knew, the summer sun was blazing down upon turrets and towns, forests and fields. Ponds shone like mirrors. Fish and frogs lazed in warm water, where ducks and geese bobbed and quacked. He wondered if Harry, Victor, and Annie were thinking of him. Maybe they made a game of it. Where was he? When would he return? Where had he been? What had he seen? He hoped he'd be able to tell them someday. *What will the story be like when it is done?* he thought sleepily. As he drifted off, he seemed to hear familiar voices calling: *Come home, come home, come home.*

In the morning the skies were clear, the wind gusting and blowing. A band of gold blazed along the horizon. It would be a sunny day, and a good thing too. All the gear was, as Ardwin had feared, cold and wet, and the ground was soaked and muddy, the yellow grasses sopping. The sun's warmth would be very welcome.

"Good morning!" called Horse, raising his muzzle from the wet grass. "A delicious morning."

"Yah," grumbled Ardwin. He stood and stretched and remembered the voices he had heard calling from the edge of sleep. Yes, in time he would head home. He yawned loudly. "First I have to find firewood," he reminded himself.

He set off to look for dry twigs beneath the boulder and ledges. If he found some, he might be able to restart his fire.

In an few minutes, Ardwin held a large armful of sticks and twigs. He was bending carefully down to pick up one more stick — it would just fit under his chin and complete the pile — when *zzzzzzzzzt!* something falling from above flew by his ear. What was that?! He jumped back, letting his bundle of sticks fall, and saw an arrow quivering in the ground beside his boot! He drew his sword and looked, but saw no one. The arrow was standing nearly straight up. It had to have fallen from a height.

He looked up and saw a second arrow dropping straight down on him! Before he could leap aside, a snow owl swooped from the sky and caught the arrow in its claws. The owl circled in widening arcs away down the slope. Then, still high, it dove, releasing the arrow, which dropped as if shot from a bow. Ardwin now saw three men much farther down the mountain. One held a bow. The arrow struck the bowman, who dropped his bow, clutched his throat, and crumpled to the ground. The others fled.

Ardwin charged down the hillside and found the dead man covered in blood, the arrow struck through his throat.

Horse came galloping up. "What is it? Oh," he whinnied. "What a mess! All this blood is bound to draw wolves," he added nervously, "or . . . worse. Let's go!"

"You are right," said Ardwin, sheathing the Hunter

and looking around. "It is bound to draw something. But, Horse, he shot at me! This must be one of Ulfius's men, sent to kill me."

"Why do you sound so surprised?" said Horse, sniffing uneasily at the blood and wrinkling his lips in distaste. "You told Belarius that Ulfius might be after you, didn't you? I know you talked about it."

"Yes. But an owl caught the arrow in midair, then killed the man with his own weapon."

"That sounds like magic to me," said Horse. "And good luck for you."

"But whose magic? Belarius is far away." Ardwin looked around uneasily. He saw and heard nothing. There was only empty wilderness and silence.

"Well, you're right about one thing: It was very lucky," he said at last, turning back to Horse. "And, assassin or not, we can't just leave him here as food for vultures. We'll have to bury him."

"*I* could leave him," said Horse. "The sooner the better. Let's just go."

"Enough, Horse," said Ardwin. "Here, grab the collar with your teeth and let's get the job done."

Together they dragged the body from among the rocks. The dead man seemed immensely heavy. The helmeted head hung at an angle and knocked against the stones with a horrid *clunk clunk*.

Ardwin dug a shallow grave in the rain-softened earth. They laid the body in it, covering it with soil and rocks.

"There," Ardwin said, straightening his back and wiping the mud from his hand on the pine needles. "It's probably not deep enough. Something with teeth and claws is bound to come along, sniff him out, and dig him up."

"Please," said Horse. "Spare me the details. Let's pack and go. Of course he's going to be someone's food. What difference does it make whether it's worms or something bigger with teeth?"

They returned to their campsite and packed. Horse kept raising his head, looking around and sniffing the air nervously. Ardwin was watchful too.

As they rode away, Horse asked, "Are you sure you don't want to go back up the mountain rather than down?"

"I'm sure," said Ardwin. "Though this is certainly not the best omen for my return to the world."

"It's not so bad," said Horse rather sagely. "After all, he's the one who's dead, not you."

Footprints in the Snow

Late that afternoon Ardwin and Horse came to a sunlit meadow still high up on the mountain. Horse sniffed and stopped. He lowered his muzzle to the grasses and earth. "Look!" he said, parting the grasses with his muzzle.

There in the damp soil was the mark of a paw. "That murder was bad," he groaned, grinding his teeth with suppressed tension. "But this is terrible! I told you things worse than wolves prowled these mountains."

Ardwin loosened his sword in its sheath and looked carefully at the paw print. "The edges are clear," he said, "which means that it passed this way not more than an hour ago."

Horse's legs muscles started quivering. He lowered his head and nervously sniffed at the print once more. "The shape announces 'leopard.' The tufted edges whisper 'snow leopard.'

Something drew it down from the heights," he added nervously. "I hope that 'something' wasn't us."

"Whatever it was, I've got my sword," said Ardwin. "And the spear that killed the lion. Most of it, anyway. We'll be all right."

"Certainly, O Lion-Killer," said Horse. He shook his head and muttered something that sounded to Ardwin suspiciously like "famous last words." But they started forward again.

On the other side of the meadow the trail led upward again, and up they went with it, ever higher.

White mist rose around them. The air grew colder, and Ardwin had to wrap his cloaks more tightly around himself for warmth. Heavy snow began to fall, thick and wet. Horse trudged steadily beside the stream that now ran splashing down between snow-covered banks.

They were riding through snow-muffled aspen, birch, and juniper when a snow owl appeared again. Soundlessly flapping its wings, it silently wove its way among the maze of bare, snow-covered branches, snow softly tumbling from the blanketed tree limbs as it passed. Trees and boulders rose out of the mist and fog, eerie as ghosts. A dying sun peered dimly down.

"What?" muttered Ardwin uneasily.

"I didn't say anything," said Horse, cocking his ears back toward where Ardwin sat cloaked and mounded with snow. "Why?"

"I thought you said, 'Birdwing,' and then something else I didn't quite catch."

"Why would I do that?" retorted the little horse. "Who's Birdwing?"

"It was — is — me. I am Birdwing."

"Humpf."

A few moments later, Ardwin said, "Horse?"

"Yes?"

"Did you hear anything?"

"Like what?" Horse asked nervously, pricking up his ears.

"I thought I heard it again. Maybe it was just the wind."

"It wasn't," whispered the little horse, stopping dead in his tracks. "Look!"

A human figure, silent, hooded, and cloaked in white, stood beside the stream. The snow had stopped. There was no wind. The ghostly white, snow-muffled trees were quiet. The only sound was that of water, rippling and flowing downstream. The figure stood unmoving, its face hidden by its hood. A few last flakes of snow drifted, glistening, through the still air.

"Birdwing," the cloaked figure said slowly and softly. "Ardwin Birdwing."

Ardwin drew his sword. The sound of the blade being pulled from the scabbard was like a shriek in the awful stillness.

The cloaked figure suddenly vanished.

Horse reared in shock. Ardwin flapped out his wing for

balance and almost tumbled from Horse's back as pots and pans and cooking gear clanged and clattered.

"Whoa, Horse! Whoa!"

"I'm doing my best!" neighed the little horse, trembling, rolling his eyes, and turning his head every which way. "Who or what was that? And where did it go?"

"I don't know where it went," Ardwin said. "But I know who it is. It is just who I'm looking for."

"Who you're looking for!" exclaimed Horse in dismay. "Well, it's not what *I'm* after. Maybe the time has come for me to head off on my own, back the way we came. That was the deal. I never vowed 'through thick and thin.'"

"No, you didn't," admitted Ardwin. "I assumed we would be partners for a good while yet. We've got a long road ahead of us, Horse. I was counting on you. I could never make this journey alone. It's much too far."

Horse snorted uncomfortably. "You are counting on *me*?" He stood mumbling to himself, chewing on his rope. "Forward," he muttered, "and face it. Back, and *it* trails *us*." He swung his head to look back. He shook his mane and stamped. "I don't like it. I don't want it creeping up on us! Forward, then, for practical reasons, you understand. This has got nothing to do with sentiment. I don't care whether you count on me or not, understand?"

Ardwin nodded. "I understand."

They rode on. When they came to where the cloaked figure

had stood, they found footprints in the snow. With Ardwin leaning from Horse's back, peering down, they followed the prints deeper into the forest. The trail wound along the stream and among the trees, which grew ever more closely together. Horse muttered unhappily, "It's getting too tight in here. I need room to run!"

Ardwin whispered, "Look."

The footprints had shrunk. They were small and broad. The heel and boot-toe imprints were still human, but, only paces ahead, they changed and became the paw prints of a wolf.

An owl hooted from among the trees, *Whooo! Whooo!* And a woman's voice, soft and low, murmured again, "Birdwing. Ardwin Birdwing."

"Yes," answered Ardwin with a shiver, feeling as if he were in a trance or a dream. His hair rose along his spine, and his heart began to beat slowly and thickly, as if sludged with ice. She had named him. Now she called.

Standing not far ahead, at the end of the trail of prints, was the slender figure cloaked in white. They could not see its feet. Now it threw back its hood and long, dark hair flowed down.

"Evron!"

"Of course, dear boy." She smiled. "But you knew, didn't you? You sensed it. Haven't you been calling me? I certainly have been calling you. I have come to see my own little *Thing,* my own dear Birdwing. So, tell me, have you learned to appreciate the *Gift*?"

"It's not a gift," he said slowly, "it's a curse."

"Hmmm. Curse, is it? Too bad. I went to so much trouble to be sure that *you* received the unfinished shirt. Well, maybe I should I take it back, then," she said, "your 'curse,' that is, and make you *normal,* if that's what you want. I can do it, you know. Your father wanted that. You'd be strong with that clever arm, but maimed. I can make you *complete,* with two real arms of your own. Of course, there's no changing your mind. Once back in the Land of the Drably Ordinary, my dear Birdwing, there'll be no more cozy little chats with horses, or with anything else bound in fur, feathers, or scales. No foxes, horses, birds, or snakes, no interesting *voices.* Woof, quack, chirp, hiss, growl, neigh is all you'll hear, just like the rest of your dull-witted kin. And whips, reins, leashes, and spurs are all you'll need, for you'll be Man the Master. Yes. I could change you. But it would make even me terribly sad to do it."

Ardwin's throat clenched, and his mouth was dry. He trembled, so that his sword shook in his hand. He slid down off Horse's back and, from between chattering teeth, asked, "What am I to do?"

Horse backed up several paces and stood watching the unfolding scene with wide eyes.

"Do?" she answered. "Why, all you need *do* is make a

decision. 'Useless wing,' you've called it, and worse. Oh, I've heard you complaining to the darkness. Don't blush. Sorrow is never shameful. I could even make you all bird if you like! Such fun! To fly forever." She laughed. "To soar above the world, free and godlike and elegant as a . . . why, as a *swan*! To never be outcast or misfit again. To know your place in the eternal scheme and be *accepted*."

"How did you know?" he gasped, startled that she could so easily read his secret thoughts and know his despair.

She threw back her head and laughed raucously as a raven or crow. "A little bird told me! Oh, how I labored to make you wise. I tried so hard to give you opportunities, and grant you my special blessings of loneliness and sorrow. Didn't I make you *different*? *Unique?* Not one of the crowd? Isn't that what you all want — to be *special*? Then why haven't you learned to enjoy it? I've given you so many chances.

"Well, let us not dawdle. I give you a choice now: man or bird? Each one offers gifts and limitations. Either way you'll have your wish to be whole. Which shall it be?"

Ardwin could not speak. He felt as if he stood on the edge of a precipice. One false step and down he would fall.

Now that the opportunity to change his life was before him, Ardwin could not make up his mind. Either decision meant terrible, irrevocable losses. To fly again would be wonderful. But to be a swan? He had seen what they were like. Or to choose to be a man — human, ordinary.

Who was she to offer such choices? Where did she get such power? How dare she use it to toy with him? He had come to her for the arm, his own real arm. Now she held it out to him; all he had to do was take hold. Why couldn't he do it?

Evron tapped her foot impatiently in the snow. She looked up at the sky and at the dwindling light of the late afternoon. She looked at Ardwin and blinked, looking like a great bird of prey, maybe an owl. "I'm waiting,"she said. "It's getting late. What, still no answer yet? Has the cat got your tongue? *Meoow. Me. Ow!*"

"What *are* you?" he managed to stammer at last, stalling for time, trying not to lose this chance, yet so confused. "Are you even human, or —"

She didn't wait for him to finish. She whipped her white cloak around so that its hidden lining was now on the outside and it was as black as her raven hair. Dramatically stark, she stood against the whiteness of the snow.

"What am I?" she scowled. "I am both sides — the hunting dog and the hare with the broken back; the cubs that feed and the doe that starves; the swan that flies away, lovely against the sunset, and the one that gets tangled in the net among the reeds, dies in brackish water, and is consumed by fish and worms. Evron is Evron. And that is everything! I wait no longer. Farewell, my half-winged child. Dare to wish what you would be, and you will be as you wish!"

Evron flapped her black cape and became a great black raven that stood darkly upon the snow. The raven turned its obsidian eyes upon Ardwin and croaked:

"Do not care.
Have no care.
Ka! Ka! Carrion!
Ka! Ka! Carrion!"

Then Raven-Evron crouched down, flapped her glossy black wings, rose up into the sky, and flew away. The sun broke through the clouds and glinted on her wings, momentarily turning the shiny black feathers gleaming white. Then *flap flap flap*, she was gone.

Ardwin felt he had been released from a spell, and in that moment, the image of Stephen and Skye asleep together, their shoulders exposed in an embrace, flashed before his mind. Suddenly he knew what he wanted. "Don't go!" he shouted. "I . . . I . . . a man! I want to be a man!"

It was too late. Evron was gone.

"Wheeeeeeeeew!" whinnied Horse, prancing in the snow. "And she is your . . . ?"

"Stepmother," said Ardwin, bitterly disgusted with himself, once again pushing away the thought of Skye and Stephen together.

"Yes. I noticed the resemblance," said Horse.

Ardwin slung his cloak back over his shoulders and sheathed the Hunter.

"What was all that about whips and spurs?" asked Horse.

"Please," said Ardwin. "She twists everything. She is monstrous. But I'm not like her. I just want to be whole and human, not a freak or cripple, not pulled in two directions. And now I've lost my chance forever."

"Right," said Horse distractedly. "Listen. I'd like to be more sympathetic, but it will be dark soon, and it's getting cold. Can't you feel it? We need to find shelter. Remember the snow leopard?" He looked around uneasily and shivered. "And who knows what else may be lurking?"

The wind rose and the snow-muffled branches began to sway. Snow slid down, making the forest rustle and shiver as if with ghostly purpose and life. "Let's go!" insisted Horse. "And I mean *now*!"

Ardwin pulled himself together and swung up onto Horse's back. Then they rode up through the narrow, winding, rocky pass, the rock walls closing around them wet and slick with melting runoff, and green in places with moss and algae slime. They came through the pass to the other side of the narrow canyon and started down.

It was dark and very cold when they stopped at last in a circle of mossy boulders. A bitter wind blew. What had been wet was already beginning to freeze. But there were no footprints to be seen, human, leopard, or wolf, and Horse said that that was good. They camped inside the rough stone circle as the wind prowled and moaned around them in the darkness like a living thing.

Just before Ardwin dozed off, a fragment of Mr. Bluestone's odd little spear prophecy floated into his mind. Something about *Her.* He couldn't remember it clearly. He was very tired. "Blood and *it* and *Her.* And not just *Her.*" Then there had been something about wings too. He tried to follow the thought, but lost the thread as it became mixed in his mind with Belarius's prediction that he would meet Evron, maybe twice. *Tomorrow, then, I may have a second chance,* he thought. This time he would be ready.

The next morning they started down the mountain.

Apple Valley

Ardwin and Horse were riding through a pine forest along the banks of a stream. A raven glided above them, gave a drawn-out, bell-like, chuckling *croaaaak!* — then flapped its wings and flew away. Startled, Horse flinched and looked up. A flock of small birds rose twittering from the nearby bushes and shot off into the east. A heron stood fishing in the stream, its wet plumage trailing like a cloak, its long beak pointing at the water. "Birds," Horse muttered, and gave a little shudder. Then he added loudly, as if to someone who might be listening, "Don't get me wrong. I'm not complaining. I *like* birds. Birds are so much better than leopards or wolves."

The trail wound gently along the shoulders of the wooded mountainside, following the stream. Now the long, green valley they had seen from above was before them. Tendrils of smoke rose at the valley's end, where the turrets of a distant castle lifted against the sky.

"All right," said Ardwin, taking a deep breath and settling himself more firmly on Horse's back, remembering just how unhappy he had been in a place like this. "Here is my old world again," he said. "Or one probably very much like it."

Horse shook his neck and mane almost irritably and said, "It smells strange. It makes me itch, like flies are crawling over my skin."

Ardwin nodded and said, "That sounds about right."

They rode into the valley and along the mountain's root, and came to an old, untended orchard where small, greenish fruit hung from tangled branches.

"Apples!" exclaimed Ardwin with delight.

Horse said, "I've tasted such delicacies before. Belarius grew them on little trees in a room of crystal. But to see so many, rows and rows! It's like magic! It's unbelievable! This old, itchy world of yours is a wonderful place, after all! Why did I ever stay so long up on that dreary mountain?"

"Because the world is many things," said Ardwin. "Apples may have worms. Eat too many and you'll end up wishing you'd never even seen an apple tree. A stomachache and the runs will be your dues."

"Bah! Just give me the apple," said Horse. "I can mind my own stomach, thank you. I've had it all my life and I know what it needs. And that's apples!"

"All right. But when you're rolling on the ground kicking your legs in the air, don't say I didn't warn you."

"What a nasty picture you paint! Hand over that apple."

Ardwin passed two small apples to Horse and ate another himself.

"Amazing!" Horse shouted. "This is worth the whole journey so far!"

Ardwin stuffed apples into his saddlebags and the folds of his rolled-up cloaks and they set off again.

Old wagon tracks stretched before them, making a road that cut through the field and led to a pond. They rode on.

Up ahead by the pond, Ardwin saw a tall, athletic-looking girl, the sun glinting like gold among her curls. In one fist she gripped a spear. Butterflies rose from the long grass nearby and fluttered around her. Red-winged blackbirds swayed on thistles. In the pond behind her a flock of geese bobbed among the reeds.

The girl turned toward Ardwin and Horse, and as she did, her posture shifted from one of relaxation to that of readiness. She leveled her spear. Yet she seemed to lean confidently forward too, like a figurehead at the prow of a ship, stretching over the waves toward whatever may come.

As they rode closer Ardwin could swear that the grass seemed greener, and the murmur of the breeze was like a melody heard long ago. He made sure the wing was covered.

(Were her eyes gray? Yes, they were, gray as clouds in rain-filled skies.) As they got nearer, the girl's face lifted into a smile. *It must be because of Horse,* Ardwin thought. The song of the breeze rose again, and the wing tried to rise with it, as if to flap out a greeting. Ardwin held it down.

Horse looked back at Ardwin and smirked.

Ardwin hadn't seen any human except Belarius for months. The only girl his own age he had even been around for any time before that had been Skye. For an instant, Skye and Stephen came into his mind. Where were they now? What were they doing? It was too uncomfortable to think about.

This girl up ahead seemed poised and strong, and increasingly pretty the closer they got. What to say to her? He shifted nervously on Horse's back, his mind curiously blank.

"Mares," whistled Horse, turning his head back toward Ardwin as the goose girl and gleaming pond came closer, "stir up the blood."

"What?"

"I bet she likes apples," added Horse.

"Stop it, Horse," said Ardwin. "Leave off now and let me be."

Which is essentially what the girl said when they got close.

"Hello," she said. "Please stop right there. My geese may start flapping and flying and working themselves up into an awful state if you come any closer. They are not used to strangers. I suggest that you and your interesting little horse stay where you are, at least for now." She looked at Horse and Ardwin pleasantly enough, but her grip stayed firmly on her spear, which, to Ardwin's discerning eye, she handled with confidence, ease, and skill.

"All right," said Ardwin. (*She was pretty!*) "I do understand about geese and their temperaments."

"Little?" muttered Horse. "Hummph!"

Ardwin searched for a way to continue the conversation. He had the feeling that she was waiting for him to say something, yet his mind remained a blank. It was not going well, and he wanted it to. More and more, as he looked at her, he knew that he wanted it to go very well. After a long moment, he asked, "Is . . . is there an inn nearby?" *Dumb!* Inwardly he winced at his own ineptitude.

"Go straight ahead," she said, not seeming to notice, "and follow the wagon tracks. In a mile or so you will come to a road. Follow it another five miles and you will come to The Roost. It's not the finest place, from what I have heard, but the food is said to be substantial and the roof does not leak except in the heaviest rains."

"That should do," said Ardwin. "Well, thank you." *Dumb again!*

"Your horse," she said, "is unusual. I have never seen anything like him before. He looks, well, intelligent and wild."

"I am intelligent," whinnied Horse. "And wild too! That's the beauty of me!" And he pawed at the earth and reared and lifted his head so proudly that Ardwin almost had to flap out his wing to maintain his balance. Instead he clung awkwardly to the jaw-rope, certain that he looked both foolish and unskilled.

But the goose girl only laughed happily, without any derision, as far as he could tell. "Why, he almost seems to be responding to my words! It's nice to see such liveliness in a domesticated animal."

"Yes," said Ardwin, relieved that the wing had not been revealed, and that no barbs were hidden in her laughter. He pulled at his cloak and said, "He's smart and wild and unusual. He's from the north."

"North?" she said, puzzled. "Isn't that just wilderness? Are you from the north?"

"No," he said. "But I've been there. And it is wilderness, but . . . well, it's a long story. Anyway, he *is* different. I like that about him too."

She looked at Ardwin and at Horse for a moment, then stuck her spear point down in the earth, stepped forward, and let Horse sniff her hand. Then she began to scratch Horse on the forehead, between his eyes, which he closed, luxuriating. "It's nice that not everything is *ordinary,*" she said. "Differences are good."

Ardwin brightened. He said, "Yes. I agree." He paused. "Well, thank you. Thank you, again."

"Yes," whinnied Horse, opening his eyes with a sigh. "Thank you."

"I guess we'll go look for that inn now. Good-bye." *Idiot!* he thought, and all positive feelings vanished.

"Good-bye."

"Well, thank you!" said Horse sarcastically as they ambled on through the field. "Why did you just up and leave?"

"I didn't know what else to say," Ardwin confessed. "I wish I did, Horse. But I got tongue-tied and just blurted out the first thing that came to mind."

Horse turned his head back and sniffed at Ardwin's leg. "Yes. That's true," he said.

"What do you mean?" asked Ardwin uneasily. "How do you know?"

Horse sniffed at Ardwin's leg again. "The nose knows. Odors are a sophisticated language for us horses, my small-nostrilled friend. It is part of our 'smartness.' A gift from the ancestors. I smell your interest. It wafts off you like perfume."

"You smell how I *feel*?" said Ardwin.

"When I put my mind into my nose, I know what I know," answered Horse smugly. "Take a bath," he added with a nickering laugh, "if you want privacy. Horses swim to cool off *and* to have our own thoughts and feelings. Water washes away the scent so, for a time, we have our thoughts to ourselves. It's like when humans close a door so they can talk in private. Ah, well," he chortled, "too late for you. No chance of that now."

"Enough! Now, giddyap!"

"What's 'giddyap'?" asked Horse innocently.

"It means, 'pick it up, get going!'"

"Oh, yes sir," snickered Horse. "Definitely. Anything you say, sir!"

And he ambled on at the same, slow, steady, leisurely pace.

Schemes and Swords

"Evening," grunted the innkeeper, a big, dark, unshaven man going to fat. He eyed Ardwin curiously. The young man standing before him looked fit, strong, and barbaric. Broad shoulders stuck out through what looked like a lion-skin vest. He had a tousled, well-traveled look, and there was a cloak draped over his left side. An old, heavy sword hung at the youth's waist, and a tooth big as a dagger dangled from a thong around his neck.

The Roost was near the borderlands. The innkeeper had seen strange sights before.

"I'd like dinner, a room, and stabling for my horse," the young man said.

"Certainly." The innkeeper nodded. "Traveling, are we?"

"We are."

"Not from these parts?"

"No."

"Heading . . . ?"

"To supper and bed."

"Certainly," said the innkeeper again. "Stable's out back. For your horse." Then he continued smoothly, "Roast tonight, and ale. I'll have it ready for you."

Ardwin went back out to Horse. "It's set," he said. "Let's go."

But Horse stood unmoving when Ardwin took the rope. "I'm going to get fat and stupid," he moaned. "I can feel it. Once things get too comfortable, it's the end of all my hard-won fitness and keen-eyed wisdom. I should have never left my wild, windy mountain. I was wrong to go." He sniffed the air uneasily. "Besides — I smell disaster."

"What you smell is greasy cooking and unwashed bedding. The inn, as the goose girl said, is not the finest. I can smell it too. Anything can mean trouble if you let it," said Ardwin. "You know that. And you're good at sniffing out disaster in almost everything. No. Don't tell me! It's your *intelligence* at work. Nervous horses are smart horses. But this won't be so bad," he added. "If it's comfort you fear, let me reassure you: It's not going to be all that comfortable. I can almost guarantee it."

Ardwin left Horse in the stable, morosely munching oats and an apple. More horses were tied outside, and men and horses passed Ardwin on his way back to the inn. When he reentered, he found a group of merchants seated at a table in the corner. The innkeeper's promise had been good: Food and drink were waiting for him. Ardwin sat down, took a long swallow of ale, and set hungrily to his meal.

Four big men swaggered in and sat nearby. Three were very large and darkly bearded; the fourth was smaller than the others, though still larger than Ardwin and, unlike the others, had pointed features and sandy-colored hair and beard.

Beneath Ardwin's cloak the wing ruffled. It didn't seem to like these new guests.

"That goosey girl," drawled the smallest man, lifting his tankard, taking a long, wet swallow, then smoothing down his reddish beard. "Ah! That's good. Washes the dust away. So that goosey girl, as I was saying. Shall we go back after dinner and ruffle her feathers? What do you say?"

Ardwin's eyes narrowed. They were talking about the gray-eyed girl by the pond. His heart grew hot and his chest tightened. He could feel the stiffened skin along his lion-scar pull taut and tight.

One of the three dark-bearded hulking giants laughed aloud, drank a long swallow himself, wiped his mouth with the back of a meaty hand, and nodded. "Aye, Sniccan." Then he giggled. "Hee hee hee hee!" It was an oddly unsettling sound coming from such a big man.

"Perhaps, brother Snorg," gruffly mused another. "But I

may have a better idea. Innkeeper!" he boomed. "Bring more ale and another platter of meat. Rare, this time, with the blood dripping! And be quick about it!"

"Meat," repeated the largest of the giants in a growl like thunder. "More meat!" And he pounded the table with an immense fist. *Boom!* Ale sloshed as the mugs danced and shook.

Then Sniccan grabbed his ale off the shaking table, took another swallow, and said, "I want to kill that ugly little horse when we go. I hate misshapen things. It tried to kick me when I cursed it. Well, it won't soon forget the stone I hurled at its ribs."

The middle giant turned, looked down calmly at him, and said, "Find the owner, pay him for it, and then you can kill it."

"Kill," repeated the largest giant, nodding his head happily as he gnawed a slab of roast.

"Hmmm. Yes, I guess you're right, Wearg. Do it proper and all. You know, strangling might be nice," mused Sniccan, lifting a slab of roast and chewing thoughtfully, as if picturing wonderful possibilities. "Slower than a spear thrust. That's good. Drags it out. Less blood that way, of course. Would miss that. Still, I'd get to use some muscle. I might need some rope, and a stick to twist it. Be pleasant to kill such an ugly beast nice and slow."

Ardwin's hand dropped to his sword hilt. His wing unfolded farther, lifting the cloak angrily.

Sniccan caught Ardwin's eyes upon him and sneered, "Something you want, *boy*?"

"You can't buy the horse," said Ardwin through clenched teeth.

"And why not?"

Ardwin thought, *Because he owns himself. No one can buy him.* But what he said was, "Because he belongs to me."

The smaller man threw back his head and began to whinny, making horse sounds. The three giants laughed.

"Oh, what a nice horsey!" said Wearg, clearly their leader.

"Hee hee hee!" giggled Snorg.

"Horse," rumbled Narg.

Sniccan stopped his horse imitation and said, "Then I'll buy it from you so I can kill it legal. Isn't that right, Wearg?"

"That's right," grumbled Wearg. "If you own it, you can kill it anytime and however you choose. That's the rules. Isn't that right, Narg?"

The largest of the giants nodded his huge, shaggy head, licked his bloodstained fingers, and almost blubbered for joy as he carefully repeated, "Kill."

"You can forget it. I won't take your money. The horse stays mine."

Wearg smiled. "Pity," he said. "So, if we want the crooked

horse, which we do, we'll just have to kill *you.*" He nodded at the others.

All four of the big men rose. A chair teetered and fell with a crash. The merchants gawked anxiously; the innkeeper stood frozen in the doorway, a full tankard in one hand, a big platter of meat in the other.

Wearg drew his sword first. Then Snorg drew his too. Narg straightened up, huge and hulking, grinning and cracking his knuckles with a sound like stones breaking. Sandy-haired Sniccan drew his blade and circled to Ardwin's left, stepping smoothly from Ardwin's line of sight with well-practiced efficiency.

Ardwin stood and drew the Hunter. His heart was racing, but curiously, there was nothing he could name as fear. A swan warrior's strength and sureness were flowing in him. The wing was wide-awake. He had always been a strong swordsman, with an arm that few of his peers could match. But he had never faced grown, experienced men before, nor had he ever been outnumbered. Nor had his opponents ever been so big. Nor had any of his fights been to the death.

Wearg swung a heavy blow at Ardwin's head. Ardwin blocked successfully, making the large man grunt with effort. Then Snorg's sword sliced at Ardwin's neck. Ardwin dropped the cloak, revealing the wing, and the broken spear met the sword's edge with a decisive *clang!* Belarius had prepared him well!

"Wha . . . ?"

"A trick!" said Sniccan, circling to the left, never taking his eyes off Ardwin, or his sword's tip from pointing at Ardwin's chest. He licked his lips like a fox staring at a goose. "A clever boy's trick. The feathered cloak of this dandy will be just the thing to wrap our goosey girl in. After we've killed him and his ugly horse."

"Aye," agreed Wearg, circling to the right as the others drifted left. "Right you are, Sniccan. Here's a plump goose to carve between us."

Ardwin smiled grimly and said, "You are mistaken. It is no trick." And he raised the wing openly, blowing the fire aflame halfway across the room with the draft of it.

Their eyes widened at that. They saw now that it was not a feathered cloak, but his own body. But they were angry and committed to the attack. They looked at one another and, again, Wearg nodded. Sniccan smiled crookedly and said, "Misshapen, is it? A freak, is it? We'll soon put an end to that!"

Ardwin had overplayed his hand — even he saw it. It was four against one. A more experienced man would have worked them skillfully, cutting down the odds by surprise or by taking them one by one. Now he might have to pay for his rashness with his life. He gripped the Hunter with his one hand, flapped his spear-bearing wing, and prepared for the worst — when, with a crash of shattering wood and splintering glass, something tawny dove into the room. Its neck was out, its ears laid back, and its mane a-bristle. Sniccan's sword was at Ardwin's back about to strike when Horse's teeth sunk into Sniccan's shoulder. Then Ardwin's spear was against Snorg's throat, and his sword pressed into Wearg's gut. Horse lashed out with a terrific kick that caught Narg on the knee, tumbling him to the floor. Two tables and all their chairs and mugs of ale fell with him.

"Get out!" cried Ardwin in fury. "All of you! Now! If you so much as look at the girl, I swear I will find you and kill you all!"

And when the men had fled (Sniccan dragging his sword arm and trailing blood; gigantic Narg hobbling, holding his injured leg) and ridden away, Ardwin turned to the tavern keeper angrily and said, "I was outnumbered and one was at my back, yet you stood mutely by. This damage is yours."

The tavern keeper, eyeing the bold, winged figure before him and a ferocious, bloody-mouthed, bigheaded, bristle-maned little horse snorting beside him, gulped and said, "My master, I was afraid. I meant no harm."

Ardwin took several deep breaths and calmed himself. "If that is so, this is for your troubles." He tossed some coins onto the table. Then, as the innkeeper and merchants watched, awed, he led Horse out of the tavern.

"You came for me!" exclaimed Ardwin, astonished and grateful when they stood alone outside, with only the night looking on. "You stood by me and risked your life, Horse! I'd be dead by now if it weren't for you."

But Horse didn't seem to be listening. Instead, he stood muttering, trembling, and shaking.

"What's this?" asked Ardwin, surprised.

Through chattering teeth, Horse groaned, "Stop your silly chatter and listen to me, will you? It was horrible, I tell you. Horrible."

"What was?" asked Ardwin, taking a deep breath and feeling his own legs start to shake, now that the fight was over.

"I was in the barn. They brought in four horses, a mare and three stallions. At least I thought they were stallions. Oh, I was right about the dangers of this place! Those horses were big, fat, and stupid. They smelled funny too, as if all the fire had been drained out of them. Even old Dust and Ashes had more life! Those horses had been fed their whole lives and ordered about, I could see that. That wasn't it. Then I saw what it was. They . . . they weren't stallions. Not anymore. Their . . . maleness, their stallionhoods had been cut off! Castrated! It was horrible! When I saw *that,* I bolted from the stable to find you. And look at what I had to go through just to get in a few words!"

"They're called geldings," said Ardwin slowly. "They do that to keep them tamer and more rideable. They call it being 'fixed.' It's the way of civilization."

"I'll bet it is," said Horse distastefully, spitting Sniccan's blood from between his teeth. "Fixed! How very like men! As if those horses had been broken before, and now they were . . . *fixed*! Ugh!" He spat. "That tastes so foul! That blood in my mouth is just awful! How can anyone eat meat? Get me an apple. A juicy one! And I mean right now. Be quick about it!"

Ardwin did.

As Horse munched his apple he stamped his leg in anger and fear. As they walked to the stable, it was Ardwin's turn. He stopped and began to shake again, then leaned his face against Horse's shoulder. Breathing in the familiar, wild horse smell, he flapped his wing to release the pent-up tension that remained, making the dust and straw swirl around them.

"All right. Thanks," he said when his fit had passed. "I'm ready. Let's go."

"Achoo!" sneezed Horse. "You raised a lot of dust. Now, what about sleeping in a bed?"

"My mistake to want to roost. We should be traveling. I want the stars above me and the earth beneath me and a friend I can trust nearby," said Ardwin. "And that's all. That's plenty. It's the best."

"All right, then," said Horse. "But let's get another load of apples tomorrow, just in case."

"In case, what?"

"In case you try to head off without them," said Horse. "There must be compensations for difficulties. Apples will do just fine for now."

That night, rumors raced through the valley of a champion and hero, or of a winged warrior and magician, riding a fierce and magical tangle-coated horse, though some said it was a lion. The merchants told the tale too as they traveled, and the innkeeper told his customers, "Yes, this is the window the, uh, lion tore through. He and the winged boy seemed to talk to each other. Like something out of old legends, it was. Whets the whistle, it does. Another pint? Certainly, sir."

The tale was carried on the wind, and rose to the castle that looked over the valley, where two princesses sighed, thinking of a strong, winged youth traveling nearby. But when the third and youngest sister said she thought she might actually have seen and spoken with him, her two older step-sisters laughed and mocked her, saying, "Silly child! What do you know of heroes? Don't fill your featherbrain with dreams. Go back to your geese, you goosey girl. You like their company well enough, heaven knows, and they're quite at home with you! Like seeks like!"

And the youngest sister, whose name was Alene, straightened her back, flashed her gray eyes, and said, "As you wish, my . . . sisters." And she left, taking with her a backpack containing cheese and bread and a warm cloak too. She tied a dagger to her waist, took a spear in her fist, and went out to drive the cackling geese from pond to pond. She did not plan to return to the palace for many days, preferring, as was often her way, to sleep out in the windiness and wild, beneath the stars.

Alene

It was the wolf's howling that woke her. *Just as well*, Alene thought. *I've had enough of the old nightmare*. The wolf's eerie, wavering cry continued rising, falling, then sank down and vanished. Alene yawned loudly, put out her hand to find her spear, and drew it closer. The stars were bright and the wind was up. Her fire was nearly out, so she rose and added more branches.

In her recurrent dream, or nightmare, or whatever it was, she was trapped in some kind of den or burrow underground. It was stuffy and she could hardly breathe. She smelled dank, sour earth. The light was dim, too dim to see much detail; the wind moaned outside. She was a little child, and she was scared, crying. Then something big and hairy wrapped great furry arms around her, drew her close, and comforted her. There were powerful odors of fur, of a great, warm, enveloping body, and the sweetness of . . . milk! Then she was nursing, drinking the great beast's milk, which seemed heavy as cream, rich as meat. Hot breath blew across her face. A soft, wet tongue licked her cheek, nose, and brow. She heard a deep grunting, moaning, *unnnh unnnh unnnh* sound, a rhythmic crooning that soothed all her fear away. As the body of the beast rocked calmly, tenderly, from side to side, the child Alene stopped crying. The crooning rose and fell, perfectly matching the pulse of the wind. Everything seemed to be back in harmony, and she was no longer afraid.

But there had been much, much fear. There had been terror, chaos. She remembered darkness, fire, shouting voices, and swords like iron teeth gnashing; she remembered groans, the thud of bodies falling, and the smell and taste and sight of blood. Then came the nightmare time of wandering, held too tightly against an iron shoulder, swaddled in a sweat-stained, urine-smelling cloak. She, who had lived so delicately — bathed in rosewater, fed on cakes and honey — had been filthy and hungry. And then the beast, big and dark and covered with fur, had reared up at the forest's edge, roared like thunder, torn off her captor's head, and carried her away.

She sat up from her old dream and fed the flames. The wolf howled again, filling the night with its lonely song. "Howl," said Alene to the darkness, "growl and snarl all you like. I don't care. If you are hungry, I might even toss you some scraps. But try to steal one of my flock, and I will kill you. Be warned. I have met and killed your kind before." She began to braid her hair. If it came to a fight, she did not want her long hair blowing in her eyes, blinding her.

When the wolf howled, Ardwin awoke. Horse was standing alert and still, ears erect. "Maybe half a mile," he said, "moving parallel to us, not coming closer." Horse's nostrils dilated as he sniffed the wind. "And there's someone else out there."

"What? Who?" asked Ardwin, sitting up in concern. "Not those idiots from the tavern?"

"Near the pond," said Horse. "Listen."

"I don't hear anything," said Ardwin. "Except the wind in the trees."

"Listen."

Again Ardwin listened. He shook his head. "No. Nothing."

Horse laughed.

"Good night," muttered Ardwin, puzzled. He laid his head back down on his rolled-up cloak and was soon asleep again.

Horse stood awake, alone in the darkness, breathing deeply of the wind rising from the east. The sky was being scrubbed clear of clouds, and the stars shone brightly. The wolf howled again, farther off now, and much more faint. But the little tangle-coated horse stamped his leg uneasily. "Wolves and leopards," he muttered. "Leopards and wolves."

In the morning, they heard geese.

"Now, who could *that* be?" asked Horse innocently.

"You are acting very disrespectfully. Do you know that?" said Ardwin, toasting his breakfast of bread and cheese over the fire.

Horse chomped an apple. "Am I?" he answered. "I don't think I noticed. Or maybe I did. Eat up and get on my back. Let's head to the pond for a drink and a dip. It's a fair morning and promises to be a warm day. I want to cool my hooves, wash the dust from my mane, and stretch out in the water. Leave your gear. Let's just go."

"Breakfast and a swim. What a smart Horse you are!"

"You don't know the half of it," nickered Horse, shaking his head and chomping a second half-green apple.

When Ardwin had eaten, he jumped up on Horse's bare back. They trotted into the old orchard beneath the twisted branches, through an untended lane, then down an alley of trees and out into the tall grasses of the overgrown fields. Ardwin held his wing out to the side, letting the wind ruffle the feathers and blow his hair back. It felt good to be freely himself.

The cackling and gabbling of geese grew louder as they came trotting out from the orchard, headed toward the pond.

Alene was wringing out her long hair. She had swum and

bathed and just dressed. As the horse and rider came closer, she stretched out her hand for the spear that leaned near at hand against a rock.

"I should have worn my cloak," muttered Ardwin. "Whatever possessed me to go without it? I should have guessed she would be here. I can't believe I was so foolish."

"Come on," said Horse. "Trust your decision! Maybe you sensed it would be all right. Maybe you wanted her to know the truth. Now, buck up and be a man, a winged man. Which is, after all, what you are. Ha, ha, ha."

Ardwin sought to turn Horse's head and ride away back to their camp. He could return once he had his cloak. But Horse would have none of it.

They were still a distance away when the girl's spear flashed as she leveled the point. Then, "You!" she exclaimed as they got closer. She raised her leveled spear. Cackling loudly, her geese flapped out into deeper water, churning up the surface of the pond.

Horse and Ardwin were still struggling, Horse going forward, Ardwin trying to tug him and turn him aside. Horse stopped short, planting his hooves at the pond's edge, and skidded on the wet, muddy shore. Ardwin lost his grip and tumbled from Horse's back — *splash!* — into the pond. He rose spluttering.

"You *are* winged!" exclaimed Alene. "Wonderful!"

"Wonderful?" repeated Ardwin as he stepped, dripping, onto the muddy shore, feeling like a traveler in a new world.

"You are just as I thought when I first saw you on your little horse," she said. "Something splendid, at last."

"Not so little," whinnied Horse as he waded out knee-deep into the pond, delicately dipped his muzzle into the water, and drank. "Tell her to stop saying that, Ardwin. Not so little at all."

But Ardwin was preoccupied. "Splendid?" repeated Ardwin-in-the-New-World.

"Not boring. Winged. Winged is . . . is different. It's *wonderful.*"

"Oh," said Ardwin. Then he said, "Your eyes are gray."

"My eyes?" repeated Alene. "What's that got to do with anything?"

"Like the sea," he said. "Like clouds and rain-washed mornings."

"Oh," she said. "Like that." And she looked at the wet, muddy, winged, broad-shouldered youth in his snow-lion vest and tooth necklace, and she smiled.

Like the sun.

The geese were bobbing and ducking in the water. Horse was out in the middle of the pond swimming, his broad head just above the surface. His eyes were closed and his nostrils were opened wide. He was humming. The geese lifted their heads and turned to watch him swim by, gabbling excitedly to one another.

Alene and Ardwin were resting on the grass. Ardwin was drying his feathers in the warmth of the sun after having washed off the mud. His clothes were cool and wet, quite comfortable in the day's heat.

"Is he *humming*?" asked Alene, amazed.

Ardwin was chewing on a grass stalk and watching her, not Horse. He nodded. "He's not an ordinary horse," he said.

"Clearly. He's very enthusiastic," nodded Alene.

"Very."

"And you, Ardwin. Not so ordinary, either, are you? It's a nice name, by the way. Unusual. *Ardwin.* I like it. It sounds like *ardor.*"

He blushed.

She didn't seem to notice. "And the wing . . . how?"

"There were . . . family difficulties," he said with monumental understatement, and told her his story.

"Ah," said Alene, nodding when he had finished. She fingered a pearl earring. "So when you were a swan, you actually *flew*?"

"Yes. I flew. Once upon a time."

She sat up and looked at him. "If I could, I'd fly off like the geese in the fall. I'd fly away and travel and see the wide world. Tell me, *Prince,*" she said, "for that is what you are, isn't it? What is it like to fly?"

He closed his eyes, remembering. He opened them and said, "It's like leaving everything. The world drops beneath your feet and you're free. You become part of everything. You see how your own little grove of trees is woven into the nearby fields and river. You go higher and see how your little river flows from the mountains, winds through forests, runs past your town, makes for the sea. You see how everything is connected, how any one thing is part of something more, and that 'something more' is everything there is. From up high, all our precious borders and boundaries and fences mean nothing at all. When you fly, the smells of field and marsh, ocean and woodland come freely to you. The wind lifts you, as if you are riding an invisible horse. When you come back down to earth at last, you finally understand that the ground is simply the bottom of the sky."

Alene sighed. "It's the way I dreamed it might be. You make it real." She studied his face, her chin in her hand. Then she seemed to wake from her reverie, for she suddenly asked, "Did you really beat up those men?"

"What?"

"I heard that you beat up a gang of toughs at The Roost."

Ardwin blushed again. "Horse saved me. There were four of them — hardly a gang."

"Do you fight a lot?"

"No, I don't think so."

"Then what about the scar?" she asked. "I saw a scar across your chest when you swam."

"Oh, that," he said. "I was attacked by a lion up north. The tooth I wear is from it. I was lucky then too. It pretty much impaled itself on my spear." Then he told her about Belarius.

"You *have* had adventures!" said Alene. She added, "I'd like to meet a wizard someday." She brushed a bit of dandelion fluff from her face. "I want to go places, see things. And I will," she said. She sighed again. "But I've never even been inside a tavern yet!"

"Really?" he exclaimed. "Why not?"

"Mother and Father forbade it. They said it was beneath us. (I have two sisters.) It was beneath me, a . . . a princess."

"Ah," said Ardwin. "Aha."

"'Aha,' what?"

"Nothing. I was just thinking, 'So, you're a princess.'"

"Yes. But you mustn't hold it against me. I insist that they let me tend the geese. I've had enough of my cackling sisters. I'd rather be outdoors. I hate feeling shut in." She paused and brushed the hair back from her eyes, considering. "Though taverns seem . . . intriguing. That's where dark plans are hatched in smoky corners among pirates, cutthroats, and thieves. That is how it is, isn't it? Oh, do tell me! Taverns must be so exciting!"

"I hate to disappoint you," answered Ardwin, "but all you usually find in taverns are quite ordinary people, doing nothing more unusual than eating and drinking."

"Oh," she said. "So why the fight?"

He couldn't tell her that she was one of the main reasons he had fought. It would seem too boastful, as if he were seeking her admiration or thanks. Though deep down he knew that he would like to have her admiration and her thanks, this didn't seem either the right way or the right time to get it. "I don't know," he said vaguely. "There were a few . . . well, they didn't like Horse or . . . wings. They said some unpleasant, threatening things. Next thing I knew, I'd opened my mouth in response. It all gets kind of blurry after that. But you know how it is," he added. "One thing leads to another and then, well, it just happened."

"You mean you got into a fight in which you or . . . someone might have been killed," she exclaimed, "and you don't even know *why*?"

"It made sense at the time," he protested.

Horse stepped from the pond and shook himself, the geese angrily flapping away from his noise and splutter. He rolled on the grass. "Tell her," he whinnied. "Tell her what a hero you are. Tell her how you stood up for her so bravely, and all alone. She's what really set it in motion. Tell her. She'll like it. Trust me."

Instead Ardwin sprang to his feet and blurted, "I . . . have to go. Will you be here tomorrow?"

"Yes," she said, surprised at his abruptness. "I'll be here."

"We're camped on the other side of the orchard," he said. "Do you like apples? They're still hard, a bit unripe, but I'll bring you some."

He ran to Horse, who was standing now, jumped up on his back and, waving and flapping his wing very gallantly, said, "I'll bring the spear that killed the lion too!" And he rode away.

As they trotted back to camp, Horse said, "You are an idiot."

"I know," lamented Ardwin. "It wasn't the way I wanted it to be. I don't know what happened. Everything was going well. Then she asked about the fight. The next thing I knew, I was jumping up and running away. You can call me an idiot all you want and you'll be right." He hung his head, his feet bouncing against Horse's ribs.

"Thanks for the permission," said Horse. "*Idiot*! You were about to reveal yourself a hero. Instead, you came off the fool. Talk about missed opportunities! 'I'll bring apples. And my spear too!'" He snorted. Then he said, "Well, relax, winged boy. Maybe your instincts were good. Heroes don't boast. Who knows, it might pay off. Love is *so* mysterious," he added slyly. "Did you at least get her name? I was out in the pond and missed that."

"Yes. It's Alene."

"Not bad. I like it."

"She's not just a goose girl. She's also a princess."

"Really!" said Horse, grinning. "My, my. I never would have guessed."

A Severed Wing

Ardwin awoke from a restless and uneasy sleep. He had dreamed that he was flying, but not flying with his brothers, nor was he a swan. In his dream he was simply himself. His wing and his one arm were spread out to either side, and the earth was far below. It was impossible. He knew that, even in the dream. Yet there he was, nonetheless. And someone familiar was flying beside him, though he couldn't see who it was. Together they soared and banked through billowing clouds and bright sunlight.

Then the dream changed and he seemed to be at home. Someone was throwing stones at a small animal, maybe a cat, or a wounded bird. He became enraged at this injustice and rushed forward, his wing out, ready to deal a bone-cracking blow.

Which is when he awoke, bathed in sweat. From the

dark sky overhead came the raucous, terrified cackling of geese.

Horse was wide awake, muttering, "I don't like it!" His ears were up, his tail stiffly out, and he was sniffing the wind. Through chattering teeth, he exclaimed, "My skin is crawling! I'm going to have to kick and bite. Watch out!" And with that, he let loose a terrific, double-hoofed kick behind him. "See! I told you! Something is definitely not right."

Ardwin stood up, his wing flapping in the darkness as if trying to beat its way into the sky. His heart was beating loudly too. The wind came roaring. Thunder rumbled. And now the geese were circling again, frantically screaming, *"Help, help, help, help, HELP!"*

"Alene!" exclaimed Ardwin. Quickly he belted on the Hunter, slung on his mail shirt, tied on his spear, and set his helmet on his head. If it came to a fight, he would be armed and ready. He swung up onto Horse, who was bucking and prancing with nervous fury. Together they galloped through the old orchard, Horse's hooves pounding the dirt, then out across the high grasses of the dark, windswept fields toward the pond. Lightning flashed, illuminating the field of long, blowing grasses with an eerie and sinister light. Off in the distance again came the rumbling growl of thunder.

When they came to the pond, Alene was nowhere to be seen. But her spear was there, stuck point down in the mud, pinning a goose's severed wing to the shore. The tip of the wing pointed west. Out on the pond a dead goose floated like a sodden lump on the water. The shore itself was torn and trampled by horse's hooves.

"Four," said Ardwin with a shiver. The sight of the red, raw stump of the severed and bedraggled wing was ugly and disturbing.

"Yes, the tracks are clear," neighed Horse in agreement. "Four horses were here."

Ardwin pulled out Alene's spear and, with it, pushed the severed wing out into the water. It floated, then sank, heavier end first, until only the gray, feathered tip showed above the surface. "We may need this," he said, gripping the spear.

Horse breathed deeply, drawing air through his nostrils in great breaths. Ardwin closed his eyes and put his mind in his wing, out among the feathers, nerves, and hollow bones. "West," he said, opening his eyes. "As the severed wing points."

They rode from the pond into the night, following a trail of odors and impulse, hoofprints and broken grasses that each flash of lightning revealed. They were heading toward the mountains and the rumbling thunder, straight toward the lightning that flickered again. And again.

"Shrew!" shouted Sniccan, flinging a stone into the darkness. "Devil-shrew!" He turned back to the fire and gripped his arm where Alene's dagger had sliced his muscle to the bone. Blood seeped through the fresh bandage. Dried blood was also caked on the wide swath of cloth wrapped tightly around his wounded shoulder, where, at the inn, Horse's teeth had torn his flesh. The three brothers sitting by the fire only laughed.

"Don't worry. You can buy a whole new arm with just a bit of your part of the ransom. And with the additional money we'll make on Duck Boy, you can hire a servant to carry it for you too, if you like. So be careful. Don't damage her — *yet,*" said Wearg, amiably enough.

"She is a king's daughter, is Miss Goosey Girl," added Snorg. "A little gold mine, she is. Or soon will be. Ha! Ha! Right, brother?" He looked at Wearg.

Then monstrous Narg chimed in. "Gold," he gurgled. "Yellow gold."

Wearg smiled and patted Narg on his arm. Narg became quiet. "Two birds with one stone," said Wearg. "Money, lots of it. And we get to kill Duck Boy, and sell his wing to Ulfius too. He'll add to our hoard. Those two cowards who worked for Ulfius had big mouths and should have kept them shut. They will now, permanently, eh? Still, they gave us just the news we needed. Everything is working perfectly."

Sniccan wrapped another layer of bandage around his arm. "Yeah, perfectly," he said. Wearg seemed not to notice the sarcasm. Sniccan added, "Gives me the creeps. They blabbed all right, true enough, but what was all that about the owl?"

"Relax, Sniccan," admonished Wearg. "They were drunk.

We gave them lots to drink. It loosened their tongues, didn't it?"

"Maybe," agreed Sniccan dubiously. "But they blubbered in such terror about that bird. They said it killed their partner."

Wearg laughed and tossed another stick onto the fire. "Maybe they guessed what was about to happen to them. If they were scared, they had good reason. Good reason and good riddance. We got the news we needed. For now, let's just be careful around our valuable little Miss Goose, all right? *Understand?*"

"Sure, sure," groaned Sniccan, cradling his bleeding arm. "But don't forget! I get to kill Duck Boy's ugly little horse. Me, alone! I'll rip out its lungs. That's how I'll do it. I've made up my mind on that."

"Yes, fine. Good. However you want. Kill his ugly little stupid humpbacked horse," nodded Wearg agreeably. "The message we pinned by the pond should bring him soon, maybe even by midmorning. A wing for a winged boy. He'll be hot on our trail. All we have to do is let him come, and then we'll have them both. Snip, snap, snout, his tale's told out."

Snorg began giggling, delighted with the brilliance of his brother's plan.

"Aye. Let him come," Sniccan said. "He's more misshapen than his horse. They're not natural, either one of them. They give me the creeps, they do. That freak shouldn't be allowed to live. He'll hatch out monster-children, duck-winged as himself. We'll earn our money ridding the world of him, I can tell you. But will we live to spend it, I wonder?"

Snorg stopped giggling and grew suddenly serious. "He has a point. Abducting a king's daughter is risky." He dug with his dagger in the earth. "There may be an army on our trail soon. Catching bears, robbing travelers, murder and mayhem were a lot safer, to my way of thinking." He looked at Wearg. "Weren't they, brother?"

"Safer to your way of thinking? Then stop thinking!" growled Wearg. "For they were much less profitable, not even close to what's now afoot."

"What if we just kill Duck Boy and the ugly horse, then have some fun with the girl? We'll still have done all right for ourselves," grumbled Sniccan. "That way, we miss the worst of what might come from hanging around for the ransom. That's where it all gets sticky." He tore the bandage with his teeth and tucked in the loose end. He shivered and drew closer to the fire, which flared and gusted in the wind. "Why not forget the ransom and have fun? Ulfius will still pay us well once we get him the wing with some shoulder attached for proof, like those two said."

"No one touches the girl," growled Wearg with quiet menace. He drew his sword, laid it across his knees, and began honing its edge with a stone. "No one, you hear? Not till we get our money, *all* of it. No half measures. Right, Brother Narg?" He turned toward the huge, hulking form.

"Right," growled Narg, clenching and unclenching his great fists.

"See? The ransom note has been delivered," said Wearg. "We stick to the plan. We'll get all that's coming to us, for the girl *and* for Duck Boy. No army will find us. Stick to the plan and we'll be safely away, over the mountains, and very rich. Maybe we'll take her to Ulfius once we get her ransom. Or maybe we won't, heh? Maybe we'll be done with her by then." He nodded menacingly to where Alene lay bound and gagged against a saddle in the darkness, back from the fire. Her eyes blazed at him. Her hair was tangled, matted with leaves and dirt and dried blood. There was a dark bruise on her forehead, and a line of dried blood ran from the corner of her mouth.

There was a sudden crash of thunder. "Narg," said Wearg, looking up from his sword to the mountains where lightning flickered. "The storm is coming. Drag that big dead branch over there in close so we can block the wind with it, will you? We can rig a tarp from it too, and make a bit of shelter. It looks like we're in for a blow and some rain. Take Sniccan, he can give you a hand."

Snorg began to giggle. "Hee hee hee! A hand. That's all he's got! Give a hand, that's a rich one. Hee hee hee! He's only got one that works now. Hee hee hee!"

"I hate wet weather," whined Sniccan. "I really do. And my arm *is* hurt. Why can't Snorg go?"

"Sniccan!" snapped Wearg roughly, holding his sword before the fire and sighting along its new gleaming edge as he polished it with a cloth.

"All right," said Sniccan. "I see your point. I'm going."

"Hee hee hee! Sees the point! That's rich! Of a sword! Hee hee hee."

"Shut up, dear brother," said Wearg, sliding his sword back into the scabbard. "Let's enjoy this night, shall we?"

The Road to War

Ardwin and Horse could follow the kidnappers' trail even in pitch-darkness. As long as the rains held off, the scent was clear enough for Horse, and though the thunderclouds rolling over the mountains threatened to unleash a storm soon, the lightning helped. Now it flashed again, luridly illuminating their trail.

"Blood," muttered Horse.

"I'll kill them if it's hers," vowed Ardwin, tightly gripping Alene's spear.

"Steady!" said Horse, galloping on and rolling his eye back to the winged rider bent low over his back. "Saving Alene comes first. Remember: Horses aren't predators. This is all unnatural for me. I should be running *away* from danger, not chasing it."

"You are a brave horse," said Ardwin encouragingly. "A

stallion protecting the herd. But you're right. We'll do what we must to save Alene. Everything else follows from that."

As they galloped on, rain began to fall, large drops driven on a gusting headwind. Just before it became a downpour, Horse slowed and sniffed. He blew out, his breath rising like steam in the rain-cooled air. "Wood smoke!" he said. "There's a campfire ahead." He trotted to the right. "We'll circle."

"Slowly," said Ardwin. "They're not far ahead. And . . . Alene *lives*."

"You *know*?"

"I know," said Ardwin, eyes closed, focusing in through the bones and fibers of his wing, tracing down along the fine, feathery nerves to his heart. "She is hurt, but not badly. She is frightened, but brave."

"Good," said Horse. "I'm impressed. I didn't know you could do that."

"I didn't, either," said Ardwin. "But I can, and I think it's because it is Alene. Let's get closer and see about our plan. The rain may help. They'll be less attentive, and the sounds of our approach will be muffled."

"The lightning will reveal us," warned Horse.

"Yes. It can't be helped. Six of one, half a dozen of another. Rain helps in one way, but makes the ground slick and treacherous. The lightning can reveal them, or us." He tightened his grip on Alene's spear. The shaft was cold, slippery, and wet in the rain. "Her spear may help from a distance.

Then it will be sword-work and the short spear, wing, and fist."

"Hooves and teeth," sighed Horse. "I'll be the first horse ever to creep up, stalk like a leopard, and attack. I'll be famous, if I live."

"You'll live."

"Till I die," muttered Horse.

A wolf howled in the rain. The sound wavered and climbed, then sank, warbling down into one, long, steady note. Then it was gone.

"What was that?" exclaimed Sniccan. The rain hissed into the fire, only partially protected by the tarp, which was already sagging under an accumulation of rainwater.

"What do you think?" scowled Wearg sitting beneath the wet, dripping cloth and peering into the rain-filled dark. "A wolf, of course. We have weapons and we have fire. Let it howl. Who cares?"

The wolf howled again, even closer. The kidnappers' horses started nervously, whinnying in the cold rain. They lifted their heads and tugged anxiously at their picket ropes.

Snorg nervously put his hand to his sword. "That's getting close, hee hee hee." He giggled anxiously. The smoke from the fire coiled around him, blown back by a gust of wind. He choked, and the flames momentarily flattened by the wind retreated, then rose again in a sudden, savage dance.

"Bah," exclaimed Wearg, coughing. "What a bunch of babies! A little cold, a little wet weather, a lone wolf, and you start sniveling. Buck up! We're about to make our fortunes."

Suddenly, from the darkness nearby rose the long, drawn-out, high-pitched, coughing, whining snarl of a hungry leopard on the prowl. The horses, mad with fear, pulled and tugged at their picket ropes with great, frantic strength. The wooden pegs tore from the wet earth, and the horses, wheeling, raced off into the silvery, rain-slanting dark.

"Bloody hell!" yelled Wearg, leaping after them and disappearing into the darkness. "Come on!"

The four men raced out from their little shelter after the terrified animals. After a few minutes they stopped and stood panting, muttering curses, totally soaked, their beards, hair, and clothes all dripping.

"Keep to the plan!" exclaimed Snorg in panic. "Keep to the plan! We need horses for the plan! What now, eh? Wolves and leopards! How, pray tell, do we keep to the plan?"

"Shut up, brother," said Wearg coldly. "Let me think."

When the men disappeared into the night and rain, Alene saw her chance. She was tied to a saddle in the corner of the little shelter farthest from the warmth of the fire. The saddle leaned against a broken tree stump, which helped keep off at least some of the rain. Now she saw a dagger lying half hidden beneath a cloak that had been tossed aside when they raced away. She slid onto her side and inched toward it, turned, the ropes cutting into her wrists, and, with her hands tied behind her back, grabbed the knife. She lay on the ground panting, flushed with a fierce elation. Then she inched her way back and half rolled the heavy saddle into place against the stump.

Footsteps thudded out of the darkness and the kidnappers slid under the dripping, rain-soaked shelter.

"And what's a leopard doing out here, anyway!" exclaimed Sniccan miserably. "I've never heard of leopards in these parts."

"We're near the mountains," said Wearg in disgust. "It smelled the horses. Now shut up," he added. "I don't want any more of your wretched sniveling, hear?"

"Yeah, I hear. I just do hate the cold and wet," Sniccan sniffled. "Goose girl!" he exclaimed. "Your daddy better be getting our money!" He picked up a stone and hurled it toward Alene. It missed and hit the broken section of the tree with a *thump!* Wearg's fist shot out and caught Sniccan on the side of his head.

"Ow!"

"Leave off!" growled Wearg angrily. "I said I was thinking."

"Thinking," repeated Narg.

"Hee hee hee," giggled Snorg somewhat hysterically as Sniccan blubbered beside the fire.

"It sounds like they're losing their grip," said Horse. "When the harmony of a herd breaks up, that's good for the predators. In this case, that means us."

"Yes. And it will be morning soon," said Ardwin. "I think the best time to make our move will be when all is still in semishadow."

"What *is* our move?"

"Get closer," said Ardwin. "Throw Alene's spear and hope it hits. After that . . ." He shrugged. "Rush them."

"I always thought that predators had all the fun," muttered Horse. "But this sounds like no fun at all. The odds are totally wrong. They're not in our favor."

Alene slid the dagger out of its sheath — and dropped it. She groped behind her back with tight-bound hands until she touched cold iron again, and sighed with relief. She caught herself, and once more lay quiet and still. The four were still huddled, talking by the fire, and seemed not to have heard a thing. Upending the knife, she turned the blade's edge from her and tried to slip it between her bound wrists. Too tight! The rope was tied too tightly! She fumbled, turning the blade the other way . . . and dropped it again. And again lay still, sweating and anxious that she would be found out. Still the four men talked on and fed the fire. Again she found the heavy knife with her cold, cramped fingers, turned its edge toward herself, and began to draw the blade across the topmost coil of rope. She made small movements, slow movements, back and forth. She could feel the knife sawing into the rope, cutting through it fiber by fiber, strand by strand, though it was hard to exert enough pressure without driving the blade too far forward and slicing into her wrist. *Who cares?* she thought, wincing as the blade nicked her flesh again. *As long as I'm free!*

"So, what's the new plan?" ventured Snorg uneasily. "I don't want to disturb you, brother, but you've been thinking a long time now."

"Eh?" answered Wearg, looking up from where he stared into the flames. "Plan? Why, it's just common sense. We set out *now.* Narg will carry the girl. We will need speed. And we get into the mountains, where there is shelter and we can watch for the rider with the ransom, and for the approach of Duck Boy. We'll leave a clear enough trail for him to follow from here. The plan is the same. We just must be stronger, tougher, to pull it off. Agreed? Because we don't need deadweight," he added, staring at the wet and miserable Sniccan. "And I do mean *dead.* Now, agreed?"

The three nodded.

"Then let's start packing," said Wearg, looking grimly at his drenched companions. "Morning is almost upon us and we must be on our way."

Alene heard. They would soon be coming for her. Her hands had to be free by then, or else. She pressed the blade harder, flinched as it cut her wrist again, but held it tight, didn't drop it, and sawed steadily on.

Gray light began to seep across the plains. Mountains loomed from the shadows. The rain was steady, though the growling thunder and flickering lightning had passed into the east. Horse's breath rose in clouds from his nostrils. Ardwin's wing was tight against his side, and his heavy, wet cloak was wrapped over him. He was hunched on Horse's back, Alene's spear upright in his fist, its butt resting on the earth. He hardly noticed the cold or the wet. Rain dripped across his eyes and slid down his body beneath the cloak. He was drenched. But all he was aware of were the twin puffs of Horse's breath rising before him and the mountains taking shape in the early light.

Horse's ears pointed forward, fully erect. "They're moving," he whispered. "They are packing up."

"They are about to leave," Ardwin said, and nodded. "It is not quite light enough, but . . ." He remembered when he and his brothers, still swans, had swooped down to save Rose. Not perfect then, either, but the time, nonetheless, to do what had to be done. "If we wait any longer they will already be traveling and alert. And it will be too light. We could never surprise them." He flung back his cloak and stretched out his wing in the rain. He loosened the Hunter in its scabbard and cinched the straps that bound the short spear beneath his wing.

"I should file my teeth sharp," whispered Horse. "Like your tooth."

"I wish we had time," agreed Ardwin, patting Horse's neck. "I'd do it for you, gladly. We will need all the help we can get." They set off at a trot through the rain toward the dark shapes now just visible, moving like shadows ahead. As they rode, Ardwin leveled Alene's spear.

"Wait," said Ardwin. Horse slowed. "I thought we might just rush through and, on the first pass, spear one and, with luck, disable another. That would leave us two. They're big, but . . . we've stopped them before. But it's still too dark. And if we wait, it will be too light. And if we just rush in now, or if I hurl the spear, it might be Alene who gets hurt. I can't chance it."

"We will have to go quietly and separately, then," said Horse. "Leopardlike, one from each side. I feared it might come to this."

"Good luck, Horse," said Ardwin, dismounting. "I hope I haven't brought you too much trouble."

"Good luck, Ard," answered Horse. "I've had a good, adventurous ride and have seen things not one of my far northern horse people has seen before."

"We'll see more together."

"That we will," said Horse. He laid his square head lightly on Ardwin's shoulder. For a moment their breath rose in the cool air together, billowing like steam.

"So, what will our signal be?" asked Horse, lifting his head.

"Stay here. Be alert, and listen," said Ardwin. "Your ears are the best. I'll circle to the other side, then sneak among them quietly as I can. When I strike, you'll know it. There'll be noise and shouting. Then —"

"All right," said Horse, nodding. "I'll be there, fast as I can. You have my word."

Then they went their separate ways to war.

Blood and Fire

As things turned out, it was not Ardwin who struck the first blow.

The men were packed. Wearg sauntered toward Alene, bowed mockingly before her, and drew a knife. "Time to cut your bonds, Princess," he said. "Little brother Narg can carry you faster than you can walk. How lucky for you to not have to tread the earth like us ordinary folk, eh?"

Wearg squatted down before her and raised his blade. Suddenly Alene struck, slicing her knife across his face. Wearg screamed loudly, dropped his weapon, and stumbled back, his hands pressed to his face, blood dripping from between his fingers. The gash was deep, but she had missed his eyes. Now he straightened up, wiped away the blood, grabbed his knife, and came furiously at her.

At that moment, a snow owl glided silently out of the gray

morning and, before Wearg could strike, buried its talons in his throat. He screamed — a horrible, gurgling, muffled sound — dropped his knife again, and staggered backward, desperately trying to tear the owl from him. But despite all his wrenching blows, it refused to loosen its grip, and only clenched tighter, pecking at Wearg's eyes with its sharp beak, buffeting his head with its great wings. Even as Wearg's eyes rolled up whitely in death, even then, with a final, superhuman effort, Wearg at last tore the owl free and flung it away. Then he collapsed in a heap.

Ardwin heard the screams. Charging in close and fast, he hurled Alene's spear at Sniccan, who was running forward, sword in hand. The spear caught him beneath the shoulder, piercing his heart, and he died instantly. Before Ardwin could draw his sword or retrieve the spear to strike again, the giant Narg grabbed him and lifted him high overhead. The wing struck down at Narg's head and face, the spear strapped to it drawing blood. Narg hardly flinched, and only raised Ardwin higher so that the spear couldn't reach him. Then Ardwin tried to pull the Hunter from its sheath, but Narg saw what he was up to, and before the blade could be drawn, he shook him furiously back and forth until he dangled limply as a rag doll. Then, with a murderous scowl on his blood-dripping, rain-soaked face, Narg hurled Ardwin to the ground with all his monstrous strength.

Ardwin lay stunned, almost broken, hardly able to move or

even breathe. The wing was oddly bent. It was numb. He couldn't feel it. He couldn't feel anything but pain. He tried to crawl away, but the ground was too muddy and slick, and he was too hurt and dazed to get his legs to work properly. For a few seconds, his legs and feet slid helplessly, pedaling in the mud. Narg, towering immensely above him, was lifting a huge, spiked club, ready to pound Ardwin into a bloody paste. "Die, freak!" burbled Narg as he swung the club high.

And suddenly everything fell into place.

Thoughts and images flashed through Ardwin's mind. He saw Stephen and Skye, Bran and his brothers, Rose and Conor, Annie, Harry, Victor, old Marjorie, Belarius, his father and grandfather — all who cared for him just as he was. He saw Alene. *Alene,* coming toward him, opening her arms, saying, "Differences are good." And in that moment, he thought, *What a fool I have been! I am not cursed at all, but blessed!*

Fierce and entirely unexpected joy surged through him as he hovered at the knife-edge of life and death. He pushed himself onto his feet and stood swaying unsteadily, looking up at the gigantic club still somehow hurtling down toward him. He had been gone only an instant; he had been gone for years. But now he was back, and the club had not yet fallen. He raised his wing and his grandfather's sword against his doom. "Come on!" he shouted defiantly. "Just try it!"

"Good-bye!" laughed Narg. "Ha ha ha!" His club was

about to smash through the winged boy's frail defenses like a boulder tearing through a bush.

Whang! The spear point hidden beneath the wing flashed forth and embedded itself in the wooden club, the sturdy shaft halting the weapon's terrible descent. Narg's eyes grew big, puzzled by this delay. Enraged, he raised the club back up, now lifting the spear with Ardwin strapped to it, preparing to smash the winged creature attached to his club into the mud.

Ardwin struck first, the Hunter biting deep into Narg's chest. Narg roared like a wounded lion. If he threw the club away Ardwin would go flying with it. But instead, with failing breath, he only blindly sought to raise the heavy club again to crush Ardwin into the ground.

Ardwin gathered his strength and swung the Hunter back to strike again, knowing that if this stroke failed, he himself would die.

But before he could strike, something big, dark, and hairy, grunting *unnnnh hunnnh unnnnh,* rose up out of the grass and tore off Narg's head. Hardly pausing, the great beast dropped back down onto all fours and shambled off through the long grass, making for the mountains. Narg's headless body, its arms still upraised, the spiked club still gripped in its hamlike fists, spouted blood like a fountain as it fell slowly backward onto the muddy earth, dragging the spear and Ardwin with it.

Meanwhile, Horse galloped, neck outstretched, toward

Snorg, the last man standing. Snorg was waiting, giggling madly, his sword arm back and low, and as Horse raced by he spun away, letting his sword's sharp edge tear along Horse's ribs. "Hee hee hee hee!" Horse's rush carried him along the blade and past. Then Horse spun around and staggered. "Fire! Fire!" he screamed. "It burns! It burns!" He bucked and kicked, maddened in agony, one lion-colored side now half dipped in red.

Ardwin saw Horse's wound and the blood, and screaming, "No!" stood up, set his boot on Narg's club, and pulled the spear free. Then he stumbled toward Snorg, who stood panting, a sickening, bewildered grin on his face as he surveyed the havoc that had so suddenly burst upon them. Then Horse was there again, biting and kicking. One minute Snorg stood erect, bloody sword in hand. The next he was down, his skull caved in. It was over.

Horse's head drooped. He trembled and slowly he sank too, until he lay stretched out on the bloody ground.

The rain stopped falling. The rising sun spilled its red light upon the awful scene.

Alene was on her knees sobbing in terror and relief. Ardwin dropped beside her. He wrapped his wing and his arm around her and saw that, except for some bruises and the madness of it, she was all right. And the wing was too. The spear had acted as a brace and saved the bone from shattering. The pain, he could manage.

Alene sobbed and wrapped her arms tightly around him.

Ardwin held her very close. Then he said, "Horse!" and got up and, with Alene by his side, ran to where Horse lay.

Horse was stretched out, breathing slowly, his nostrils dilated like great dark whorls drawing in an invisible world. His eyes were open and his chest slowly rose and fell. His side was laid open, ribs and flesh revealed, blood welling up, drenching his yellow tangle-coat and staining the wet grass and sodden earth very dark.

Ardwin put his arm around Horse's neck and the wing beneath it. Horse lifted his head and looked at Ardwin. "We won," he whinnied softly.

"We did," wept Ardwin. "Now we will get well."

"All right," said Horse. "Whatever you say." He laid his head back down. Then he raised it slightly again. "*She* helped, didn't she?"

"She did," said Ardwin. "I will look to her, after you."

"I'm glad she came. Say hello and thank you," said Horse, and he put his head back down with a great sigh and closed his eyes.

"Horse!"

Horse opened his eyes. "I'm not deaf, you know," he said mildly.

Then Ardwin grabbed handfuls of wet grasses and with his hand and wing pressed them against Horse's wound. Alene gathered more grasses and strips of cloth, and together they bound Horse's side tightly so that the dark and awful flow of blood at last stopped.

"Now if I only could breathe," gasped Horse, "what with the tightness of this bandage you've put on me. Still, I forgive you. You may have saved me." And he laid his head back down on the earth and feebly moved his hooves. Ardwin found a somewhat dry blanket among the kidnappers' gear and Alene draped it over Horse and sat beside him, stroking his head and neck until he closed his eyes again.

"Evron," said Ardwin. He wiped his eyes, and awkwardly holding his hurt wing, all red now with Horse's blood, he walked toward her.

Owl-Evron lay on her back where the dying Wearg had flung her. Her wings were spread wide and her yellow eyes blazed. Her beak was clacking slowly open and shut and her head and neck were bent, twisted oddly to one side. A breeze ruffled the soft, white feathers with their black-and-gray edges. Ardwin knelt down, helmetless, half winged and bloody beside her. "Thank you," he said. "Without you, we would be dead."

"Perhaps," answered Owl-Evron. "One can never be . . . sure as to what . . . *might* have been. Only what *is*."

"You helped us. Why?"

"Dear *Thing*," she gasped. "I told you I have been . . . watching. No one ruins *my* . . . experiment and spoils *my* fun!

Especially not . . . *amateurs.*" She spat out the word. "Playing with . . . forces . . . as if *they* . . . I would not have it . . . insufferable."

"You are dying," said Ardwin. Despite himself, his tears fell. He had never imagined he might one day weep over her. It surprised him even now.

"*This* dies. But I am . . . Evron, the Never . . . Ending, the Ever On, the Ever One." She paused and chanted:

"I am the owl with a
Robin as son.
Red breast of blood,
Now sing! *and be done.*

I am the Lady of Wild Things.
Evron am I,
The Ever-On,
The Ever-One."

"My death verse," she said evenly. "For now. You saved me once, long ago, when you were still just a child. You ran bravely between Bran and myself and stopped his sword before he could strike. I named you *Birdwing* then. It stuck, didn't it?"

"It stuck, like the shirt."

She nodded feebly. "Words have power. Now, we

are . . . even. Your curse," she whispered, for her voice was failing, "alone . . . remains. Good-bye." The beak clacked shut. The fierce, golden eyes drooped.

"No," Ardwin said.

The yellow eyes blazed open.

"I am not cursed. Not anymore."

"So, you have . . . chosen?" she murmured, looking intently up at him.

"Yes. I will be a man, a man with a wing."

"No," she said. "Not 'will be.' You *are* . . . a man," she said firmly. "You have found . . . your way. I knew . . . hoped, you would." Her owl beak opened in a mysterious smile. But was it a look of irony or . . . *love*? Ardwin could not tell. It was the same unfathomable smile he remembered from so long ago, when she had first named him.

Her voice gathered strength. "I *created* you. To be a sign of the old magic . . . that is fading now and soon will be gone; a remnant, a reminder, so the world would not forget. You were the bridge between my world and the new." She began to fade, her mind wandering. "Then I . . . I gave . . . foolish . . . gave you a choice. Your own life. Final . . . indignity. Never wanted a . . . heart. Too heavy . . . for magic. Foolish. Against my . . . principles. Joke on . . . me. Farewell, dear *Thing*. Tell them . . . your father, your family. Tell . . . Rose . . . tell her sorry. Win a few . . . lose everythi —"

The light died in the owl's eyes, and a film came down across them like a twilight haze, or like a shutter closing forever on a window. The proud head fell farther to one side, the beak stopped, frozen in mid-*clack,* and the owl lay still.

Ardwin brushed his wing over Evron's owl-corpse, leaving a smear of blood among the white and black feathers. "Goodbye," he said softly. "In the name of my family, the House of Peredur, I accept your apology. And thank you."

The owl form lying on the grass before him faded. In just a moment a beautiful, pale, black-haired, ageless woman now lay there, wrapped in a cloak of white- and black-trimmed feathers. Then she was translucent as glass. Then she was gone.

They burned the four corpses and much of the kidnappers' gear. "I wish we could just leave them here as food for wolves," said Ardwin after Alene and he lit the pyre. "That way some benefit might come from all this. Let wolves and bears, ravens and worms, have their fill."

"It's better this way," said Alene. "Nothing but air and ash passes on. It's cleaner. I, for one, have no desire to live beside a wolf-feast while we wait for Horse's wound to mend and for him to become strong enough to travel again. No, let it end here, like this. But" — she shook her head — "that she-bear — it was a she-bear, wasn't it? I do feel almost certain of that! Weren't we lucky she appeared! Without her . . ."

Ardwin shrugged. "I might be dead," he said, finishing her thought. "Narg and I both. The bear showed up just in time, the bear and my stepmother."

"Yes, your stepmother. But Ardwin, what *was* she? Was she . . . human? She could become things."

"She was left over from an older world, from an old tale. An enchantress. A real one."

"She became an owl!"

"She was the wolf too, the one that howled, and the leopard that drove the horses away. I think it was all part of her . . . *play*."

"She certainly terrified their horses and disrupted their plans. Without her, your rescue might not have worked. But the bear was an amazing stroke of luck! Or do you think that was your stepmother's doing too? Some friend of hers, perhaps?"

"I don't know. My stepmother could be full of surprises. More than I ever knew or guessed." He paused. "I met a caged bear, months back. She had been mistreated, and her cubs stolen away. She was ill and sorrowing. I freed her. Maybe . . ." He stopped. There was nothing more he could yet put into words. He shook his head, wondering.

"And I . . . I . . ." Alene paused and looked puzzled too. Then she brightened. "Well, safe journeys and blessings on our wonderful bear savior. Three cheers for strong, brave, and very timely Mrs. Bear!"

Ardwin looked at Alene and suddenly became quiet and very serious. He unfolded his wing, wrapped it around her, and drew her to his heart.

A few days later, Horse lifted his head and whinnied. There was an answer from far off. Four horses came galloping over the plains. As they came closer Ardwin could see that they dragged picket ropes and shredded wooden stakes. Alene explained that these were the four horses that Evron in her wolf and leopard forms had frightened into the night — three geldings and a bold little mare.

Horse kicked off his blanket and rolled back and forth until he had enough momentum to swing to his feet. He stood weak and trembling, but with head held high, and said to Ardwin as the other horses approached, "Get me an apple from the saddlebag, will you? My mouth tastes like . . . well, it just tastes *awful.*"

Horse was munching an apple as the horses rode up, and though Horse was weak and little, Ardwin could see that the four were awed by his wildness. Seeing the geldings again caused Horse another bit of shiver. But life seemed to flow into him as he turned his body to face the little mare.

She said to him, "Are you a king?"

And Horse, swallowing the last of his apple, said, "If you are queen." And the little mare giggled and the geldings laughed and bowed their heads and sniffed and said, "Apples?"

"One for each," said Horse grandly. "My, ahem, attendant, will serve you." Then he added, "Actually I am not a king, but maybe, one might say, a chieftain. For, where I am from, we have no need of kings and all that foolishness."

And the little mare sighed and said, "Well, *that's* a relief."

And Horse pricked up his ears, for he liked her tone. It was oh-so-familiar.

A week later they set out, Alene riding the mare, Ardwin on the smallest of the geldings, and all their gear piled on the other two horses. Horse trotted beside them, wrapped in a clean bandage, which he seemed to wear proudly like a badge of honor. The wind was blowing from the north and they were heading with it, south.

Ardwin had asked Alene to come with him. They had been sitting on the grass not far from where Horse was resting and healing. "He'll soon be ready to travel," Ardwin had said quietly, looking down and twining his fingers among the grass blades. "When he's strong enough, I've decided to go home. There is unfinished business I must attend to with my father. There are things to be sorted out, decisions to be made. I hope. . . ." He paused and cleared his throat (something seemed to be stuck in it). "I want you to come with me,

Alene. I feel that you and I are . . . connected. We have so much in common!"

She had looked at him then, her brow arched and gray eyes flashing dangerously, he thought. "Is that all? So much in common?" she had demanded. "*That* just sounds convenient." She paused. "You're not one of *those,* are you?"

He looked up from where he had been staring at the grass as if somehow greatly interested in watching it grow. He swallowed noisily. "One of what?"

"Do you fall into things, or do you choose them?" she had asked, tapping the sole of her sandal with a twig. "I'm not the path of least resistance, you know, and don't ever want to be. If you just follow the flow of the river, you always end up downstream. I think it's time for you to say exactly what you mean."

The clouds raced overhead. The grasses rippled and blew as if some wonderful message were being inscribed among the swaying green blades. The old music began, but there was a pounding to it now, for it had the pulse of Ardwin's heart.

Where to begin and how to say what he meant and wanted? "Alene," he stammered. "Alene . . ." Some dam within finally burst. "There is music playing, can't you hear it? The music is so old and beautiful, I can hardly describe it. And it says my real life has just begun, and I cannot imagine it now without you beside me." He broke into a sweat. He wanted to run, to hide, and to fly all at once. "I love you, Alene! Marry me, please! Come with me. I see a little cabin in the woods, a fire's cozy warmth, and my sword hung on the wall in peace. It is home, and you and I together in it. Do you see what you have done to me? You've given me such words! I don't want to lose you. Not now, not ever."

Her eyes grew wide. She nodded, took a deep breath, and tossed her stick aside. Then she burst into tears and wrapped her arms, strong ones, around him and kissed him again and again, saying, "You, you."

Now Ardwin remembered that day and looked at Alene riding alongside him. She felt his gaze and smiled back. "What are you thinking?" she asked.

"Of what it's like to leap into the unknown."

"Really?"

"Yes," he said. "I was thinking of the day I found my tongue."

She laughed, remembering too.

He laughed with her. But he was also thinking of Stephen and Skye and of his dismal parting from them. He remembered with amazement his past anger and hurt. Now he was only glad for them, and for what they had discovered. He wanted to see them, and hoped it would be soon. "I was thinking too of some friends I'd like you to meet."

"Friends of yours?"

He nodded.

"It would be a pleasure," she said.

They stopped at midday. "You're a quick healer," said Ardwin, nodding approvingly as he inspected Horse's wound and changed the bandage.

"Where I'm from," Horse answered, "you have to be. You don't get many second chances."

They ate by the roadside, then set out again. Alene's geese flew honking and circling overhead. The goose girl was leaving, and whether she was a princess or not didn't matter to them. She had treated them kindly. Now they followed her.

"And your sisters, your mother and father?" asked Ardwin as they jogged along. "What of them?"

"My sisters can manage quite well without me, thank you. As for my things, they can take whatever they want. All but these." She pointed to her earrings. "These are mine. They'll stay so.

"In time, I'll write Father and Mother and let them know where I've gone. There is change in the air, not all of it good, I'm afraid. There are rumors of war." She looked quizzically at Ardwin, a brow raised. "We heard it is rising in the south, but Father fears it may soon draw us all in. Ulfius and Lugh may soon be at it. Ulfius is dangerous. Do you know anything about it?"

Ardwin sighed, "Yes, I know." He paused and drew a breath. Time to remove another cloak and reveal what was still hidden. "Lugh is my father, the one we are returning to. And I may have precipitated the war you speak of." Then Ardwin told her about the arm of gold, Ulfius, and why he left. He concluded, saying, "I will run no longer. If war is coming, I must help. Belarius told me things about Ulfius that might prove useful. I may have something, I don't know what, some information, perhaps, that might turn the tide. As to what awaits with Father . . . well, we shall see. But I won't let him take the wing. I won't give it up, no matter what. And I'm certainly not marrying that girl! So, shall we still go on? Is that what you want? We may be heading into the storm."

"Yes, of course. Let us continue," said Alene easily.

"You don't seem surprised at any of this," Ardwin said, puzzled by her lack of dismay or even concern.

"No," she said, and laughed lightly. "I guessed much of it already. We had heard tales, though some said they were only fairy tales, of a winged prince of the House of Peredur. My father's kingdom may be small and isolated, but word spreads. Ard, if you know something that might save lives, it is your duty. You must go back."

"Yes. All right. We shall let the wind carry us home."

The little mare whinnied, "Did you hear that, Chieftain?"

Horse answered, "It is a wind, but not yet my wind. My wind blows north."

"North?" repeated the little mare, puzzled. "I have long heard that there is nothing there."

"Am I nothing?" snorted Horse.

"Yes, and no," snickered the little mare.

"You," he said, sniffing deeply in her direction, "are a very interesting little horse."

"And you," she replied quietly, sniffing back, "smell like no other horse on this earth. And that is good enough for me."

They traveled all that day at a steady, easy pace, giving Horse time to rest along the way. The next day, where the road passed through a dark forest of oak and pine, three heavily armed riders overtook them. The leader's horse was loaded with saddlebags. As the riders came close, the front rider reined in and cried out in amazement, "Lady!" his eyes opening very wide as he saw his princess — and Ardwin's wing. "Hold, knave!" he ordered, and though facing a marvel, something that seemed to have wandered from out of an old tale into the daylight, he bravely drew his sword. The two beside him wheeled in close and leveled their lances.

Ardwin drew the Hunter in reply, but Alene commanded, "Cease!" adding, "This is the man who saved me, not one who means harm."

At once the lead rider sheathed his sword, dismounted, and knelt courteously before them, saying, "Princess!" The two others lowered their lances and then both did the same, kneeling in the dusty road before Ardwin in his lion vest and with his tooth necklace and white wing. Trying not to stare, they said, "Lord, we are very grateful."

"Why are you traveling here?" Alene asked.

The leader answered, "We come with tribute, my lady. We bring ransom from your father, the king, to save you."

"I thank you. But it is no longer needed. The kidnappers are dead. This good youth has released me from danger. His horse was wounded in this service. Now I travel with them."

"For how long, lady? Your father and mother grieve. What shall we tell them?"

"Tell them, 'Grieve no more.' As for how long, I cannot say. I shall send a message in time, telling them all. You may go. But give us a pouch of gold for our journey. Do not fear. I will sign and seal a receipt with my ring so my father will know that you have neither lost his gold nor stolen it."

When all had been done and the receipt signed, along with a note in her hand proving to her father that all was well, the riders set off back to the castle in the valley.

After they had gone, Alene tossed the pouch of gold coins in the air and caught it deftly. "So much for formalities. Now we can eat and drink as we please."

"Yes, that is enough to buy us cheese and bread for a hundred years," Ardwin said. "Come! There is a merry old inn I know where we can drink good ale and eat good toast to our heart's content."

"Ale? Toast?" repeated Alene, mystified.

"Follow me, king's daughter," said Ardwin. "And you will see."

One pale, perfect evening, as swallows swooped over the fields, Ardwin and Alene stopped before the carved and painted sign that proclaimed THE RACK: SAMUEL AND LEONORE BLUESTONE, PROPRIETORS. Behind the inn, immense and distant mountains rose against the sky.

"Should I wait out front? That way I can dive through the window if you need me," said Horse drily, "again."

"No." Ardwin sighed. "You and the other horses will go to the stable. The Rack is not The Roost. There'll be no fights here. You'll like it. And so will we," he added, smiling at Alene.

"Well," said Alene, sliding off Mare's back and straightening her tunic. "Are we just going to stand here? Let's go in." Her eyes shone with excitement.

"Right," said Ardwin. He swung his leg over the gelding's

back and stepped from the stirrup. Slipping his arm beneath Alene's own, they strolled toward the stable, Horse and Mare and the others ambling behind, the geese waddling noisily after.

Mare flicked her tail and sniffed the air distastefully. "It smells of burnt things," she said.

"What did Mare say?" asked Alene.

"She said the cooking smells well done. Very well done. Uh, Alene, I recommend the toast. *Only* the toast. And the ale. We can take apples and cheese in with us. But, please, don't order any food."

"Why?"

"The cooking is awful."

"Oh, but this is an inn!" said Alene. "People eat and drink here all the time. You must have arrived on an off day. Anyone can have them."

Ardwin shrugged. He wasn't going to argue. He would let experience be the best teacher. In the end, it always was.

Alene set out grain for the geese. Ardwin pinned his weather-stained traveling cloak over his wing. "Onward," he said.

"Rack your spears," said Mr. Bluestone when they entered the inn, hardly glancing up from a large ledger spread on the counter before him. "I'll be with you in a moment. Rack your spears," he repeated, nodding vaguely toward the polished wooden spear rack that hung on the wall. Three spears were already in it, and places remained for nine more. Alene placed her spear in an open slot below the others, then returned and stood at Ardwin's side.

"Now then," said Mr. Bluestone. He closed the ledger with a loud, dusty *snap!*, opened the registry, and looked up at them at last with a friendly smile. "Just the one spear, then, is it? Very good. Sign here and we'll get you settled. Wait a minute! Why, it's . . ." He clapped his hand to his forehead and exclaimed, "*Mr. Birdwing!* Hello, sir! Leonore! Dearest!" he called. "Come, see who's here!"

"In a minute!" came her reply from the noisy bustle of the adjoining tavern. "I'm quite *odious* at the moment. Totally *helpful.* Things are in a *triumphant* whirl."

Mr. Bluestone wearily raised his eyebrows and looked at Ardwin and Alene from beneath his bushy brows. "I . . . I . . . *understand*, dear," he called back patiently. "Just as soon as you are able.

"My, my," he said then, looking Ardwin up and down. "But you do look a sight. And the missus, is it?"

Ardwin looked at Alene and smiled. "Soon," he said.

Alene laughed. "I'm Alene," she said, holding out her hand graciously to Mr. Bluestone, who took it and shook it heartily.

"A pleasure. Samuel Bluestone at your service, miss. Or perhaps, it should be my lady." Then he turned to Ardwin.

"But where is *she*, our special guest? Not lost? Not destroyed? Not gone forever?"

"No, Mr. Bluestone," answered Ardwin. "She is not lost. But she is *changed,*" he added mysteriously. "She is *transformed.*"

He raised his cloaked wing, released the straps, and slid the spear out into his hand. "Here."

Mr. Bluestone's jaw dropped. Were those feathers? Was that a wing? The cloak made it hard to tell. "But . . . but," he spluttered in agitation, "why have you cut her so short?"

"That," said Ardwin, "is a long story."

Soon they were eating and talking and drinking companionably together. At one point Ardwin told about the spear, and about the bear that had saved them, and Mr. Bluestone agreed that if one good turn deserved another, why, then, it was very likely to have been the bear they had freed. "That's the way things should be, isn't it?" he added, taking a swallow of ale. "Good enough for me. Well, my dear Leonore is busy. Let me get us more . . . toast." He went to the kitchen.

"How do you like it?" Ardwin asked Alene. "The tavern? Mysterious as you hoped?"

"No. Dreadfully tame, actually," she answered with a sigh, looking steadily around. Most tables had mugs of ale and platters of toast on them too, though some people were gamely eating potatoes and roast — or trying to. Many of the diners, Alene could see, were furtively wiping their potatoes and slices of roast with their napkins before chewing quickly, amid great swallows of ale.

"The only plots being hatched here," she added, "are those of kindness. How to eat Mrs. Bluestone's food without letting her know how awful it is! You were right. I admit it. The food is terrible! It's salty as the sea, and burnt and herbed to death." She sighed. "Another mystery gone. Taverns are not the wonderfully romantic dens of iniquity I had so richly imagined."

"Well, there are taverns and taverns, I *expectorate,*" said Ardwin, and lifted his mug.

"What's that?" asked Mr. Bluestone, setting a platter of buttered toast on the table and sitting down again.

"Oh, nothing, really," said Alene, "that toast and cheese and apples can't cure."

"And ale." Mr. Bluestone winked. "And lemonade and ginger beer and cups of tea and water, water, water!"

They raised their mugs together and drank to that.

When the toast and cheese were nearly gone, Mr. Bluestone looked around the room, leaned in close, and whispered, "I have a *proposition.*"

Ardwin and Alene, mystified, leaned in as well. "Yes?" they said.

"You, my lady, are from foreign parts? Not from the immediate locale, as I understand?"

"Correct, Mr. Bluestone," nodded Alene. "My home is many days' ride to the north."

"Ah," he said, wiping his brow with a handkerchief. "Well, I was wondering. You must know some recipes from your own land. Unsalted things. Casseroles, baked potatoes with butter, cakes and pies." He closed his eyes and seemed to drift into a trance. Then he opened his eyes, looked around the room, mopped his brow, and continued. "Sweet things, full of taste and flavor. Do you?"

"Some, Mr. Bluestone. My mother enjoyed cooking, though it wasn't necessary for her to cook at all. Yet she was considered a good one. I learned from her."

"Ah," whispered Mr. Bluestone thoughtfully. Then he asked, "Might you like free room and board at The Rack, and free stabling for your horses? And all the food, uh, toast and cheese and drink you could want, for as long as you want. For both of you?"

Alene looked at Ardwin and wrinkled her brow, half smiling.

Mr. Bluestone, seemingly growing desperate, blurted out, "*Forever!* For all time! Every time you stay. Totally, entirely *free.* Would you?"

Alene looked at him, surprised by this sudden intensity. "Certainly, Mr. Bluestone."

"Of course," agreed Ardwin, nodding.

"Ah," said Mr. Bluestone, visibly relieved, mopping his brow again. "Good, good."

"Please continue, Mr. Bluestone," said Ardwin.

"Well, it is this. What I mean to say is, in exhange, *please, please, please* might you teach my dear Leonore some of your less salty recipes? Teach her to measure *all* her ingredients carefully? Especially the salt. Urgently impress upon her that with such *foreign, northern* recipes, this is absolutely crucial. Just think of the good you will be doing for so many people. For us all," he added with heartfelt conviction.

Alene laughed warmly. "Of course. I shall be happy to teach her, Mr. Bluestone," she said. "It will be an honor and a pleasure. We could stay for, maybe, a few days, anyway."

She looked at Ardwin for confirmation. He thought for a moment, then nodded in agreement.

"Oh, that is so kind of you," exclaimed Mr. Bluestone happily. "I am grateful. I really am."

He lowered his hands, opened his eyes, raised his handkerchief, and dabbed at his wet eyes, which had become quite teary with emotion. Then he heaved a sigh, looked gratefully at Alene, and blurted out, "Would you start tomorrow? Before breakfast?"

Jiggity Jig

One fall morning neither late nor early, two travelers rode up to the gate of a well-fortified castle of a certain small kingdom. They were tanned, and their clothing was travel-stained. The youth's hair was tousled. He was comely, with broad shoulders and a strong right arm. But on the left side, the heart side, where his other arm should have been, was a great, white wing. The young woman who rode beside him was also handsome, with pleasing touches of wildness in her dress and manner. A dark blue cloak was across her shoulders, a spear was slung on a thong across her back, and there was a dagger in her belt. Beside them pranced a strange little horse. A gaggle of geese flew above them, and two packhorses loaded with pots and pans, panniers, and saddlebags followed behind.

The riders were laughing and talking.

"Well, we should let them know we are here," said the

youth as they approached the castle gate. "There is work to be done and it starts now."

"Yes, that is so," answered the maiden.

"Halloooo!" called the youth in a strong voice. "Open the gate!"

The guards looked down from the castle walls. "The winged boy!" they exclaimed. "Lady Rose Red's brother!"

"Opening, sir!" called the gatekeeper.

With a screech and a groan, up went the gate and down came the drawbridge. Then, with the small flock of geese waddling behind them, the strange little company passed under the arch and entered within the stone walls of the castle.

"Uncle Ardwin! Uncle Ardwin," called Victor and Anne as they ran down the stone stairs into the courtyard. They stopped, surprised. "But where are Stephen and Skye? What happened to them?"

"They had to go . . . home," answered Ardwin, uncomfortable with even this half-truth. "They were very sorry to have missed seeing you again."

Harry hung back, remaining halfway up the stairs. He wore a cloak over one arm, the edges of which had been cut and sewn so they looked feathered.

Ardwin was surprised to see that all three children seemed almost a head taller than when he had seen them last. Then he realized that there was nothing unusual in that. Some miracles were obviously quite ordinary.

"So, my bold cygnets!" called Ardwin. "Come down! Harry, you too! Come! Come see!"

Soon all three children, even reluctant Harry, were leaping around him. Rose and Conor rushed forward and Alene was properly introduced and hugged and admired and kissed and passed from arm to arm. The geese flapped their wings, cackling and honking. Horse pranced, leaped, and whinnied. Mare reared up and chomped on her bit, then settled down and nuzzled Annie, who was petting her nose. Harry ran with his wing-cloak held out. Then Victor was somehow up on Horse's back, chasing after the running boy. And so, in short, chaotic order, Ardwin and company came out of one sort of wild into another.

That night over dinner Ardwin told of his travels. He showed them the shortened spear and told of Belarius and the lion. Later, when he and Conor walked along the high parapet where torches flared, Conor said, "I can well believe that any creature who thought to face only a downy wing would have his eyes opened upon finding that little beauty pressed into his gut." He chuckled and said, "Strategy and surprise. That's the secret." Then, more soberly, he added, "Your father needs you, Ardwin. We may all be called to war soon."

Ardwin nodded and said, "I have returned because of it. As to my father's need —" He shrugged. "Well, we shall see."

The next day, with Ardwin's permission, riders were sent to notify his brothers and the king of his return. Ardwin was edgy and restless after that, and, as he walked in the orchard with his sister, Rose Red asked, "What is it? What bothers you?"

"Nothing."

"Really, Ard, *nothing* does not fidget so. You have something on your mind. I know. I too have carried such nothings that weighed tons."

"Soon Father will know where to find me. I ruined his plans. But he . . ."

"Ruined your life? As did I?" she said, with a touch of bitterness.

He took her hand. "Once I thought so, Rose, but no longer. How blind I have been. I appreciate your sacrifice and see how much it cost you. But you need to know that the unfinished shirt was destined for me. It was Evron's plan. She chose me to be different. You could not have completed it, no matter how hard you tried. Besides, what I thought was a catastrophe had purpose and meaning after all. It made me who I am. Forgive me for blaming you."

"How do you know all this?" Rose asked, stunned.

"I met Evron."

"What? When?"

"Not long ago," he said. "In the north." He ran his hand through his unruly hair. "She died saving Alene and me, and as she was dying, she apologized for the pain she'd caused. She called me her 'experiment.' She especially apologized for what she's done to you."

"I am shocked," Rose said, her face pale.

"I was too. But she said it clearly. And she said I was to tell you, Father, Bran, and the others. Those were her final words — as far as I can tell."

Rose looked quizzically at him.

"Her neck was broken. She faded before me like ice melting, and then she vanished. Yet I can't be certain she is finally, truly gone." He looked at his sister. "She was an enchantress, and stranger than we dreamed. More complex. She told me she was both of the darkness and the light. I believe it. Evron was like a storm that kills and at the same time brings life-giving rain." He paused. Then he said simply, "In any case, I no longer believe I am cursed."

Rose wiped her eyes — there were tears starting — then rubbed her hands lightly together. "I knew it!" she said. "I am so glad, Ard! The spell is broken. You used to smile like that when you were a boy. This is your real face. It's wonderful to see it again."

She grew serious. "You know, I don't think Father intended

to betray you. He sought you, and yes, Ulfius has been acting up, but you may not actually have needed to —"

Ardwin interrupted her. "Are you sure? Father could be hiding something."

"Maybe. Of course, I could be wrong. His men did come. We told them that you had headed home with Skye and that Stephen went north. I doubted they believed us. I'm sure you've guessed that Stephen and Skye were found — Father was furious with them! But they revealed nothing. You have good friends."

"Yes, I believe I do. Or may, if I can patch things up." She looked at him oddly. "We didn't part well," he said. "But that is another story, not for now. Well, whatever the truth, I am no longer running. So, after a few days to rest and catch up with you, if that's all right, we'll go."

"All right?" said Rose. "It's perfect. And so is she."

The children came running, Alene walking behind them. "Tell us a story, Uncle Ardwin," they clamored.

The sun was dropping. The faces looking up at Ardwin were lit by its glow. He felt grateful to have made it to this moment, to be alive and well, and inside his own story.

Ardwin raised his wing, making the last of the red-and-gold leaves rustle overhead. "All right," he said. "Now, listen. I will tell you about the time that Horse and I went after the giants who had stolen Alene. A wolf drove them, a leopard frightened their horses, and an owl sank its claws into one giant's throat. The owl, the wolf, and the leopard were really all one single enchantress, my own stepmother, the one who gave me this wing." He paused. "How does that sound?"

"And then what, Uncle Ardwin?" called Annie.

Ardwin looked into their eager faces. "And that's when the trouble *really* began."

A few days later Alene and Ardwin stood in the courtyard, cloaked and muffled against the chill. Conor and Rose and the children stood beside them. Light snow was falling. A crow flew, cawing, overhead. Ardwin said to the children, "Do you still have the feathers I gave you?"

"Yes," said Annie and the others.

"Good. Keep them. One day — who can say when, but when the time is right — a wind will come and it will lift you where you need to go. For now, prepare," he continued. "Learn all you can. Study maps and books, music and stories. Grow strong. You will have wings, not like mine, but your own. Those feathers are the sign."

Horse bowed. Mare whinnied. The geese flapped.

"Remember us," said Alene.

"Farewell, Chieftains and Princess! Till we meet again!" said Ardwin, waving his wing. Then he and Alene mounted their horses and rode away.

When the Wind Blows

They rode through forests and past fields where hay was rolled and stacked, the ground bare, stubble-yellow, and dusted with snow. Ardwin was on Horse, Alene on Mare, the geese flying overhead, and the three geldings plodding behind loaded with gear (more cloaks and dresses and warm robes and apples, cheese, dried meat, and bread). Horse's wound was healed, and now he liked being in the thick of things, no longer prancing about on his own. This way, too, he got to amble close beside Mare.

The castle loomed ahead, the gate wide open. They rode into the courtyard and there stood the king, waiting.

"Just like him. He must have seen us approaching," Ardwin said to Alene.

The sun was bright. A few snowflakes glittered, drifting across the yard. The king's hair was more silver than Ardwin remembered, and he watched them intently as they rode forward and dismounted.

"It seems like only yesterday," said Ardwin, glancing around. "Then again, it seems like years. And now I am back. Time to settle things properly." He squared his shoulders, looked at Alene, and nodded. Side by side, they started forward.

"Take them," the king ordered. Ardwin flung back his cloak, exposing the Hunter's hilt. Alene gripped her spear.

"Take their horses," repeated the king, eyeing Ardwin and Alene and the weapons they gripped.

The men looked at Horse, wide-eyed. They took the horses from Alene and Ardwin. Horse snorted and pawed the ground. "I want to stay and see what happens!" he exclaimed. "I've been waiting for this."

Ardwin ordered, "Do not take them to the stables yet."

"As you wish, my lord," said one of the men. "It is good to see you back home."

Ardwin let his cloak drop back down, nodding to the man in acknowledgment. Alene relaxed her grip on her spear but stayed wary.

"You didn't have to leave, you know," began the king angrily as Ardwin approached. "I sent those two fawning courtiers packing. You didn't have to run. You've caused me a lot of trouble. Now you're back. How nice of you."

Ardwin shook his head, held the wing down (it was starting to bristle), took a deep breath, and laughed. "Hold on. A few corrections. I *did* have to leave and I didn't run. I *escaped,* if you recall. If I had waited and discovered in the morning that you had chosen the arm, it would have been too late. I made the right decision. Many good things have come from it and, yes, also some bad. We'll deal with those. Which is why I've returned."

"Escaped?" repeated the king. "Oh, please! I just wanted to talk. There were excellent reasons to consider Ulfius's offer. It was my royal duty to explore and examine them. But I said no in the end." The king paused. Ardwin wasn't shouting, which was a pleasant surprise. His own anger faded. When Ardwin responded, "Why? Because you couldn't find me?" he even laughed and said, "Maybe. But I also saw that to force you might prove my own undoing. I could have cut off the wing and made you angry enough to turn against me. I decided I'd rather face Ulfius." He paused to brush away a wet flake of snow that had settled on his eyelash.

"Not being able to find you helped. It gave me time to think. Though I was furious with Stephen and Skye when I couldn't get my hands on you." He ran his hand through his gray hair. "I wanted you here."

Ardwin was touched by his frankness. "If I had waited, who knows?" he said. "I might have been tempted by that arm and the possibilities it offered too. So I left."

The king looked at his son. "Think things through, decide for yourself, then act," he said. "Find out by doing what you need to do; discover your road by walking it. If you make a mistake, try again. All my life, I have tried to follow this path."

Ardwin said, "We are very similar."

The king brightened. "You think so? It means . . . I'm glad you see it that way."

"Definitely."

The king rubbed his bearded chin and looked at Ardwin again. "My father's old sword? It served?"

"Yes. It served well."

"Good," said the king. "It's a heavy blade, but you've got the arm to wield it, son, as if it were meant to be." He paused. "Maybe you've already heard, but Ulfius is not taking rejection well."

"Rose mentioned."

"War may have been his plan all along." The king frowned. "He is hard to read, Ard, and he is dangerous." He looked Ardwin up and down carefully, really taking him in now: the tanned face, tousled hair, and broad shoulders; the lion tooth; the short spear; the cloaks and mail; the heavy-bladed, well-oiled sword, and lion-skin vest. And he grinned, his weary, lined face becoming for the moment almost young, as if the years fell from him like a cloak. His son looked strong, capable, and quite grown. "It's good to see you, Ard. Very good," he said. And he reached out and clasped Ardwin to him.

"It *is* good," said Ardwin. Then he laughed, shaking his head happily as he gripped his father back. "And . . . but this is terrible! Alene, forgive me! Father, this is Alene. Alene, Father."

"Alone?" said the king.

"No, Father. *Alene,*" he said, raising his eyebrows, rolling his eyes, and looking at Alene in apology.

"Ah," said the king. "It is a pleasure to meet you, Lady Alene." He bowed. "Please excuse my lack of courtesy and manners. I should have welcomed you at once and brought you into the warmth of the hall instead of keeping you out here, standing in the snow. For that, I ask your pardon."

Alene said, "Of course. And the pleasure is mine, Sire." She looked him in the eye. "As to standing in the snow, I like being out in most any weather. And your conversation with Ardwin was important. Now we can go into your hall together, at peace."

The king looked at her appraisingly. Alene stood at ease, tall and beautiful, a dagger at her waist, a spear in her hand, snowflakes sparkling on her dark blue cloak like stars.

"Yes," he said. "Yes, a very genuine pleasure. We have all been out in the cold long enough."

So Ardwin, Alene, and the king went in together from the snowy courtyard to the great hall, where a fire was already blazing.

Horse and Mare and the big geldings were given comfortable stalls of their own in the king's stables. All the horses with them were munching hay and chatting amiably, switching their tails back and forth in a friendly way.

"Now, Ardwin, my wing boy," Horse began, and all the horses swiveled their ears and listened, "killed a snow lion single-handed, and they're big, let me tell you. That's its tooth he wears around his neck, and a swath of its skin is on his back. And then with some help from me, of course, he killed the bad men who had stolen the princess."

"Good for him," said a stallion. "Kicked 'em, did he?"

"No, he speared one and . . . er . . . a bird, though it wasn't actually a bird, exactly, it was . . . well, she looked like an owl and, whatever she was, she killed one."

"Kicked 'em good, did she?" neighed the stallion.

"NO!" whinnied Horse. "Taloned him and tore out his throat, if you must know. And a bear tore off the head of another, and I killed the one who cut my side open. You've all seen my scar, haven't you?"

"Yes," answered all the horses, "we have! It's a beauty! We noticed it right away, as soon as you walked in!"

"Good. Well, I killed the last one."

"Bit him?" asked the stallion somewhat hesitantly.

"No. Kicked 'em, actually," sighed Horse. "Caved in his head."

"Where'd he get the wing?" broke in an old mare, several stalls away.

"Why, why . . . oh, it's a long story!" snorted Horse, pawing the floor of his stall. "And, madam, it's not . . . what I'm trying to tell you is not *where,* but *what*—what he's done with it! That's the point! Haven't any of you *lived*?"

"I have," said one of the geldings quietly. "And from what I've seen, this has got to be the best place in the whole world. The men I knew were cruel, and made us carry them while they did awful things." He looked around. "I like it here and plan to stay."

"Apples!" neighed Horse. "Oh, how I will hate to give up the blessed fruits of civilization. But what has happened in this tame southern land to my dear horse people? I'm going back north as soon as I can. Where a horse can be a *horse*!"

"And I'm going with you," said the little mare.

"You are?" exclaimed Horse, ceasing to paw the floor and standing stock-still, his legs all aquiver, stunned.

"Of course," said Mare. "It's what I was made for."

Horse lifted his square head until his nose rose just over the wall of her adjoining stall. He closed his eyes and sniffed, his black nostrils growing soft and wide. "You're right," he exclaimed. "You and I are destined to run together. Now I see it! The purpose and meaning of my journey has at last been revealed! Oh, Belarius, here is the ending of the tale! You were right. It has become my own! Celebrate with us, good horses! My mare and I are met."

"We met long ago," interrupted Mare.

"Yes," said Horse. "But it was not yet *the Meeting*."

"It was for me," said Mare.

In the great hall Stephen and Skye were waiting uncomfortably, fidgeting, holding hands, fingers tightly entwined. Ardwin entered with Alene at his side, saw them, and immediately ran forward as Alene stayed behind. Stephen and Skye flinched as he came at them, arm and wing spread wide. But Ardwin grasped Stephen and then Skye, and blurted out in a rush, "I'm sorry for the way we parted. I was hurt and angry but my behavior was childish. Please forgive me. I'm so glad to see you!" He beamed at them. "And thank you for being such good friends and for bearing the brunt of Father's rage."

"We should have been more open with you," Skye said.

"Or we should have kept things better hidden," added Stephen.

"I hope you know we never meant to hurt you," Skye said, looking at Stephen for confirmation. He nodded.

"I do now."

Alene approached and Ardwin turned and introduced her to his friends. Then he took Stephen aside and said, "Stephen . . . Raven is dead."

"I was afraid of that. I watched from the ramparts when I learned of your return. Even from a distance I could see that you weren't riding him, and I feared the worst."

"He was a great horse," said Ardwin, putting his arm on Stephen's shoulder. "He got me to the swans. I can't think of another horse who could have done it."

"How did he die? Tell me. What happened?"

Ardwin told him about the snow lion. "But I killed it, Stephen. Raven was avenged."

Stephen nodded. "Thanks," he said. "Only a lion could have taken him. He was so strong, I think he could have fought off anything else. For Raven, maybe it was a good death."

"I believe you are right. But come now." Ardwin turned to Alene and Skye and to his father the king, who had gone off to the fireplace and was quietly adding wood to the fire. "All of you, come, sit down. Alene and I will tell you everything. There's so much to catch up on. And now we will."

The king watched as a servant put a last log on the fire. "Good!" he said. "Now let's hear your tale."

They drew up chairs. Ardwin took a breath, about to start, when a voice called out, "Wait!" and the king's ministers trooped into the hall.

"We want to know everything too," said the chief minister, Stephen's father. "We have been waiting, and face war with Ulfius because of you, Prince Ardwin. Don't start till we are seated."

When they were settled, Ardwin took another breath and was again about to speak when, "Wait!" a frail voice ordered.

Now old Marjorie hobbled into the hall, leaning on a cane. She took a seat, then, impatiently tapping the flagstones with the tip of her cane, demanded, "Well, what are you waiting for? Begin!"

Before anyone else could interrupt or say anything more, Ardwin at last started in and told the whole tale, all the way through. He left out the details of his flight from Stephen and Skye, which was the courteous thing to do. After all, no one needed to know about that. From time to time Alene added bits of her own to the story, especially about how she and Ardwin met, and of the fight with her kidnappers and what followed.

Those gathered listened wide-eyed. Even the serving men and women set down their trays and leaned against the wall or sat on the stone steps, absorbed in the tale. When Stephen heard the details of Raven's death, he covered his head with his cloak so no one would see him weep.

"A grand tale!" exclaimed the king when all was done. "Magnificent." He looked meaningfully at his ministers. "Welcome back, Chieftain. And welcome, Princess." Then he said almost to himself, "She apologized, did she? Well, well." He looked at Ardwin. "And so, Evron is dead," he said quietly. "You say you actually saw her die?"

"Yes. That is, I saw her fade away and vanish. But is she gone? I don't know. When one of her forms dies, do they all?"

Old Marjorie stood up stiffly and wagged a bony finger at Alene. "From now on, if he has nightmares," she said, "don't call on me. He's your problem. Welcome home, Prince Ardwin. Now maybe we can all have a little well-earned peace, thank goodness!"

Prophecy

For Ardwin, it was like the very best of old times, only more so. His wing didn't flash out as it used to, smashing into people or things. Belarius's training had paid off, allowing Ardwin to be much more relaxed, at ease with himself and with others. And he was truly part of things now. He and his father and the ministers reviewed maps and planned strategies of attack and defense together. He told them everything Belarius had said, and shared all he had seen while on the wizard's mountain. They went over it all, seeking any clues, no matter how seemingly insignificant, that might help them successfully oppose Ulfius. They found much of interest, but nothing decisive. Finally Ardwin said, "Time is short. I suggest we send for Belarius himself. Maybe we can get him to join us. He has no love for Ulfius and he has some grief too, knowing that his weapons might be restored by that madman and used for harm. He and I got along well. Let us see if an invitation will bring him."

One afternoon, Ardwin was hurrying to another strategy meeting when he ran into Conrad laughing with a friend. Ardwin heard him say, "Oh, it is just too ludicrous! I mean, the swan boy and the goose girl! Can you believe it? We won't run short on eggs, anywa —"

He never finished, for Ardwin grabbed him by the collar and, tall as Conrad was, lifted him till his toes dangled. "By the tooth of the lion!" Ardwin exclaimed angrily, looking up into Conrad's shocked face. "When are you going to grow up? And don't even think of reaching for that knife! I have already killed much worse than you."

Turning to the astonished youth, who stood openmouthed beside him, Ardwin said, "Remind your friend here, when I put him down, what he looked like dangling from my hand like a puppy." He looked at Conrad. "I am tired of you and I will nail you to a wall if you can't keep your mouth civilly shut. These are sad and perilous times. Lives hang in the balance! At least try to be useful! Stop being such a selfish twit and finally act your age."

Ardwin dropped Conrad and wiped his hand on his cloak as if he had held something slimy and rotten. He looked at Conrad again, shook his head, and left.

But a week later Conrad was gone, off to Rotterdale to

further his learning, it was said — though what learning that was, no one could precisely say. Even the king admitted privately that he was glad to see him go. "He was always whining and spying. It will be a relief not to have him slinking around underfoot."

Old Marjorie, however, was wrong in thinking that Ardwin's return would make life more peaceful. There was no peace at all. Ulfius was striking deeper, his raids becoming more swift, cruel, and constant. A pall hung over the land, especially along the borders. Even in the heart of the realm, in the central towns and in the king's walled city of Ludon, everyone could feel it. It was becoming clear that the raids were preparatory. Soon there would be all-out war. Lugh's spies brought reports that Ulfius was massing his forces.

Ardwin began to have a recurring dream. Night after night he saw a certain isolated border spot. He and Horse were standing alone at the bottom of a steep, snow-covered hill, with dark woods behind them. A band of raiders, wearing Ulfius's colors of black and green, were charging down the hill through the snow, straight toward them. The leader of the raiders was thin, his face hard, with a prominent scar running across his forehead and cheek. A voice soft as the wind in the pines, soft as the ruffling of feathers, repeated, "The last day of the year, midmorning; last day, year's end," over and over, always the same. The voice also sang, whisper-quiet:

"When broken C finds dead G
Kings will dance
And a world set free."

Ardwin would awake, look at his wing, and ask, "What are you trying to tell me? It is you, isn't it? And what does this mean?"

His feathers only rustled softly, roused and rustled, then lay flat and still again. And the wing offered nothing more.

Belarius on the Mountain

Belarius held the note that Ardwin's messenger had delivered. He tapped its stiff edge on the tabletop. *Tap tap tap.* Ardwin was asking him to come and help. That would mean taking sides. It would mean leaving the security of his fortress and exposing himself to possible failure. There would be serious consequences if he should be on the wrong side, the losing side, when Ulfius won. And working for kings was . . . well, it meant creating what *they* desired. He had seen where *that* road led! Missiles with brains and men, women, and children blown to bits! Potentially of course. None of that had happened, at least not yet. And if he had destroyed enough of his models and plans, it wouldn't, not for a long time.

The choices we make — the choices I *make,* thought Belarius, correcting himself, *are important. None exists in a vacuum.*

There are always consequences. He saw that he must build things that mattered, things that actually had consequence, that is, meaning, purpose, and — what was the word? *Ah, yes. Value.*

And now here was Ardwin, asking for his aid. Belarius sighed. Giving help in person might be better than sending it from a distance. Guiding that bear while staying seated in his fortress far away had been tiring but not terribly hard. The poor thing already hated those crooks. How her fur had bristled at her first whiff of them! She must have met them before. He had felt grief in her too, but rage had been the keynote. And so he had used it, letting it draw her to the task at hand. Interestingly, the bear had felt kindly toward Ardwin and the girl, wanting only to protect them. But the others she wanted only to tear apart. And then the Enchantress arrived, just in time too, as if the larger pattern, the plan not of his devising but one already set in motion long ago, was completing itself.

The only really hard thing had been his own recovery. For three days afterward he had lain in bed exhausted, able to eat only apples and honey, like a bear. He had had to fight a temptation too, to set off into the woods and rip logs apart, searching for grubs — the thought of white, wriggling, juicy grubs had been positively mouthwatering at the time. Ugh! Now, he was back to normal, thank goodness, and grubs seemed properly disgusting. Bears! Fortunately the side effects had only been temporary, though it had taken a full week for the fur that had grown on his arms, back, and hands to fall off. Yes, working invisibly, from far away, had its risks. Sometimes you could take on too much. Of course, he hadn't actually *become* the bear. But their minds, his and the bear's, had become linked; his spirit and the bear's had joined. He was lucky he hadn't lost his ability for human speech! He could just see himself growling out orders to Stephano and Trinculo as he lay in bed, mending.

Belarius rapped the note on the tabletop again. And again. It sounded like a distant hammer chipping steadily away in some deep mine shaft. He sat thinking. *Tap, tap, tap. Tap, tap, tap.*

Then, "Stephano! Trinculo!"

"Yes, Mas-ter," came the replies.

"Gather provisions for several weeks on the road. Load the wagon and hitch up Dust and Ashes. We're going on a journey."

"Yes, Mas-ter."

It was time to take sides. He was getting rusty sitting up here in solitude on his lonely mountain. It was all so . . . *protected.* Ulfius must be stopped. He was mad, insane, and people were going to get hurt. *All right, Ardwin, hold your horses,* thought Belarius with a shiver of excitement. He rubbed his hands together gleefully. *I'm on my way, lad. Belarius is coming.*

Midmorning at year's end, on a snowy day, Ardwin sat alone on Horse, under gray skies, along a lonely forest border of his father's kingdom looking up at a steep, snow-covered hill. He loosened the Hunter in its sheath.

Horse asked nervously, "So this is going to work, yah?"

Ardwin reached down and patted Horse's neck. "Yes. They'll be here. I'm sure of it."

"But it all works out as planned, right?"

"I only have a wing, Horse, not a crystal ball. We'll have to see. Anyway, you know as much as I do."

"Alene's mad at you, isn't she?"

Ardwin sighed. "She'll get over it. Fighting wolves is one thing, battles with men another. I couldn't have her come along. Not to this."

Horse pricked up his ears. "What's that?" he whinnied nervously.

Ardwin listened. "I don't hear anything," he said. "Except the wind in the pines and the whirling snow."

"I hear hooves," said Horse. "And the jingle of reins and armor, and the panting of tired horses."

Ardwin narrowed his eyes and looked. Still he saw and heard nothing. Then, far off at the top of the hill, he saw them, what looked like thirty riders coming down the slope. "Bravo, ears," he said, and reached forward and patted Horse's neck again.

"Bravo, whatever you please," said Horse. "I just want this to work. That will do, as far as I'm concerned."

The riders came closer. The colors they wore were black and green, the colors of Ulfius.

The approaching riders stopped on the snowy hillside and sat on their horses looking down to where, far below, one lone rider sat looking up at them. They turned to one another and seemed to be conferring. Several of their horses pranced restlessly. The leader pointed. Then he made a broad motion with his arm, signaling *Forward!* The riders spurred their horses and headed more rapidly down the snow-covered slope.

Horse's back grew tense. He stiffened his legs. Ardwin threw back his cloak, exposing the wing. "Closer. Closer," he murmured.

Horse stamped a leg, impatiently. "Aren't they already close enough? I'm a runner, not a waiter!"

"Easy," answered Ardwin calmly. "Very soon now."

They were so close that Ardwin could see their faces and the designs on their tunics. Beneath their weathered traveling cloaks he clearly saw an upright bear, black, on a field of green — Ulfius's mark. He could even make out a long, white scar running across the leader's whip-thin face.

"All right," said Ardwin. "Now!"

"Definitely now!" whinnied Horse.

Ardwin shook out the wing. He saw surprise and then cruel recognition on the faces of the rapidly closing riders. They were about to get what they needed to start their war.

Ardwin saw the flash and glitter of weapons being drawn. "Yes," said Ardwin with a smile. "They have taken our bait."

"How very nice of them," said Horse unhappily.

Closer came the raiders. They were almost upon him when Ardwin at last raised his wing high.

From the dark woods directly behind him, and on either flank, a small band of armed riders burst from among the trees. Two iron figures walked stiffly after them. *Creak creak creak, rumble rumble rumble, clank clank clank.* One of the iron men wore a chain-mail shirt over his coat of steel.

Horses neighed madly. There were fierce cries, oaths, groans, and the resounding, ringing clash of iron weapons striking as the two warring parties met. The raiders seemed confident. In a few minutes their work would be done.

But somehow the raiders' attack began to go terribly awry. The two armored knights strode among them, yanking mounted soldiers helplessly from their saddles and flinging them to the ground. Many of the attackers already lay stunned and groaning on the snow.

"Charge them! Kill those two!" shouted their leader, furiously wheeling his horse and pointing his sword at the two strange, stiff-jointed knights in their heavy, blocklike armor. The raiders spun their mounts from the attack and massed around the two iron warriors. They slashed and hacked and stabbed, but no sword or lance or ax could slow them. Nothing seemed to injure them. Not even a dent appeared in their armor. Instead those pitiless iron hands just kept reaching up, breaking swords, tearing ax heads from shafts, ripping shields apart as if they were paper, and flinging soldiers down from their horses, left and right.

"Halt! Surrender! You are surrounded!" called Ardwin.

The leader of the raiders looked, and was shocked to see that it was true. More than half his men were injured or down. Many of the others had been disarmed. Those who remained fighting were so intent on bringing down the iron men, they hadn't noticed that they themselves were surrounded.

The captain of the raiders licked his lips, seeking some way out. Then an iron fist lifted him from his saddle and a hollow voice said, "Yield . . . or . . . die." He had no choice. Stunned, he said, "I . . . we yield."

The trapped men looked at one another, then at their leader. He nodded, and they dropped their swords.

"See to the fallen and wounded," ordered Ardwin. Many men were groaning, rising groggily to their feet. Some were limping, others holding shoulders, elbows, or heads. Stephen put up his visor, dismounted, and knelt beside a rider who lay sprawled awkwardly on the snow. "He's dead, Ardwin."

"Take up the body and return to your lord Ulfius," Ardwin said to the raiders. "Once you bandage and splint your wounded, we shall let you leave."

"Release him, Trinculo," ordered Ardwin. The iron hand let go. The captain of the raiders dropped back onto his saddle with a *thud.*

When he had regained his breath, and with an uneasy glance at the iron warrior standing eerily silent and unmoving beside him, the captain said, "My lord, we shall do as you say." Then he added, "But . . . how did you know to await us here? We ourselves only decided on this crossing late last night, while still on route."

Ardwin answered, "Tell Ulfius that the House of Peredur has powers greater than can be imagined. Now," he continued. "Tell us your purpose and do not lie. Was it your plan to harass a village and cause harm?"

"Yea, Lord. We were sent to burn, to pillage, and slay."

"Your path home would have been bloody," said Ardwin grimly. "And war would surely have come. Go back and tell your king to desist, and come no more as a foe but, rather, as a guest. Or tell him, if it is not friendship he seeks, he should come in full force, prepared to battle to the bitter end. But by my power I tell you, should he try, he will lose utterly! Tell him of our invincible iron warriors. And tell him too that when he has lost, I will take his precious arm of gold and melt it down to make children's toys of it. We have no need of such baubles here. Now, do you have food enough for your return journey?"

"No, Lord," said the leader. "We planned to take what we needed by force from those we met along the way. We are raiders, and travel light."

Ardwin motioned with his hand. A smallish rider rode forward, untied two large sacks that hung from the saddle horn, and handed them to the raiders' chief. "Cheese, bread, meat. Two skins of wine," said Ardwin. "Enough for thirty thrifty men. Twenty-nine shall find it even easier going."

The raiders' eyes opened wide. They looked at one another and muttered darkly, "The precise number! He knew the exact tally!" The leader tied one sack to his own saddle and handed the other to the man beside him. He said graciously, "We had heard, Lord, that you were different. But those who said so did not do you justice. You *are* different, but if so, all men should be as you. We shall eat your food gratefully and spare those we meet."

"Go, then," said Ardwin. "And swiftly."

The chief of the raiders bowed courteously. He pointed to the dead man and said, "Take him up." Two riders dismounted and hoisted the dead man over the saddle of his horse, tied him on, then swung back up onto their own mounts.

He nodded. "Let's go."

The small soldier, the one who had carried the sacks of food, raised his visor. A strange look was on the young, smooth face. Then the helmet was pushed back so that it fell with a *clunk!* onto the snow. Long, gold-brown curly hair tumbled free. There sat Alene, gazing fixedly at the captain of the raiders.

"That voice," she murmured. "That scar! Your face was cut that night defending *me*! Blood and fire!" she suddenly exclaimed. "I . . . I *know* you. I *remember*! I was . . . oh, it all comes back. All I had forgotten!" Alene buried her face in her hands.

Ardwin cried out, astonished, "Alene! What are you doing here? What are you saying?"

The captain's face turned white. The scar burned lividly red across his forehead and cheek. He trembled, slid from his horse, and stumbled through the snow toward Alene, who sat helpless, her face still buried in her hands.

Ardwin spurred swiftly forward, drawing the Hunter as he came. "Defend Alene!" he shouted. "Defend her!"

The voice of Belarius rose from among the trees. "Protect Alene! Full strength! Now!"

Trinculo and Stephano, red eyes glowing, lumbered swiftly forward.

But the captain of the guards got there first. He looked up at Alene, gasped out, "The pearl earrings! Princess Gwennethfar!" and dropped to his knees in the snow by her stirrup.

"Yes," said Alene, looking up and speaking like a dreamer waking from sleep, "I remember everything now. That was my name. And you are Cyric, the brave champion who fought all alone and unaided against desperate odds to save me. You slew two of the ruffians as I screamed for help. Then you sank down, your face bloodied beneath a terrible blow from a third attacker. A cloak was flung over my head, I was lifted up on an iron shoulder and . . . knew no more. Now I am come back to myself at last. But I am no longer that lost princess named Gwennethfar, younger sister to Alisoun, and King Ulfius's own daughter. I am, and shall now forever be, Alene."

"Yes, Your Highness," said Cyric, looking up at her with joy on his fierce, scarred face. "You are back. All shall be as you say."

Ardwin had leaped off Horse, prepared to cut Cyric down.

Now he paused, sword upraised. Stephano and Trinculo were reaching for Cyric with iron hands.

"Stop! Do not harm him," ordered Alene. "This is my brave, good, and loyal protector," she said. "And he has found me at last."

Ardwin lowered the Hunter. "Do as she says," he said to Stephano and Trinculo. "Let him be."

Then he turned to Alene, who sat regally above him. "And you, you are actually the daughter of *Ulfius*?" he said, stunned. "I have only one word for this," he added, sheathing his sword, "and that is *unbelievable*!"

"Yes," said Alene with a tearful smile. "It does seem so."

The Story That Shortens the Road

Well," nodded Horse, shaking his bristle-mane and stamping his hoof, "things rolled along at a merry clip after that, I can tell you. Old, broken, cut, and scarred C did meet dead G. Cyric is our brave C, and the long-thought-dead Gwennethfar, our lovely G. How did the wing know? That's the puzzle. Maybe it wasn't the wing at all. Maybe it was just Ardwin. Sometimes we all know more than we think we know, and no one can say how. But all's well that ends well."

"Indeed," agreed Mare, swishing her tail. "Actually it all unfolded at such a gallop, it was not easy to keep up. Even our winged lad, Ardwin, was hard-pressed."

"Hard-pressed?" whinnied Horse. "He was amazed! The two kingdoms were to be allied by his own marriage to the daughter of the very king he'd run from. After several days I had to ask him to stop saying *unbelievable*. It was getting on my nerves."

"Thank you, dear," said Mare. "It was getting on *all* our nerves. Even Stephano and Trinculo were becoming jittery. We're all quite grateful."

The other horses in the stables were listening wide-eyed, their ears pricked straight up.

"And so Alene is really Princess Gwennethfar, who had been stolen from her father, King Ulfius, long ago?" asked a young stallion respectfully.

"The one," nodded Horse smugly.

"The same," nodded Mare.

"But wait! I thought she was the daughter of a *different* king and queen," added an old mare, also clearly confused.

"She was adopted," said Mare. "She had been found wandering naked and alone in the woods, a little girl lost, without any memory of her past. The kind queen found her and brought her to the palace, where she named her Alene."

"Ah," said the old mare. "That explains it."

"But, oh, my friends, you should have seen the grand reunion of father and daughter. It was so moving, I almost cried," said Horse grandly.

"You *did* cry," whinnied Mare.

"Perhaps," nodded Horse agreeably. "What a moment! There was the one crying, 'Father!' and the other, 'My lost daughter, *found*!' And, then, the two kings, who had come so terribly close to a war in which many humans, and horses too, would have died, came together, fell on each other's necks, embraced, and swore eternal friendship. And Ardwin's father," said Horse, "King What's-His-Name?"

"King Lugh," put in one of the old stallions.

"Yes, him," said Horse, "began crying, 'It's a miracle! The wing! If we had cut it off, none of this would have happened!' "

"And the other, Ulfius," said Mare, "exclaimed, 'The scheme rejected, saved us! It brought my daughter home, us kings to peace, and me back to my own right mind. I had fallen into such darkness! But good can come as quickly as bad. I swear by the clear sky above that I am healed. I shall offer recompense to all I harmed in my madness. Who would have thought it? The wing I wanted cut has saved us all!' "

"And then the two kings embraced again, and laughed and cried, stunned by the wonder of their mutual good fortune. Yes," said Horse sagely, "that was quite a moment. Of course," he added, shaking his head and bristly mane, "it is puzzling to think that so much good came from a curse. Did Evron plan all of this, or would she be as surprised as the rest of us to learn what happened? In any case, it was her very own Birdwing who saved the day!

"But it wasn't just the wing that did it," continued Horse.

"It was the boy *with* the wing. That's what I'm trying to say. It's what he's *done* with the wing that makes the story. If Bran had had the wing, it would have been all quite different. No peace, no reconciliation, no finding of the lost princess, no healing of the realms. My boy did it single-handed. Literally." He smiled at his own wit. "Credit where credit is due. Three cheers for the one-armed, winged boy, I say."

"Winged *man,*" said Mare. "He's not a boy anymore, dear."

"That's true," said Horse. "Very true. I just knew him when. Anyway, this was all just prologue. The high point was the wedding."

"And quite a wedding it was," nodded Mare. "And it was so nice of Ardwin and Alene to invite us."

"We stood near the door," said Horse. "The best place, I can assure you. The head ushers, my old friends, Stephano and Trinculo, guided us there, hard by the threshold, out beyond the stuffiness of the crowded . . . what do they call it?"

"Chapel, dear," said Mare.

"Yes, just outside the chapel door, out in the fresh air. And the king, what's his name?"

"Lugh," sighed the old stallion.

"Yes, that one. He had complained so," snickered Horse, "saying, 'Horses! No! No animals can come to a wedding! The chapel is not a barnyard or stable!' Oh, how the crickets on the hearth, the spiders behind the stove, the mice in their passages, the bats in the rafters, the ants in the floor, the snakes in their holes, and even the old dog and cat laughed at that!"

"Yes," nodded Mare in agreement. "It is amazing what kings, the poor dears, don't know! Well, he agreed in the end and, so, there we were. Along with both kings and Ardwin's brothers and their families and his sister and Conor and the children."

"And Alene's sister, the beautiful Alisoun," said Horse. "And her new husband, Borvron. (Ulfius hadn't waited. He'd already married her off.) And Alene's stepparents and sisters. And Belarius, of course. And the loyal Cyric too!"

"Yes," sighed Mare happily, remembering. "All in all, it was the grandest wedding that ever was."

"Indeed," agreed Horse, lifting his square head and nodding happily. "Trinculo wore white gloves especially for the occasion. How the crowd outside the chapel and lining the streets cheered when the happy couple at last emerged! They cheered and they shouted, 'Long live Prince Ardwin and Princess Alene!' (Though some were shouting 'Princess Gwennethfar,' so it was a bit confusing.) 'Health and long life!' they cried, tossing their caps into the air."

"And guess who caught the wedding bouquet?" asked Mare.

"Who?" asked the other horses, entranced, picturing the tumultuous scene.

"Was it you, Mare?" asked the young stallion.

"No. Not me. Though that was a good guess," said Mare. The young stallion looked pleased. "It was Skye. Though later she gave me the bouquet to eat," added Mare, looking shyly at Horse.

"Ahem. Yes, that's right," said Horse. "Then a guard came running and said that a great she-bear was outside the walls, moaning and clawing and wanting to get in, and he asked should they kill her or what? And Ardwin, very forthrightly and kingly, I would say, said, 'No! We must let her in,' and though they were astonished, they did. She ambled right in like she owned the place, went up to Alene, put her great paws around her, and moaned and cried so pitifully. Then Alene cried, 'It is *she*! My very own bear mother! The one from my old dream!' And Ardwin exclaimed, 'The collar mark! It *is* she!' Then Alene, wiping her eyes, told the story of how this very mother bear had saved and protected her when she had been abducted and before she'd been found by her stepparents. And Ardwin exclaimed, 'She saved us from death later too. This is the bear. I'm sure of it!' Then Alene's real father, King Ulfius, declared very graciously that this bear from now on was to be a royally protected beast and that she should always have apples and honey as long as she lived, and that she should always roam freely and never be hunted or captured. All the other kings and queens who were there said it should be so in their realms too. And all the people cheered 'Hurrah!' to that.

"Mrs. Bluestone's apple pies, northern style, I must tell you, were the best food I have ever eaten, or shall ever eat, in my whole life. And we, we," whinnied Horse triumphantly, "*we* are the very first horses in *all of history* to ever attend such a spectacular event as guests, mind you, *guests*! As well as to be granted the privilege of eating such magnificent food. Have I told you all *that*?"

"Yes! You have!" loudly neighed all the horses in the stables.

"But we don't mind," added the old stallion shyly. "Tell it again, from beginning to end. And don't forget to include the pies. Northern style."

All the horses in the royal stables swished their tails and shook their heads and cried, "Again! Tell it again!" so loudly that the stable boys ran in and cried, "Whoa! Whoa! Hush now, all you crazy horses! Hush!"

The winter passed with sledding and parties, with dances, feasts, and celebration. There was music in the hall, stories by the fire, eye-opening magic performed by Belarius and his two remarkable iron assistants, and there was peace and happiness and friendship everywhere. There were falconings and winter hunts and feasts and more feasts. Then, at last, when things had finally settled down, and all the wedding guests, even the last, including Mother Bear, had gone, and all the riding gear had been mended, and all the armor polished, and all the tattered clothing resewn, and the endless socks knitted and darned, and everyone, *everyone,* from the king and the newlyweds, to the horses and hounds, had begun to tire terribly of endless snow and clouds, and lying by the fire, and snow, and reading books, and snow, and feasting and more snow, and all had begun to yearn deeply for spring and buds and green grass and breezes that gave delight and not shivers, and for air that did not make them cough from wood smoke, and for yellow sunlight rather than gray clouds, then, one day, like the eternal miracle it always is, sunlight and buds and warm breezes finally came again. Crocuses pushed boldly up from beneath the wet earth and shone above the snow in bright yellow sunlight. Everywhere there was the perfume of budding, changing, growing things. Cloaks and mufflers were thrown off. Boys and girls and dogs went racing out of doors again, and the mares began to think that soon, soon the world would again see the truly greatest miracle of all: new colts.

It was on such a mild, early spring day that the king went into the dining hall in a jovial mood and walked vigorously to the big wooden table. He sniffed the air hungrily, smelling oatmeal bubbling in the kitchen nearby and bacon frying in the black iron skillet. He rubbed his hands in expectation and sat down in his place, lifted his napkin — white as a swan's wing — and found this note:

Dear Father,

The spring wind is blowing. We'll leave the geldings. They like it here. Watch for us, though I make no promises, in the fall. And watch over Alene's geese until then, will you? We're off for now.

Your son,

Ardwin

The king sighed and shook his head. *Oh, Ard,* he thought. *Not again!*

Out on the road, spring breezes blew. Young trees, green with new leaves, caught the wind and even the tops of the old trees swayed back and forth. Ardwin and Alene, Horse and Mare ambled along happily, laughing and joking, eager to see what their journey would bring.

The swans and geese were migrating. Their calls drifted down to where a young man stood alone on a hillside in the darkness. The coals of a little fire glowed nearby, where two horses stood side by side, nodding and dreaming. A young woman lay wrapped in a cloak, asleep by the fire.

The youth looked up and raised an arm and a wing toward the starry sky. "Good-bye," he said to the flocks flying in the darkness overhead. "You were unkind to me once, but I forgive you now. I have found what I was looking for, my true home. May you always fly freely back and forth through the seasons to yours."

A young swan, flying low, heard him. It banked its wings and circled above him. "Winged boy!" it called down. "Swanwing?"

Startled, Ardwin answered, "Yes?"

"I saw you up north. But Mother told me about you when I was still just a cygnet! A human with a swan's wing, she said, one who was brave and strong."

"Your mother?"

"You saved her when some nasty boys attacked her with stones as she sat on her nest. You saved me too. I was one of her nestlings, then. She's . . . dead now. I know she would have spoken up for you if she had been alive. I wanted to talk with you when you visited us at Swan Home, but the others wouldn't let me. They were thoughtless and stupid to drive you away. You should know there are others who think like me. Come visit us again, or we'll visit you. There's so much to talk about, so much to learn. I have to go now. Maybe in the fall, when I return, we could meet."

"I'd be delighted," said Ardwin. "Honored, even." His heart leaped at this unexpected gift. "I'm sorry about your mother."

"Yes," said the young swan. "So am I. Now I must hurry and catch up with the others. Till next time!"

"Yes, till then."

Then the swan flapped its wings and flew away.

Ardwin shook his head, amazed at how things circled

around. Belarius was right: There were consequences always. They could be bad or good. It all depended on what you did and what choices you made. It all depended on what kind of seeds you planted.

He went back to the fire, where he sat up, watching the coals shimmering before him and all those countless worlds shining overhead. He added a few sticks to the fire and looked at Alene's beautiful, familiar face, lit by the fire's ruddy glow, and listened to her soft breathing, steady and rhythmic as waves of the sea. He stretched out his arm and his wing, glad — so glad — to be alive. "Swanwing," he said quietly, trying it out. "Maybe. It might be an interesting change." He smiled to himself. "We'll see." Then he curled his cloak around himself, lay down beside Alene, folded his wing over her, and, at last, fell peacefully asleep.

Acknowledgments

Various people were key to giving this book life. So here I offer special thanks to the "crew."

Arthur Levine bought Birdwing *literally on a wing and a prayer in the faith that I would actually turn an interesting idea into a living tale. Jacob Martin read various drafts and offered stunningly perceptive suggestions. (Sometimes, indeed, the child is father to the man.) Ariya Martin, following her artist's path, renewed my own ability to persevere. Linda Zuckerman tirelessly offered her editorial skill, which should now surely reserve her a place in that mythic realm — editor's heaven. My agent, Susan Cohen, gave valuable advice and support. My wife, Rose Martin, dedicated teacher, reader, and lover of good stories, remains this book's, and my own, best friend.*

AFTER WORDS™

RAFE MARTIN'S

Birdwing

CONTENTS

After Words™ Guide by Rachel Griffiths

About the Author

Rafe Martin grew up surrounded by stories. His mother read him fairy tales from the *Book of Knowledge Encyclopedia*. His father told of his adventures while flying dangerous missions over the Himalayas in World War II. His grandmothers, who had fled Russia during the revolution, fed him stories of Cossacks' swords and long Russian winters, along with many sweets and hot tea. And his large, loud, extended family loved nothing more than getting together in New York's Lower East Side to swap wild tales.

When Rafe could read, he fell in love with King Arthur; with Kipling's Mowgli; with Biblical tales of Joseph, Daniel, and Samson; and with Herman Melville's *Moby Dick*. Later, he studied English at Harpur College (now Binghamton University) and became the first student to win highest honors. After getting married, Rafe and his wife, Rose, ran a bookstore together, and Rafe won the first Lucille Micheels Pannell Award for his "unique creativity in bringing children and books together." But Rafe was in love with storytelling, so he began to write books and travel the country spinning yarns.

Rafe's now written more than twenty books,

including the bestsellers *Foolish Rabbit's Big Mistake*, *Will's Mammoth*, and *The Rough-Face Girl*. Among his many awards are three American Library Association Notable Book Awards, four Parents' Choice Gold Awards, and an IRA Teachers' Choice Award.

When not writing, storytelling, or reading books, Rafe spends his time riding his BMW motorcycle. In the last six years, he's logged more than 60,000 miles.

Q&A with Rafe Martin

Q: *What was it about the Brothers Grimm "The Six Swans" story that resonated with you?*

A: First and most dramatic was the transformation of the boys into swans. I was fascinated with were-wolves at one time and here were were-swans, boys who could fly! I always loved flying. I was born on an Air Force base a year after my father came back from overseas in WWII where he was flying search-and-rescue missions over the Himalayas into China, Burma, and India. Airplanes were a passion we shared. Every year we'd go to a little airport in Flushing, New York, and, in a tiny open-door Piper Cub, have a pilot fly us over the Statue of Liberty and Empire State Building. I loved it! In "The Six Swans" these boys can fly; I wished I could, fly, too.

The other thing that resonated with me is that weird ending of the tale, where we find out that the littlest brother ends up with a wing. It's not a totally happy ending. It's like a piece of the story is left dangling and now goes wandering out, after the tale is done, into real life. I think I identified with that boy. He's different. He doesn't fit in. I felt like that, too.

Q: *What effect did your father's stories from the Himalayas have on you?*

A: Four things stand out to me. First, that flying was a great experience. Second, that Asia, where he was flying, was made of many fascinating and ancient cultures. Third, that in war, destinies and lives could change in an instant. For example, a man could put his foot in his boot and a poisonous snake, a tiny but deadly krait, could bite him, and in three steps he'd be dead. Or, as happened to my father, someone might miss an easy mission on a chance circumstance and on that flight everyone who went could be killed — leaving the one who remained the sole survivor. Finally, I learned that stories told in words — which is how I got his stories — would form pictures in your mind.

Q: *You travel widely as a storyteller and perform before audiences, but you're also a writer. What does it mean for you to be creating stories both orally and through writing?*

A: Telling stories helps me understand the needs of an audience and the need for dramatic moments that bring a story to life. Writing reminds me of the power of words themselves and of our interest as readers in exploring complex worlds in our own imaginations. I think that doing both helps me be both a better writer and a better storyteller.

Q: *What's your "wing"? Do you have a curse that you now find a blessing?*

A: My imagination. As a child I was a dreamer imagining all sorts of things. I never saw how I would fit in. Now I see it as the greatest blessing. With my imagination I can create anything, have any adventure, make any wish come true — in a story.

A more in-depth interview with Rafe Martin is available at www.arthuralevinebooks.com/birdwing.asp

The Goose Girl: A Story

"The Six Swans" wasn't the only story from the Brothers Grimm that fueled the writing of Birdwing. *The character of Ardwin's wife, Alene, draws deeply from the "The Goose Girl," a tale of magic, mother's love, and false identity retold here by Rafe Martin.*

Long ago when wishes still had magic power, there lived a queen and her daughter. When the princess was of an age for such things, the queen arranged for her to be married to a fine prince who lived in a neighboring land. The girl seemed destined for happiness.

The time of parting came. It was a sad moment for the queen and the princess, for they loved each other dearly. The old queen said to the princess, "Here, my child, is a white handkerchief with three red drops of my blood upon it. Keep it with you always. It will be of service to you as you journey on your way."

Then the princess mounted her horse, Falada, and the handmaiden the queen had chosen to accompany her daughter mounted another, and with many a backward glance the princess set off. But the horse, Falada, was no ordinary mount, for Falada could speak.

Hours went by and the princess was overwhelmed with thirst. They came to a stream and she asked her handmaiden, whose job it was to do such things, to please dismount and bring her a cup of water. But the handmaiden answered quite nastily, saying, "Get it yourself. I didn't ask for this job."

So the princess dismounted and knelt down beside the flowing water. "Ah, Heaven," she said, sadly. And as she drank, the three drops of blood said, "Alas, Princess. If your old sick mother saw you being treated like this, her heart would surely break in two."

Then the drops were silent, for the handkerchief fell from her pocket and washed away downstream. And the princess didn't notice.

But the handmaiden saw it. And now she knew she had the princess in her power.

The handmaiden said, "Now I will ride Falada and you will take my horse. And you will give me your fine clothes and you will wear mine. And you must swear by the clear sky above to tell no one of any of this. If you refuse I will kill you." And the princess felt so lost and strange and weak and powerless now that the drops of her mother's blood were gone, she did as the handmaiden ordered. But Falada saw and heard it all.

On they rode, the handmaiden on Falada and the true princess on the handmaiden's horse, until they came to the palace where the prince awaited.

There was great rejoicing when they arrived. The prince ran to Falada and lifted the handmaiden from the saddle, thinking she was his true bride. "But what about the other girl?" asked the prince and the king. "Oh," said the false bride very haughtily, "I found her along the way. Let her work for her food so she is not lazy and idle."

The king said, "Hmmm. Conrad the goose boy always needs help." So they sent the princess to tend geese.

Then the false bride said to the prince, "Dear Husband-to-Be. May I ask a favor?"

"Of course," said the prince.

"My horse is a dangerous brute. He nearly threw me on the way here. Would you have him killed?" She knew Falada had seen everything and she feared he would tell the truth.

When the princess learned of this she gave a piece of gold to the slaughterer and asked that when the awful deed was done, he nail Falada's head up in the great dark gateway to the town. And the slaughterer agreed.

The next morning when the princess and

Conrad drove the flock out through the great dark gate, she said, "Ah, Falada, hanging there."

And the head answered:

"Ah, Princess, how ill you fare!
If your mother knew,
Her heart would break in two."

When they came to the meadow and the pond where the geese roamed free, she unbound her golden hair. Conrad was amazed with the brightness of it and wanted to pluck a strand or two. But before he could, the princess sang:

"Blow, gentle wind, I say,
Conrad's little hat away.
Make him chase it here and there
While I again bind up my hair."

And the wind heard her song, and it blew Conrad's hat off, and away he ran after it, and when he returned, the princess had bound up all her golden hair and its brightness was no more to be seen.

The next morning once more they set out through the dark gate and the princess, who everyone thought was just a goose girl said, "Ah, Falada, hanging there."

And the head again replied:

"Ah, Princess, how ill you fare.
If your mother knew,
Her heart would break in two."

Then they drove the flock into the meadow and the geese went their way out into the pond, and the princess unbound her hair. And again Conrad wanted to grab a strand. And again the princess called the breeze to blow and make Conrad run after his hat. And when he returned, all huffing and puffing, and nearly out of breath, her hair was all bound up again.

That night Conrad went to the king and said, "Your Majesty, I'm not going to work with that goose girl anymore!"

"But why ever not?" asked the old king, taking off his spectacles and giving them a rub with his sleeve.

Then Conrad told the king how the goose girl spoke that morning to a horse's head nailed up in the great dark gateway, and how she unbound her golden hair and a wind came up like magic and he had to run all over to get his hat, and he'd had enough of it.

"Really," said the king. "How interesting." And he put his spectacles back on.

The next morning the king stealthily followed Conrad and the goose girl and heard and saw everything. That night, he called the goose girl to him and asked her to explain. But she said, "Alas, sire, I cannot, for I have sworn beneath the clear sky to tell no one." And despite all his entreaties she would say no more. At last he said, "Go into the big iron stove and whisper the truth to the stove. That will not break your vow, for you will not be under the clear sky inside the stove."

So she crept into the big iron stove when it was cold and no fire was lit, and she whispered the whole truth of the handmaiden's deception and cruelty and wept at last over the death of her horse, Falada. But what she didn't know is that the king had his ear to the stovepipe and heard it all.

And when she came out of the stove he ordered that the stove-soot be washed off her. And then beautiful robes were placed on her and anyone could see now how royal and beautiful she was. Then she was led to the wedding feast. The false bride sat at the prince's side and the princess was seated in the chair at his other side, but no one knew who she was. All marveled at her beauty.

Then the king asked the false bride, "What should be done to someone who steals from another, who even steals her name, her clothes, her horse, and makes a princess do the work of a goose girl?"

And very brazenly the handmaiden said, "Such a one should be killed horribly. Roll her down a hill in a barrel studded with iron nails."

"So be it," said the king. "For that thief is you and it is your own doom you have proclaimed."

And the prince, astonished, said, "What do you mean?"

And the king said, "Here is your true bride. We thought she was the servant and made her the goose girl. But she is the real princess."

And the prince's heart leapt like a bird up into bright sunlight. For though the false bride had appeared beautiful, she chilled his heart, and he had not looked forward to the wedding. And the princess was happy, too. For this was the husband she was meant to have. At last all her dangers, trials, and troubles were past.

Then the prince and princess were joyfully married. In time, they became king and queen, and had all the happiness they could wish for as long as they lived.

Who Were the Brothers Grimm?

Cinderella, Rapunzel, Snow White, Hansel and Gretel, Little Red Riding Hood — most of the Western world's best-loved fairy-tale characters first appeared in print in an 1812 collection put together by two German professors of linguistics, Jacob and Wilhelm Grimm.

The Brothers Grimm — though always fond of a tale — didn't set out to dazzle the literary world. What really interested them was the evolution of the German language, and they found that the best way to study German sounds was to ask people to tell them their favorite fairy tales. Over the course of their research Jacob and Wilhelm collected hundreds of stories: dark chronicles of witches seducing unwitting kings, young children being sacrificed for their families, and stepmothers doling out unholy punishments. These were seldom the kinds of stories that lulled children to sleep.

During the time they were conducting their research, the Brothers Grimm were quite poor. Their parents had both died, and Jacob was supporting all of his younger brothers and sisters; he himself could afford to eat only one meal a day. Jacob and Wilhelm decided to try publishing eighty-six of their favorite stories in a scholarly collection entitled *Kinder- und Hausmärchen* that was heavily footnoted and annotated. Naturally, almost no one read it and it brought in very little money. They tried again in 1814 with an expanded collection that included ten stories specifically for children. This was more successful, but it wasn't until 1825, when Wilhelm edited the stories extensively and included illustrations from his brother Ludwig, that the collection took off.

Wilhelm had realized that the fairy tales appealed most broadly to children. Unfortunately, the original tales — so filled with blood, gore, sex, and horror — were more likely to give kids nightmares than entertain them. So he had sanitized the stories, turning them into a "manual for morals." Still, even the versions in the last collection are much rougher than the ones kids know today. Did the princess kiss the frog to turn him into a prince? Not in the Brothers Grimm version — instead, she threw him as hard as she could against a wall, and the *splat* jolted him back into human form.

Instruments of War: The Five Most Gruesome Medieval Inventions

Trebuchet: One of the most devastating weapons in the medieval arsenal, the trebuchet was a massive catapult capable of launching projectiles of up to 200 pounds and exploding castle walls. If lead and stone missiles failed to intimidate, trebuchets were sometimes loaded with dead animals or the heads of captured soldiers. The most infamous trebuchet was the "Warwolf," used by the English to end their four-month siege of Scotland's Stirling Castle in the fourteenth century.

Arbalète à tour: The soldiers operating the trebuchet had a worry of their own — the deadly *arbalète à tour*, a powerful crossbow machine that was mounted on castle battlements and shot five-foot javelins or white-hot iron bars at attackers below.

Iron Maiden: Captured warriors quaked at the mention of the bloodthirsty Iron Maiden, a wooden coffin lined with strategically spaced iron spikes that would pierce the flesh of the person locked inside without hitting any vital organs. Not only were the victims left to stand and bleed, they were confined in a soundproof blackness that swallowed their screams.

Smoothbore Cannon: In the eleventh century, the Chinese were the first to use gunpowder for war, but Europeans caught on quickly. Smoothbore cannons shooting smoking balls of lead soon appeared on battlefields to the devastation of charging armies and fortress walls.

Greek Fire: The weapon most feared by medieval sailors, Greek fire was a chemical launched in rockets or sprayed through siphons that ignited almost everything it touched. To this day, the exact chemical composition of Greek fire — a substance capable of burning underwater — baffles scientists. What is known is the terror it induced at sea and on land. One soldier in the Seventh Crusade said the following: "None can deliver us from this peril save God alone. My opinion and advice therefore is: that every time they hurl the fire at us, we go down on our elbows and knees, and beseech Our Lord to save us from this danger." Running might have been wiser.